SILVER LEY

ADRIAN HANBURY BELL was born in 1902, and began a career as a journalist on the *Observer* before tiring of London life and becoming apprenticed, for a year, to a West Suffolk farmer of the old school. In 1921 he bought 35 acres of his own land at Stradishall, and continued to farm in East Anglia until after the Second World War.

He contributed a weekly column about country life to the *Eastern Daily Press* for 35 years, and many of these essays were published in book form. *Corduroy* first appeared in 1930, to be followed by its autobiographical companions *Silver Ley* and *The Cherry Tree*, and the trilogy at once established for him a huge literary reputation. He also compiled crosswords for *The Times* for half a century. Adrian Bell died in 1980.

RONALD BLYTHE's latest book is *From the Headlands*, his collected essays. He began writing in the 1950s and his work takes in a variety of forms from fiction to the kind of personally observed history reflected in such books as *Akenfield* and *The View in Winter*—the first about his Suffolk background and the second about the mystery of being very old, something which he has watched since a child. He has written a number of critical introductions to the classics, including Jane Austen's *Emma* and Thomas Hardy's *A Pair of Blue Eyes* and *Far From the Madding Crowd*, and is the editor of *William Hazlitt: Selected Writings*. His anthology, *Writing in a War: Stories, Poems and Essays of 1939–1945*, has just been reissued. Oxford University Press recently published another anthology, *Places*. Blythe has received a number of literary awards. He has lived all his life in East Anglia.

ADRIAN BELL

Silver Ley

A Novel

INTRODUCED BY
RONALD BLYTHE

OXFORD UNIVERSITY PRESS

Oxford University Press, Walton Street, Oxford OX2 6DP

Oxford New York Toronto
Delhi Bombay Calcutta Madras Karachi
Kuala Lumpur Singapore Hong Kong Tokyo
Nairobi Dar es Salaam Cape Town
Melbourne Auckland

and associated companies in
Beirut Berlin Ibadan Nicosia

Oxford is a trade mark of Oxford University Press

© Adrian Bell 1931, 1974
Introduction © Ronald Blythe 1983

First published by John Lane The Bodley Head Ltd 1931
Hutchinson Library Services edition 1974
First issued as an Oxford University Press paperback 1983
Reprinted 1986

All rights reserved. No part of this publication may be reproduced,
stored in a retrieval system, or transmitted, in any form or by any means,
electronic, mechanical, photocopying, recording, or otherwise, without
the prior permission of Oxford University Press

This book is sold subject to the condition that it shall not, by way
of trade or otherwise, be lent, re-sold, hired out or otherwise circulated
without the publisher's prior consent in any form of binding or cover
other than that in which it is published and without a similar condition
including this condition being imposed on the subsequent purchaser

British Library Cataloguing in Publication Data

Bell, Adrian
Silvey Ley.
1. Country life—Suffolk (England)
2. Suffolk (England)—Social life and customs
I. Title
942.6'4083'0924   DA670.S9
ISBN 0-19-281408-7

Library of Congress Cataloguing in Publication Data

Bell, Adrian, 1901–
Silvey ley.
(Twentieth-century classics) (Oxford paperbacks)
I. Title. II. Series.
PR6003.E423S5 1986   823'.912   86-2393
ISBN 0-19-281408-7 (pbk.)

Printed in Great Britain by
Richard Clay (The Chaucer Press) Ltd
Bungay, Suffolk

CONTENTS

INTRODUCTION

BY RONALD BLYTHE

Silver Ley is the middle volume of a celebrated trilogy of gently novelized memoirs set in the West Suffolk countryside of the inter-war years. Along with its companions, *Corduroy* and *The Cherry Tree*, it throws a revelatory light on the English agricultural scene at a moment when, after the brief subsidized prosperity brought about by food shortages during the crisis, the whole industry sank back into the depression which had afflicted it since the 1870s. The lasting fascination of all three books lies in the contrast between the natural hopefulness of their youthful author and the economic hopelessness of the scene to which he has committed his life. *Silver Ley* describes the conjunction of the idealistic writer's "new morning" with the old-style farming's good-night. What has taken place in the East Anglian fields for centuries is coming to a muddy halt. Another war will bring the first fruits of an unprecedented recovery and wealth, but neither Adrian Bell nor the farming old-timers with whom he had thrown in his lot would in their wildest dreams have imagined this in the early Thirties, when these books appeared. Interestingly, they were not regarded then as chronicles of the great rural depression but as good green shoots in an area which was producing all manner of strange growth. Bell is the least sensational, the least dramatic of the best twentieth-century country writers, also the least probing, but he is among the most truthful. Everything in *Silver Ley* is in exact focus for his individual eye. He doesn't generalize, doesn't attempt to take in the broad economic and social picture, but by remaining perfectly parochial he manages to capture a memorable view of an entire world in transition.

The landscape of *Silver Ley* is that bulge of the Suffolk border contained by the rivers Stour and Kennett, a still fairly remote district. Stradishall, the "Benfield St. George" of the story, is a village set in the very centre of a beautiful corn-growing area whose periphery is made up of Essex and Cambridgeshire, and a half circle of market towns, Sudbury, Clare, Bury St. Edmunds, Haverhill and Newmarket. The book's names echo those on the map. There is a Bradfield St. George, a Weston Colville for the "Mr. Colville" of Farley Hall and a hamlet called Silverstreet for, perhaps, the title itself. Admirers of Adrian Bell are still able to tour the Stour and Waveney valleys respectively, for his latter years were spent in and around Beccles, and discover how well he integrated in his work everything from the atmosphere of a particular region to the character of its inhabitants. *Silver Ley* is especially successful in its creation of West Suffolk at an historic milestone, when there was no way of returning to the tried old ways, and no convincing pointer to the prosperity to come. It is the kind of story which both the historian and those absorbed in human nature stare into, surprised to discover so much. How can such a modest, if stylishly written, account of a middle-class young man's attempt to work a little farm be anything more than yet another competent country-book? A great many were being written when Bell wrote his, so why the lasting quality?

Part of the answer is that the urge which brought Bell from Chelsea to Suffolk in 1920 had nothing to do with the customary going off to write in a cottage but, far more extraordinary, to do with becoming a traditional small farmer: not even an enlightened back-to-the-land emigrant but simply someone who wanted to live as the ordinary practical farmer lived. Just too young for the trenches, ex-Uppingham School and from a literary London home, Bell's motive for abandoning the city for the village could have been the common one of the period—a quest for real values—yet there is little in his writings to suggest that he was searching for more than what his farm apprenticeship would bring him. It was the ancient pattern of toil on the land which beguiled him, man's basic occupation.

It is as well to add here that this sowing and reaping existence, and everything and everybody involved with it, was also beguiling quite a few other pens in East Anglia during these years. Adrian Bell's unique talent is only now beginning to emerge from a whole school of post-World War I writing about East Anglia as something distinctive and rare—the authentic voice of its era. Not a native voice but, because it belonged to someone who by accepting Suffolk as he did was accepted by it, a voice which is singularly honest and percipient.

Bell doesn't even attempt to go much beyond the responses of his class, and in his dealings with the fieldworkers and their families it is kindliness, rather than any deep understanding of them as individuals, which makes the connection. But that there is a genuine connection there can be no doubt. The 1920s and 1930s witnessed a great crop of country-books about every corner of these islands, and the Eastern counties' contribution was impressive. Adrian Bell wrote in good company, so to speak. Yet he wrote very much alone, better than the good rural belle-lettrists, and quite away from the conventions of the good rural novel. When in the late 1950s he wrote his autobiography proper, *My Own Master*, and took a description of himself from the first chapter of *Silver Ley*—"I was now alone and my own master, and nothing would be done on this holding until I left my bed and did it"—he could as well have been summing up his standing as a regional writer as a man who had "made it", albeit in the most modest way, on the land. During the decades which saw (for Norfolk) R. H. Mottram, Michael Home, Lilias Rider Haggard and Henry Williamson; (for Suffolk) the excellent and neglected W. H. Freeman; and (for Essex) the brilliant A. E. Coppard, S. L. Bensusan, James Wentworth Day and C. Henry Warren, among many others, Adrian Bell, by means of an accurate vision and subtle simplicity of literary style, was able to write of this much written about province freshly and originally. There was no one quite like him at the time and there have been none at all like him since.

Silver Ley is a very happy book, its happiness that of youth in progress, not of youth remembered. Life sprawls uncertainly ahead, but the war is over and the author–hero, ageing from twenty-one to twenty-eight as the tale progresses, finding his farming feet and working all hours, is buoyant. Sidling through the narrative, barely mentioned, we see the emergence of Bell the writer as well as of Bell the young ploughman, village school manager and taker-on generally of the roles which would then come the way of such as he. By the customary notion of the behaviour of foreigners, his is conventional and he is immediately accepted by his adopted community. He fits, and were he a lesser writer than he is it could have been a disaster. Instead, the acceptance allows him to work from the inside as he quite unpretentiously shares the indigenous outlook. He feels it a privilege to be able to do this, and that it is up to him to see things straight. But there is never any deadening ortho-doxy and it is the absence of this, in what to all intents and purposes often appears to be an orthodox situation, which lends the writing its edge. Bell, the newcomer to them, stands witness to the virtues of the yeomanry just when its ancient horse-powered (in the majestic four-footed Suffolk Punch sense) economy is about to vanish. Unlike the majority of artists and writers who have opted for country life, his is a love affair with the land, not the landscape. What we get in *Silver Ley*, and in all his books, is a working farmer's view of Suffolk transmitted via a fine, even elegant, literary intel-ligence.

"As I ploughed I thought", he says in Chapter I,

When I rested the horses at the headlands I looked about
me. I heard the clock in the village below strike one, but
I knew that those who put their hand to the plough did
not leave off till two-thirty. And, seeing that to-day I
was a ploughman, I continued. But I realised that my
present work was more of a gesture than a real attack on
the autumn cultivation before me. It was a mere
obedience of the first rule of arable farming: that horses
must not stand still. At two-thirty I surveyed my work.
So narrow compared to the rest of the field looked the
strip of dark earth I had been all this while making even so
wide. There was much else to be done, and that quickly;
harrowing, trimming the grass from the sides of the fields,
hedges to cut down, manure to cart . . .

"As I ploughed I thought", and its succeeding
anxious pile-up of what had to be done, not only
today but year after year until one's strength ebbed;
what countless young men alone in their first field
must have thought thus. While the farming cycle is
certainly not that of the treadmill, this initial sound
of "the plough hushing through the earth" and
being pulled along the furrow in a kind of stumbling
trot for today and for ever has always brought home
to farmer and farmworker alike a sense of being
caught inescapably in a current of toil. *Silver Ley*
opens with a concise and unforgettable description
of the writer, aged twenty-one, waking up on an October morning in the huge iron bed he bought for 13
shillings, and on the thirty-five acre holding which
he would then have purchased for a song, to the
chastening realization of his being quite alone and
that nothing would be done "until I left my bed and

did it". It is an inspired start for a farming memoir and one whose only equal in East Anglian terms is to be found in Hugh Barrett's *Early to Rise*. Barrett was only sixteen when, in 1932, he was set down in his first field, all ninety-two acres of it, and told to hoe it. It was sugar-beet, the most detested crop,

and the land was hard; each chop of the hoe jarred the wrists. Mercifully, the field had been drilled the short way, but even so the rows were over four hundred yards long and neither before or since have I met longer ones. They stretched away past breakfast and "bait" time, ended at dinner time by the wood, started back in the afternoon and finished at five. In the first two days I hoed precisely two rows a day—eight hundred yards— just there and back, and the rest of the field looked bigger each day, extending into an aching and bent-backed future.

In spite of the gruelling future before them, both writers are honest enough to recall an elation. Bell says,

My work was about me; my fields were as private to me as my own garden. My work was arduous, but my mind was easy. My hours were long, but I was master of them and did not have to live like a city man, tethered to nine-thirty a.m. like a goat to a tree. I had no reproach to fear save the silent one of my neighbour's fields should they make a better showing than mine when the time came.

The inter-war years were ones of a great dread and despising of cities and anyone who could, from those who forsook their streets for the bright properties of the ribbon developers to those seeking the simple life, as they called it, in the villages themselves, made for the countryside. Adrian Bell's work appeared to his contemporaries as the embodiment of the city-escape ideal, and not idyll—a lesson on how it should be done.

Silver Ley would not be the scrupulous confession that it is if it failed to reveal that villagers themselves frequently have reverse longings. Miss Jarvis, a local girl, asks Bell point-blank,

"But why did you come here?"

"Why, of course, to farm."

"Yes, but I mean why choose to settle right out here? You came to Farley Hall [where he was taught to farm] for your health, I expect."

"Oh, it is not as bad as all that . . . "

"I didn't mean to suggest that you were ill . . . "

"I don't look ill, do I?"

"No, not now. I think your year with Mr. Colville has done you a great deal of good. Only now . . . "

"Now the natural thing for me to do is to return to town, you mean?"

"Well, you have your life; it's not as though you were middle-aged and retiring."

It is a sharp little encounter in a farm parlour, and the writer catches his own awkwardness when confronted by someone who is mystified by his decision to leave Chelsea for Benfield St. George. The only reason for doing so would be poor health and the need for fresh air. Throughout the book, Bell allows these "point-blank" native challenges to himself and his family. For halfway through the story, impressed by what they are hearing of Suffolk, his parents themselves desert London for

Benfield, taking a large house and, although he never says as much, ruining the spartan existence of his bachelor farm. They were to remain in Suffolk, on and off until the end of their lives, and older people will remember Mrs. Bell particularly, a still pretty, amusing but rather formidable woman in her sixties, who became a familiar figure in and around Sudbury just before the last war. Also Adrian's father, Robert Bell, a bent, bookish, charming old man. Adrian's novelist's skill is uppermost when it comes to describing their descent on him, with his mother displaying the kind of panache and fortitude which carried the memsahibs and their households across India. Soon, as the educated townee often does, she is reviving many a method and attitude which Benfield itself has thankfully abandoned. Bell treats her with a kind of bemused admiration and affection, not criticism. Having his family with him, and having to live at impressive Groveside and forsake little Silver Ley, effects a total transformation of Benfield's concept of him and yet, when at last they leave him in peace and solitude once more, life at the farm pursues its way with no acknowledgement of the interruption. "In truth I felt no older than then; that I had been a little over twenty on closing the cottage door, and was a little under thirty on re-opening it, was a fact without inner confirmation, though it stared at me every time I dated a letter."

But for all that, as the quiet narrative proves, something of a maturing and impressively advancing kind had happened to Bell during this first decade in a chosen territory. By a means which only a reading of his trilogy can explain he had come into his own. *Silver Ley* is about a stranger turning into an insider and not quite knowing how it happened. The country "wasn't an escape, as I had thought at first; it was a wonderful grappling influence, like love in its depths and darkness. It wasn't delicate; it didn't tremble; it was like a blundering, uncouth mother with lovely children, one of whom by luck might survive."

Suffolk's actual children mystified him—those of the poverty-stricken labourers, that "ragged and chubby throng with angel eyes but acquisitive hands that made a procession of Benfield street morning and evening" and who were found in the fields without shoes or stockings on winter days eating mangolds, some of whose fathers were drunks and some of whose homes were condemned as unfit for human habitation, and some who, for all the hardships, shone from some undiscoverable source of good-living. And he was mystified by their mothers too, "thin and pale, as so many country wives are". All around him the new cry on the collapsing farms was, "Buy a tractor and sack some men." Towards the end of *Silver Ley*, Bell gives a wonderful portrait of these East Anglian field workers, almost the last of the 'old people', as they are now known. They had come to Groveside to ring hand-bells on Boxing Day, 1928:

The old narrow bricks used to ring with their steel-shod feet, and their voices to vibrate with an unfamiliar depth and huskiness here within walls. Somehow, seen suddenly away from their usual background of acres and sky, the texture of their lives stood out the more. The brows that one never saw save now, when their caps were off, the wiry rebellious hair like patches of standing corn that the wind had swirled awry, their clean rough shirts and collars, blue and red striped, the heavy festooned watch-chain, the thick waistcoat without points, the leather-bound cuff, the rosy cheek, the swart hand—the roughness and cleanness and well-mendedness of their clothes, the colour of them, and the slow stir that even the small movements seemed to make about them. Their cheeks had been painted by the air and light. They were touched always and all days by limitlessness—by great views, winds. And they brought the stare of it in with them, somehow: it was like the light of the snow in the room.

Such descriptions, there are many of them, are not for the fostering of an idyll but for the heightening of the predicament in which agriculture was gradually discovering itself. This gathering rural storm is what lifts *Silver Ley* from the usual run of ably written village annals and gives it its current importance, for in its quiet pages we have one of the finest records of what it was like to live through the second "coming down time", as it was known in Suffolk, or the horrible re-emergence of a slump which had first begun to ruin the fields in the 1870s. Portents of this calamity begin to be noted early on in the story, although "at present no one worried seriously". But already Farley Hall, the best farm in the village, and the one on which Bell had been trained, and which had been trim, weedless, and rich-yielding under Mr. Colville, but which had been sold to a sharp precursor of many of today's farm-industrialists, Mr. James, was in decline.

Soon, "it came upon the whole valley in the end, till even the best farmers had to allow tangled hedges behind which the harvest sheaves could not dry after rain, while the men had to load them wearing gloves on account of the thistles which the farmers had been unable to afford to hoe out." Bell's use of this gradualism is very skilful. The mainly middle-class community of which he writes, although its plight bears little comparison to that of the labourers and their families, goes about its business and social pleasures, neither heartlessly nor all that fearfully, but very much as people do when some vast altering of the world's circumstances is beyond their being able to do a thing about it. Repellent politics fill the air, even that of remote Suffolk. The young man slogging away on his few acres, assisted now by the not-so-young Simmons, turned off Farley Hall by its new owner, is openly uncontrite about his turning his back on what is happening. "The post-war world appeared to me ugly and threatening, overpopulated already with high ambitions, and would-be wresters of power." In 1918 he had listened to the government declaring, "The agriculture of England must never again be allowed to fall into national neglect", and here it was doing so after five short years before his very eyes. Being so young, Bell is compensated by the incomparable, if rather perverse-sounding delights of hard physical work in sun and wind. Quite rightly, the message of *Silver Ley* is not that of how to run away from life but how to find it.

The familiar minutiae of his situation, parish meetings and committees, trips to market, tennis parties, the fête, the church, the seasonal round, are all faithfully strung along the narrative in the expected order. Most now possess historic interest. But, unlike such observations and episodes in countless village chronicles, Bell's exist to support and explain his reason for witnessing them. It is an unusual stance for a country writer. On the whole, he is reticent on his emotional development; slight encounters with girls, faint pointers to who or what he is via his responses to his being alone in different rooms, for example, as well as in different fields. Now and then, as when the itinerant threshers arrive at Silver Ley, he rises to a descriptive power comparable to that of W. H. Hudson and Richard Jefferies. Although on the whole it is an error to judge Bell according to the standards of these or other rural masters. Those who are most like him are those who are greatly inferior to him, or who simply deal conventionally with what he deals with so inimitably. Having the perspective of fifty years' distance, we can see very clearly that *Silver Ley* and its two companion volumes occupy a literary farmscape entirely their own, but exactly how to define this honest property in comparison to all the rest it is less easy to perceive. *Silver Ley* doesn't "wear well"—it doesn't wear at all. Its strength is the strength of Adrian Bell's own youth. It ends classically in the harvest field and in a scene of traditional beauty and meditation. But just before harvest he and thousands of the farmers and farmworkers of East Anglia had packed Parker's Piece in Cambridge in a huge demonstration to draw the government's attention to the catastrophe now sweeping down on them, and it is this, the modest and unflamboyant pulling together of the practical and the dream, which gives *Silver Ley*, and indeed all Bell's work, its excitement and its authority. He didn't need time to prove that there is no one quite like him, but it has.

FOREWORD

WHEN I was living the things I wrote of in *Corduroy* and its two sequels, *Silver Ley* and *The Cherry Tree*, corduroy itself was a cloth worn only by the worker. It was hard and stiff—new trousers would stand up without legs in them—and it weathered to the colour of chestnut leaves in October.

Every tool and machine mentioned in *Corduroy*, which we worked with, is now in a museum. Except the self-perpetuating power for them, which was the horse whose bones are underground. I doubt if one man's life has ever before witnessed so complete a disappearance of everything he worked with to produce bread and butter, because farming up to 1920 had been going on exactly the same as I found it for over 200 years (I even saw the same tools in a "pioneer farm village" in Canada).

Even more strange to me now is the fact that of all of us who lived and worked in the parish of "Benfield St. George" (which was Stradishall) not one of us had a premonition that we were living in history. "This will go onward the same/Though dynasties pass", wrote Hardy: but he was wrong. Every week we took a tumbril-load of our grinding barley to the windmill, had a glass of the miller's home brew while the mare stood unalarmed by the pouncing shadows of the sails, and drove home with a load of barley meal for the pigs.

When wheat fell in price till we could hardly sell it at ten shillings a sack (a quarter of what it fetched 100 years previously) we still did not know what had gone wrong, neither the old farmers nor the young farmers. We still had no recipe for getting more than a day's work from one man in a day, nor for ploughing more than one furrow at a time with our horse-power, which was the power of horses. There was not a single power-machine in the parish, apart from an old steam engine used for threshing, and even that had to be pulled by a horse from farm to farm.

England was two races (perhaps still is), town and country. Suffolk in 1920 was vaguely known in London as being flat and full of turnips, which county is now commuted to and from. To me, therefore, a new world at the time. The usual liberal education of my youth ignored completely the life of the land since the Georgics of Virgil. So the life and social manners of "Benfield" were as strange to me as Erewhon. The clay-land vernacular, genuinely and unconsciously Shakespearian, when I learned it, became a new philosophy, its rhythms almost psalm-like. Tradition in every act.

What determined me to be a farmer? Perhaps the array of heavy horses paraded in the grand ring of the Suffolk Show in 1920—the most opulent sight I have ever seen. I do know well that at a certain hour of a certain evening in June of my first year on a farm, as I returned from a visit home and clicked the latch of the last gate of the gated road to the farmhouse, I said to myself, "This is my home from now."

I don't think I have been outside Suffolk for longer than four consecutive weeks ever since.

1974   ADRIAN BELL

I

I AWOKE, and heard a wind soughing at the gable-end where the greying window was. It seemed far and unexplained to me in the stillness of the room, and the trance of sleep hardly cast off. It was just light enough to see the wooden ribs of the Gothic ceiling inclining up to each other, like fingers meeting at the tips in thoughtful poise. I heard a thud or two; but nothing seemed to break a sense of the absolute solitariness of my little chamber, not even my watch ticking.

I lay blank-minded, enjoying that delightful reprieve from knowledge and responsibility, that minute of the opening of the eyes from sleep, wondering where I was and what hold I had on the life to which I had returned, or it on me; yet knowing that in a moment memory would come surging back like the tide into a cave.

Another thud; and suddenly I remembered that for the last year I, a young man from London, had been learning farming with Mr. Colville of Farley Hall, Benfield St. George, Suffolk, a big farmer and one of a big family of farmers who lived like a ruling clan in the neighbourhood, co-operating and conferring. Another thud, and I remembered that I had left Mr. Colville's and had just wakened to the morning of October 13th, after the first night in a fifty-acre farm of my own on the outskirts of Benfield. Another thud, and recollection concentrated on the immediate fact that, whereas all my wakings hitherto had been to the cheerful sound of the feet of twenty men walking into a farm, leading out horses, opening fowl-houses, milking and feeding cattle, I was now alone and my own master, and nothing would be done on this holding until I left my bed and did it. For those thuds were the sound of my horses stamping in the yard, while the sun rose and the hens cackled in the hen-huts. There was a little heart-failing at the thought, and at the sense of time bearing us all along, as the ticking of my watch insisted. The knowledge, too, that nothing stood still on my demesne, but went forward or back. For the blank fields of autumn, erased of their last season's tale, waited for me to plant them with corn, or the wind would with weeds. There was no sealing them to the *status quo* as a house, nor drawing down of blinds as a shop, but always day and night the wakefulness of vigil, and a stirring through all the expanse. I was aware of it, the unceasing continuance and change, in the wind that had been playing about the house all night as I lay in my cast-iron bed under the strong suppliant beams of my chapel of a bedchamber.

I took heart that I was not altogether ignorant of the business, having been at it a year under Mr. Colville. So I rose, and all the brass knobs of the bed clattered cheerfully as I got out. I presumed once they had been tight, and had not announced one's getting in and out with a tambourine flourish. It was a double bed, and when I bought it for 13*s*. at a sale it had been hung with some faint feminine material, which I had detached as ill-befitting my use. I had no doubt that it had done bridal honours in its time, but now, sated with the mysteries of birth and death, it had grown old and loose, seemed pleased with this young bachelor for a tenant, and chattered cheerfully every time I moved a limb. As much as to say, " Having already the land and the weather to coax and contend with, what a fool a man must be to marry also a woman."

The hens flocked out when I opened their doors, indignant that the sun should be up before them. The cocks, stammering and strutting, proffered their side-long attentions, but were disregarded. The other sex was already intent on grain. It was ever so, my bed would have rattled out ; while man is sentimentalising, the woman is thinking of the next meal.

I fed my horses, Darkie and Dewdrop, giving them, I believe, too much oats to their chaff. There were many unforeseen gaps in my education. Judgment of quantity in farming is a whole subject in itself which Schools of Agriculture seem to neglect, relying on weights and measures. But in practice the farmer has no time to weigh and measure ; he speaks to his men of " double handfuls, siftings, forkfuls," and they understand by practice what those terms amount to.

I had not yet acquired the ploughman's skill in the manipulation of harness, and was still liable to get into a Laocoön pose in my struggle with the chains, thongs, and plough-cords which together made up the tackle. However, I got the horses harnessed without much difficulty, the chief trouble being to get the collars on ; they being disinclined to lift their heads from the manger for that purpose, and my cries of " Hold up " not having a gruff enough intonation to be compelling. I rode them out to a field which I must lose no time in ploughing up for winter oats, as

Mr. Colville had advised, and there made a start. I cut two sticks from the hedge, peeled them to show up the better from a distance, and planted them one in the middle of the field and one at the farther side. I eyed them well that they were in line with my team, to which I then returned. I had coupled the horses well apart that I might get a clear view of the sticks between them. Tilting the plough into the ground, I braced myself and drove straight for the first of the sticks, gazing on that only and leaving horses and plough to my arms alone. I heard the plough hushing through the earth, and the stubble crackling over: it desired to leap to right and to left, but I crouched over it and held it to the course. The horses passed one on either side of the first stick; the plough caught it and bore it over. I felt it crack beneath my feet. I had eyes only for the second stick, which we came to without much wavering and trod down. Then I turned and surveyed my work. I sighed with relief: it was nothing to be ashamed of, the first furrow I had ploughed on a field of my own.

The first furrow is the most difficult to draw out: the others have it and each other for guide. I continued then to and fro about it with easy rhythm. I found the day bright about me, though the too-clear dawn had yielded to a fleet of clouds that threatened to close their ranks across the sky. At present there remained those jagged fragments of blue that water-colourists like to paint. Starlings quickly learned that ploughing was going on, and came and made a hopping, fluttering procession of my progress.

At eight-thirty I returned to the farm for breakfast. I had bought some provisions the day before. I had, amongst other things, some bacon, a frying-pan, and some coffee. My cookery knowledge was slight, but equal to this occasion. It included a maxim that it was unnecessary to melt fat in the pan for the frying of bacon. A chopped faggot and some logs soon made a blaze, to which I sacrificed a whole candle, as I was hungry. I put the rashers in the pan, and after a minute of silence, they began to splutter companionably. Making the pan balance itself, I next turned my attention to coffee, which I made in two mugs, not having a jug to spare. Encouraged by these authentic mingled fragrances, I determined on some toast as well, and fixed a fork through the fender in such a way that that too " did itself." Meanwhile I laid the table for my simple meal, keeping one eye on my automatic cookery. As I sat at it, the postman came with a letter from home in which they hoped that I was getting on all right in my new abode. A well-timed enquiry. The coffee was excellent (wood-smoke being no drawback) ; the bacon done to a turn. Though my mother might have found certain things to take exception to—a drop or two of spilt fat, fork prongs tarnished with the fire—to a man's skimming eye it was well enough.

After breakfast I returned to the fields. As I ploughed I thought. When I rested the horses at the headlands I looked about me. I heard the clock in the village below strike one, but I knew that those who put their hand to the plough did not leave off till two-thirty. And, seeing that to-day I was a ploughman, I continued. But I realised that my present work was more of a gesture than a real attack on the autumn cultivation before me. It was a mere obedience of the first rule of arable farming : that horses must not stand still. At two-thirty I surveyed my work. So narrow compared to the rest of the field looked the strip of dark earth I had been all this while making even so wide. There was so much else to be done, and that quickly; harrowing, trimming the grass from the sides of the fields, hedges to cut down, manure to cart. I must, of course, have help ; a man, perhaps two for a time.

I am always one for settling into comfortable rhythms, swift or slow, according to the demands that life makes, coping with things with the help of an ordered day. That to me is half the battle : if jolted out of it, a sudden anxiety magnifies the affairs ahead into mountains. So, until I had discovered and engaged labour adequate to my needs here, I was quite at sea and knew not which way to turn, my own activities seeming but to nibble at the edge of the problem.

I felt strangely alone with the birds and the clouds on my plot of earth, as I rode the horses homeward. But I was not to lack visitors. In fact, I had not got fairly into the home meadow before the first of them made his appearance—a young man in blue overalls with a spanner sticking out of a pocket just above the knee. His complexion was pale, and his having last shaved yesterday gave it a tired shadow. His knuckles were scarred and his nails were squarely outlined in a grime that did not come from dabbling with earth. Blood showed at a recent graze, more brilliant for the ingrained oil; an exclamation mark of humanity in those hands that were the colour of machinery. Anything that I wanted in the way of petrol, oils, or tyres for my motor-cycle he would be pleased to supply :

he lived just in the next village, and was, in fact, my nearest motor-engineer. Ah, yes, I knew his place, I said, being as willing to give my orders to him as to anyone else : but I said wrong, for the group of signs near the post-office I mentioned as being my idea of his place was the store, it appeared, of a mountebank of much more recent standing than he—an ignorant meddler who had been through no proper tuition, who was only fit to tinker with pedal bicycles. Whereas he, J. Stockforth—he paused to hand me a card signed with his thumb—had been apprenticed for years to I-forget-what famous firm. By the defensive arrogance of his tone—he spoke almost as though I had been championing the other fellow—I gathered that he was trying not to have to admit to himself a rivalry, and that there really was a certain leakage of customers, by chance or otherwise. And later I found that the other man had the advantage of position, glaring all into the road, whereas J. Stockforth stood back rather, and more to the end of the village of Sarrow. As I sat on my horse assuring Mr. Stockforth that when I wanted a new tyre I would come to him, I felt somehow that he had the germ of a complaint against life, the one certain thing to sap a man's soul from within and make him an underling.

When I came out of the stable from feeding my horses, I saw a car drawn up by the house, and a man coming round the corner. He was a merchant, insurance agent and small millowner from the next village. He was mock-hearty, and tried to blarney me into buying a ton of barley meal there and then. He would impress me with the need of immediate insurance also : but at the moment I was needing my dinner. I think Mr. Sumner saw a hungry glitter in my eye. He had expected a full man and found an empty one ; so, without more ado, he was off into his bustling little car with a wave and a three times " Good day." But hardly had his dust died down and silence resumed its sway than with a swish and scrape of a sliding foot another stood at the gate. I was within-doors now, and had at least seized on bread and cheese, so was more in a mood to greet the newcomer cheerily ; which I did by opening the window and calling to him as he began to make his way circuitously to the back door. Country folk find something abashing about a front garden, as though it were a piece of Sunday they were treading on. However, he turned at my voice, and I recognised his face over the hedge as that of a friend : he was the pink, round-faced miller of Benfield. I had gone to his mill many times with orders from Mr. Colville; had drunk the formal glass of home-brewed ale with him when I had brought a cheque in settlement of an account. After a little diffident fumbling with the front gate he came across the narrow lawn to the window. He was as dawn to dusk compared with Stockforth, the motor-man : the day's work whitened him that blackened the other.

" I'm sorry if I'm disturbing you at your dinner," he said, pausing half-way.

" You're not," I answered, taking a bite. " But I had a visitor a minute or two ago who was keeping me from it, so I wasn't too pleased to see him. After you've been ploughing all morning . . ."

Mr. Sumner's business card was on the window-sill,

where I happened to have laid it. The eyes of the miller of Benfield dwelt upon it for a moment.

"The land ploughs well now," said the miller, raising his eyes.

"Yes, I'm ploughing for oats."

"Oats want to be in soon," he assented. The side track of farm-doings was always the gradual approach to a business matter.

"Yes, I heard you'd taken this little place. I hope you get on well. If there's anything you're wanting in the way of pig-meal . . ." he added, allowing the point of his call to obtrude. He handed in his card, floured by his fingers. "I think you'll find my prices a bit more reasonable than some people's," he said, with a glance up the road, where his rival's car had disappeared.

I could not help noticing the contrast between the miller's bearing in face of rivalry and the motor-man's. Though he knew quite well who had been there before him (in fact, Mr. Sumner must have raced past his bicycle on the road), and for all he knew I might already have placed an order, he did not betray that even the existence of another miller was known to him. Whereas the mere mistaken resting of my mind's eye on the premises of another was enough to put the motor-man in a flurry.

I groomed my horses, a little amateurishly perhaps, turned them out into the yard, fed my scanty stock, mooned for awhile over a fan-rayed sunset, and went in to tea. The adding of the remains of that to the remains of previous meals in the sink definitely made a debit balance of used over unused crockery in the house. The domestic problem was the next that must

9

be faced. As though to underline that fact, a man stepped out of a motor-car with a note-book in one hand and a bag in the other, said he represented Bidley Bros., family grocers, in the town of Share, that he always called for orders throughout the district on Wednesday afternoon, and he hoped that he might be favoured with the honour of my custom.

I saw no reason why he shouldn't. He opened his note-book. "But," I said, "I have only just settled in here, and at the moment I really don't quite know what I do want. I shall be passing your shop in a day or two, and I'll call with my order."

But possibly a commission basis made it desirable for the traveller to side-track that suggestion. He discovered my needs to me by catechism. Had I salt, had I pepper, had I mustard, sugar, jam, etc, etc.? He let fall such an avalanche of veriest essentials which I lacked, I was quite dazed, and it seemed a waste of breath to continue repeating "No." Mr. Cartwright's pencil galloped over the paper, and his spectacles twinkled jollily with the speed. At length even his invention grew out of breath: the pencil idled a moment or two at his lips, then was definitely put to bed behind his ear. "The goods are delivered on Saturday," he said: "but if there is anything you need at once, I carry a few things with me in the van to oblige customers."

He left me some apples and cigarettes. I enquired about cake. I was not sure just how many yards of his "rich Genoa" were due to me on Saturday; but until then . . .

Mr. Cartwright was sorry; he had with him only a sample birthday cake which a lady had wished to see. But of course if one didn't mind the inscription. . . . He produced it in a box with a frill and under a glass top, like a relic. It said " Many Happy Returns of the Day." But it was a cake. I took it.

In the silence following the departure of the grocer's van that inscription became almost vocal. Well, after all, this was in its way a kind of birthday. It was strangely silent in the little cottage to-night in contrast to the scene at old Mr. Colville's golden wedding the night before. But the flames of the fire leaped cheerfully and the stamping of my horses in the yard bore me company. I was about to say they were my only company that night, but I remember that later there came a knock at the door, and a young man with a scarf round his neck introduced himself as Alfred Jarvis—the brother of Miss Jarvis, a girl who looked delicate and yet had ploughed and carted during the war on her father's farm, whom I had met at Farley Hall. The Jarvises were now my neighbours ; their farmhouse stood half a mile down the road ; and Alfred Jarvis, to whom his father, growing old, had handed over the management of affairs, called to say that he would be pleased to help me in any way I needed, as he knew how awkward it was, moving into a farm, for the first month or so, and every newcomer, be he never so fore-thoughtful, finds himself lacking tools at a moment when he most needs them. He sat and smoked with me for an hour or so ; I had two basket-chairs, swung a little over to one side, but comfortable enough. He was a round-faced, deep-voiced young man, and when he laughed seemed to strain the little room like a too-tight jacket. Of his complexion and the effects of the elements on it I have heard Mr. Colville say, " I've passed Alf Jarvis on his motor-bike in winter, when it was so flaying-cold that his face looked regular black-red." Horses were Alfred's pet topic; and, though I had only a skimming knowledge of the Hunt, I managed to keep him encouraged enough to continue. So that when he left it was getting quite late, and I did not return to my chair from the door; but put the fire-guard up and the lamp out. Thus ended my first day's farming on Silver Ley.

II

LONELY ? During the day there was no time to be,
and in the evening body-languor, combined with the
soon familiar grouping of my few chattels about me
in the lamp- and fire-light, and reading or gazing in
the fire and planning, made me a half-conscious
companion to myself. There was no art-tension
about that interior upon which I look back as being
one of the warmest corners that I have been granted
to occupy by Life's chances : its harmony, though not
immediately obvious to the stranger's eye, was yet
the inevitable one of amenity. The arm-chairs seemed
to be stretching backward with yawns ; the table's
single pedestal about a foot from the ground branched
into four legs which had a suggestion of courtly dance
about them, ending in brass claws such as had breathed
tales of witch-tranced animals to me as a child and had
seemed to herald imminent re-assumption of bodily
form. I had pictures, too, without which I am uneasy
in a room and cannot feel it to be home ; engravings
which pleased me by their peaceful light and haunting
shades, such as October mornings have before the
upper mist quite breaks ; a great picture, too, done in
lively colours, of the death of Nelson—all torn sails
and battle-smoke, save where in the middle foreground
the famous admiral lay back white-faced among a
group of strong men compassionate. The sailors
all had fair curly hair and boyish faces ; honest fellows

obviously that knew their catechism and had only one wife apiece.

I got the wife of Mr. Colville's foreman, Midden, to come and put in a few hours about my cottage during the middle of each day, as she had no flock of a family, as was usual, but one son, her only conformity to modern modes. She was thin and pale, as so many country wives are, lacked front teeth, and had a tone of voice which suggested she was ever at her wits' end, till one came to know her. She went with a tottering walk, yet hove in sight across the meadow every day without fail, whatever the weather. I can see her now, leaning into the wind like a ship making a difficult port, her profuse skirt bosomed out with the gusts. Once arrived, she would shed a few clothes, remark what bad travelling it was across the fields since the last rain, and how the wind was enough to craze the devil; then set about clearing the debris of my break-fast and tea. She gave me commissions for butcher and grocer when I went to a town, and when I bungled them she only sighed and somehow contrived something for lunch. Once, for instance, I was told to get 1 lb. of steak and ¼ lb. of suet for a pudding, and returned brightly with ¼ lb. of steak and 1 lb. of suet, which came in time to Mrs. Colville's ears and is a laugh against me to this day. Mrs. Midden would be gone when I returned to a late lunch from the fields and hastily opened the oven door to discover what she had left for me, and, if it were steak and kidney pud-ding, rejoice; if stewed steak, only just be thankful for food.

I engaged a labourer: I bought a cow. I went with Mr. Colville to market to profit by his advice,

and bid for a heifer due with its first calf, which
Mr. Colville considered a useful sort; and I, too,
except for an inward misgiving over a wild look in
her eye, which he did not seem to notice. I put it
down to the strangeness of her surroundings, and let
her be knocked down to me at a reasonable figure.
Next to get her home. As we walked away from the
ring, a drover who had been watching the proceedings
with an eye to his own profit touched his cap to me.
" Did you buy the red heifer, sir ? Good sort, she is.
Do you want her got home, sir ? "

I was about to reply that that was what I did want,
disposed to feel grateful that he had so timely offered
himself, but Mr. Colville, who seemed to know the
man, broke in first, " What'll you take to get her to
Benfield, Harry ? "

" Couldn't do it under seven and sixpence, Mr.
Colville," replied the man, cautiously defensive
now.

" Seven and sixpence ! Why, I thought you'd say
about five bob," Mr. Colville broke in.

The drover put on an injured look, as of one
between the upper and the nether millstone of life.

" Oh, you know that ain't right, Mr. Colville. I
shan't be there till near dark, not if I start right away.
It's twelve mile to Benfield, and you know what such
things as them are on a strange road about nightfall.
It ain't as though there was other cattle travelling
with her. A cow's a funny thing alone."

" She'll go all right." Mr. Colville laughed at his
fears.

" She may or may not—there's no telling. The
market wholly upsets some of 'em, so that they're

like mad things when you get 'em on the road."

"I'll give you six bob, then," cut in Mr. Colville, with the air of a distributor of largesse, and began to stroll on. I followed, feeling that the situation had been taken out of my hands, wondering and learning. It had not occurred to me even to ask the fee of this tatterdemalion whose only worldly property seemed to be a knobbly and erratic stick, let alone bargain with him about it. But, as usual, Mr. Colville was right and I was wrong. His business was to make farming pay, and part of his business was to know the economic value of every job—from cattle-driving to threshing a sack of corn. When it came to charity, he was second to none—but he did not give alms in the public market.

So we walked towards the market gates, the drover casting off his injured look and with a brusque shake of the head crying, " No, shan't do it for that, sir " ; Mr. Colville murmuring blandly, " All right Harry, just as you like " ; but I considerably perturbed within at the uncertain prospects of getting my beast home before dark, and inclined to be resentful at all this fuss over eighteen pence. Had we to go through a similar rigmarole with other drovers ? And, if so, with how many before a price could be agreed on ?

Mr. Colville was pointing out the merits of a bunch of home-bred calves, but I fear my appreciation was lukewarm, for I was casting anxious looks about me for some other man, and at the heifer I had bought and was apparently deserting for ever, standing in a corner pen. But my fears were vain, for hardly had we gained the gates than the drover caught up with us, calling out, " All right, sir, I'll get the heifer home for you."

" Very well," replied Mr. Colville, and, turning on his heel, immediately lost his air of leisured onlooker and bustled back to the cattle-pens, giving instructions to the man as he went, I following. The man's assent was the sign for Mr. Colville to assume authority. " You stand over there," he called to me, " and stop her going that way, and you stand there, Harry." He opened the pen. " That's it, let her go gently ; she'll go well so." We escorted the drover and his charge down one of the principal streets (" We'd best give him a start with her out of the town," Mr. Colville said), the heifer trotting ahead with bulging flanks and swinging udder, swerving with lowered head and dancing hind-legs from the traffic. " Ho Ho ! " called the drover, as she paused uncertain at a side-road or inn-yard. " Goo on there ! Ho ! Stop her, please, will you ? " A passer-by would pause, wave his stick at her, or stand and dodge before her, arms extended, and she would turn and continue down the street. Down one alley-way she scuttled, there being no one to prevent her, and a dog, thinking he had routed her thither, rushed barking after. Both in less than a minute reappeared quicker than they had gone, the dog having been turned from pursuer to pursued, fleeing for his life into a toy-shop. A child in a pram shrieked piercingly as the heifer brushed it ; a car swerved ; but she was off again in the right direction, and nobody took especial notice of a cow trotting down the main street of Stambury except to remark, " Nice heifer, that, but a bit wild." At the corner the policeman, at a sign from the drover, turned her in the right direction. Mr. Colville and I paused at the corner : he shouted to the drover, " All right now ? " The drover, half-walking, half-running, to keep up behind the heifer, waved his knobbly stick high in the air, without turning round, for affirmative answer. So we stood and watched them out of sight.

Mr. Colville, being stout, was a bit out of breath.

" True as to God, I thought she'd have that pram over," laughed he ; " the old woman looked wholly scared, too."

As we walked back he said, " Don't give old Harry any more than six shillings for that job. That's plenty."

I remarked that he didn't seemed inclined to take it at first.

Mr. Colville laughed. " I knew he'd be after us before we got out of the gates. I've dealt with these chaps before. You see, he lives next to Benfield, and it's homeward for him. I daresay he might have earned seven and sixpence off someone for taking some cattle twelve miles in another direction, but then he'd have had to get all the way back, so he'd have been worse off in the end. They're single chaps, mostly, that don't like regular work, that go cattle-driving. They like hanging round markets and picking up what they can. There's usually one in every village. The more you give Harry, the drunker he gets on Saturday nights, that's all."

At about six o'clock that evening, just as I had finished my tea—tea was my " evening meal," remember—I heard the drover's voice again. I had been feeding with my window half-open, becoming just a bit anxious about my heifer, as the sky was

growing very dim and the stars beginning to show.
I walked out to the garden gate and stood listening. I
heard footsteps in the distance, mingled with the soft
pitter-patter of her tread. Even though I was on the
look-out, the creature surprised me with sudden
nearness in the gloom, a sense of power moving
secretly; a thunderous ghost of a thing she seemed,
halting suddenly there before me, sniffing fearfully
at me, the equally sudden obstruction. Fierce, irregu-
lar jets of breath like steam; I felt them hot upon me,
the very voice of alarm.

"Well, here we are, sir," cried the drover from
behind her.

"Was she much trouble?" I asked.

"She weren't too bad," he replied. "I wish
farmers'd keep their road gates shut, though." I
guessed she had given him more than one chase over
stubble and fallow.

"Well, she can come into the meadow here for
to-night," I said, and we drove her into the home
meadow, where there was a thatched shelter in which
she could lie if she wanted to.

She stood woodenly just within the gate, gazing
into the dusk, as though wondering to herself, "What
next?" nor realising for a minute or two that she had
come to her journey's end. Indeed, what nightmare
intervals to cattle these changes of ownership must be:
snatched from the familiar green-walled pleasance that
was all their world, hustled into a crowded place
filled with hundreds of their kind, all equally in a
daze of blank bewilderment; marched round a ring
walled with human faces instead of hedges, then away
along a road for miles and miles, till suddenly there

was the soft grass beneath their feet again and hedges marked the limit of their world; a little different than before, perhaps, more or less succulent, but a world that the cow-mind understood. And of that frantic hiatus does there ever remain even enough memory to be a premonition that the present Eden isn't for ever ?

" Six shillings, isn't it, that job ? " I said, wondering if the man would try to make it more. But he didn't.

" That's right, sir," he replied.

And I'll say this for Harry and his kind : when he makes a bargain he sticks to it, he is that much independent, and one " in the trade," an agricultural branch-liner, like the higgler. If he didn't, it would imply to him that he was unable to take care of himself in business dealings. If he took the whining tone, it would class him with the old and infirm—the old women to whom villagers subscribe because their sows die, and such-like. So he gets drunk on Saturday night, and wakes penniless but vigorous on Monday morning, and if the price you offer for his services isn't adequate, he will give you to understand that there is plenty of business awaiting him at the correct figure elsewhere, and so good-day to you.

So it was six shillings exact he had from me that night, which he counted in the moonlight, and twisted into the corner of his handkerchief and put into his breast pocket. I admit, however, that I offered (and he didn't refuse) a pint of beer, in which he drank my health at the garden gate. After the first gargantuan draught, which illustrated to me a saying which I have mentioned before that sixpence isn't the same as a pint of beer when you're needing it, he paused and gazed at the moon with that air of thoughtful solemnity which so often characterises the first dip in the tankard, as though it were an elixir calculated to inspire some weighty saying.

"Yes, she's a useful heifer," he remarked, and I, too, involuntarily looked at the moon with him, as though it were Diana herself we were thus blasphemously appraising.

"She may be a bit wild at first, but she'll settle down in time," he added. "I won't say she's dear, either. No, she's not dear—for what she is." He took another drink, and brought forth a further intelligence, "I shouldn't be surprised if she don't calve soon, either, by the look of her."

"They said ten days, at the market."

"Yes, they said ten days, but I reckon it'll be before this moon's much older. The journey, too, would upset her a bit. Once I thought I see the calf kick in her belly." He handed me back the mug. "Well, I hope you have luck with her," he said. "And thank you, sir. Good night."

The next morning I saw my man Walter coming across the meadow as usual to feed the horses. It was a clear morning, and the hour of early burnished sunlight which toned with the yellowing chestnut trees of my neighbour's wood. The dew was thick upon the grass as it were a frost, and the man's steps were visible behind him as he trampled it. He was a flaxen-haired, lanky, middle-aged man, with a smile of imperturbability and small but wide blue eyes. His feet, whether he went or stood, always expressed the hour of ten to two. It may have been just his general manner which made him seem to my eye to retain something of the wandering boy on the look-out for birds' nests; a kind of go-as-you-please alertness in his gait.

Him, and the aspect of the morning, I saw from my bed, for the window gave on to the meadow. His appearance on the far side of it was my signal for rising, and soon after he had fed the horses I would be dressed (not shaved, though) and standing with him at the stable door, accommodating the work to the weather.

But this morning he came and stood beneath the window and called, " Master ! "

I looked out. " Hello, Standish."

He had the usual smile, but a little more of it.

" Seen my heifer ? " I asked. I had told him the day before I was going to buy one if I saw one I liked.

" Yes, master," he replied, " both of them."

" What do you mean, both of them ? " I asked. " I only bought one."

" Well, there's two there; you come and see."

" One must have strayed——" I began, but then I saw that of course this was the riddle that the rustic makes of a piece of news. The heifer, then, had calved in the night.

I went quickly down with him. It lay nested in the grass, asleep, with its head on its foot. Its mother stood cropping the grass near by, but ceased at our approach, sniffed the calf, and looked at us defiantly.

" It's the journey did it," said my man, " but she seems all right, and the calf too. Lucky thing she managed to calve by herself, without much trouble. We'd best get them up into the cowshed," he suggested. " They'll catch cold out here. Good thing it wasn't a rough night."

So we got them up into a closed shed, putting the calf into a cart ; the heifer, in her anxiety, following as closely as though she were tied to it by the nose.

When we had got them there, the calf was in no mind to go to sleep again, but stood upon its legs and tottered drunkenly towards the heifer's udder with the instinct of the newly born. After one or two ineffectual jabs, it found the source of nourishment, and immediately its tail became ecstatic. There it stood, head and neck stretched stiffly up, its whole little being taut as though in a trance, only its tail shivering, and there we stood, cow and all, mutely attending on the ceremony. When it had taken its fill, it lay down again, but did not immediately dispose itself for sleep, but kept its head up, gazing at us with a look of quite adult intelligence, a filmy blue in its eyes like the chance day-gleams on a tree-shadowed pool.

"Yes," said Walter, going over his discovery of the pair, "I see something lay in the grass as I come over the gate into the meadow. Hullo, what's this ? thought I. I thought maybe Master Reynard had had one of them big old brown hens. But then I see it move and I wondered to myself; surely the master would never have put a cow and calf to lay out in the meadow all night this time of the year."

"No, of course not," I added to that.

"Then I see as I come up close that the calf was still wet. Oho ! so you ain't wasted much time on the job, my lass, I thought, and it's a wonder you didn't drop the calf on the road home from market. But that's a fierce little thing, though it's afore its time; it was up and sucking almost as soon as I got to it."

Now we had to tackle the heifer ourselves, for, though the calf was filled, her udder was still distended with milk, which, if not taken from her, would be the cause of milk fever probably and her end, so seriously has man meddled with the course of nature here.

I fetched a bucket, and squatting as far from the cow as was possible still to be within reach of it, began gently to milk it, while Walter held its head. Suddenly the pail shot from my hands to the other side of the shed with a clatter, and I lay on my back, my legs just failing to turn me somersault.

"Coo! that was a rare kick she gave," said Walter. "Hurt, master?"

It was the pail that was hurt, having lost its symmetry for ever. Walter brought it from the corner.

"It's got a dent in it as big as a half-moon," he said. "If she's going to come that game, she'll be a trouble at first."

Then he had a try, and would have received a similar buffeting but that he had that remarkable alacrity which the farm labourer can show at need. He seemed to have a prescience of the heifer's intention to kick the second before she did so, and drew the bucket away with an, "Ah, you would, would you?" stooping to her again a minute later and continuing, murmuring, "You've got to come to it some time, old dear, so you may as well make up your mind." In the end, we had to strap her hind legs together so that she couldn't kick, but not before Walter had taken one fair toppler, from which he rose rubbing his shins. " Seems as though she knows I'm not her calf," he said, in a tone that implied astuteness to the cow. But by tying her legs we managed to milk her dry.

I have no hesitation in saying that that first was the wildest of all cows which I have subsequently owned, and my first premonition as I eyed her in the market was no illusion. For several months my farm was the scene of the Taming of the Shrew. Usually Walter went forth to plough and I stayed behind to deal with her. When I joined him in the fields, the first question was always, " Well, how was she this morning, master ? " The answer varied : " Oh, she was pretty fair this morning," or " Just about as awkward as she could be." " The b—— ! " was Walter's comment, as he jogged the plough-cord and the horses started across the field again. " Well, she'll have to come to it in time."

So there she sulked like an abducted princess. I had not realised until then, either, what a regalia of silver-zinc utensils was her due. My little dairy was soon furnished with pans, pails, skimmer, strainer, etc., and seemed to imply a whole herd in the meadow. I resisted the attempts of the local manufacturer to foist churn and separator on me as well. One cow, I knew, was no good by itself, but there are a number of ways of dealing with milk, and I was in no mood to muddle myself up before I knew how I stood. In any case, at present a good proportion was upset in the daily contest. When she seemed quieter, I tried without tying her legs, and time and again I rose from a knock-out blow, my clothes flowing with milk. I walked in an odour of it continually. My pails became as embattled as though they had helmeted Tweedledum and Tweedledee.

I envied Midden, Mr. Colville's milkman, his orderly middle-aged animals, as I stood in the yard of Farley Hall one day watching him driving them up. In the cow-shed, they stood in a row as though unaware that anything was in progress. But it had not always been like that, Midden assured me.

" How does your heifer do ? " Mr. Colville asked me, and I said, " She's got plenty of milk ; the thing is to get it."

He and Midden walked across the fields one evening to look at her. It was just about milking-time. Midden would test her for himself. He took the pail. " Coo-coo, old dear," he murmured, patting her neck propitiatingly, and set himself beneath her flank. He had got half a pailful with remarkable ease and rapidity, and I was beginning to think there must be something antipathetic about my personality. " Coo-coo, old dear ! " He repeated from time to time the apparently magic phrase. It was odd to hear such dove-like tones coming from that squat and grizzled old fellow ; as though he were love-making. Suddenly her leg shot out. Clang went the pail ; thump went Midden ; flop and splash went the milk. He rose slowly. " The old bitch ! " he swore.

The milking over, they stood and appraised her.

" It's a rare strong calf," said Midden.

" Yes, and she looks like making a lovely cow," said Mr. Colville. " Just look at her bag."

We looked at her bag. " Yes, I reckon she'll be a master milker, next calf," he said.

" She's pretty wild now," I put in.

"Oh, she'll get over that," Mr. Colville said.

"Yes, she'll get over that," echoed Midden lightly, as they strolled away across the fields. And she did, of course, in time.

Moreover, I had the satisfaction of seeing her offspring three years later, then herself in calf, make the highest price of any beast in the market on that day. A beautiful thing she was, and a beautiful time her purchaser was going to have with her when she calved, I guessed (for she was like her mother), as I watched her trotting away down the main street of Stambury just as her mother had done before her, turning, or attempting to turn, into every side-street or yard on her way, even having half a mind to invade the cinema, which the commissionaire prepared to defend.

It was the occasion of my cow's leaping a gate into a field of Alfred Jarvis's as cleanly as any hurdler, upon my first letting her out into the meadow after her confinement, that was my next meeting with him. He was schooling a hunter not far off, and, seeing what had happened, rode across and helped me back with her, cracking his crop as though she were a stray hound.

"Well, how are you getting on?" he asked.

"Not too badly, for a start," I replied. "How are you?"

"Oh, so-so," he said; then suddenly, "Garn, you bitch!" to his mare, attempting something fanciful. "Just trying to teach her manners," he explained, then added:

"Never do business with relations."

"No?" I asked.

"They're sure to do you. I bought a horse off my

27

uncle and it was no good, and now I've been fool
enough to buy another, and dashed if I don't believe
he's done me again. She's as awkward as you
like, and just goes when she thinks she will. He
deals in hunters up in the grass country, and I guess he
thinks anything's good enough to hunt on down here.
One ditch she'll jump as though it's as wide as a river,
and the next one she'll go and fall straight into.
No, don't ever buy a horse off a relation."

I assured him that, numerous as my relations were,
the only connection they had ever had with horses
was that once one of my uncles had been taken to the
Two Thousand Guineas at Newmarket. There,
having seen a number of horses gallop by, he remarked
of one that came past a good deal in the rear, " Well,
he hasn't got much chance." Whereat his companion,
who was the sporting editor of a paper, said, " Oh,
yes, he has ; he's the second favourite." " But he
can't win now," said my uncle. The editor explained,
" The race hasn't begun : they're only riding out to
the start."

" So you are the first of the family to take to the
land ? " said Jarvis.

" Yes."

" Ah, well, it's a good life when the trade's all
right. Perhaps I am a bit too fond of these things."
He tapped the horse's flank. " Some say so, I believe.
They shake their heads and say, 'Ah, he don't do the
land like his father used ! ' "—he imitated a dubious
nonagenarian—" but, dash it, if you can't get a bit of
fun out of life, what's the good of being alive ? That's
what I say. Now, my old father—you haven't met
him, have you ? Not many do nowadays. Why, he

28

hasn't slept away from this farm more than twice in
forty years. And those times were his brothers'
funerals. Did you ever hear the like? He's been a
wonderful farmer in his time, but, Lord! I should
go mad. Stand still, old mare!" The mare was in
no mind to stay any longer, and swerved away from
me. "Look here," he called over his shoulder,
"stroll down to-morrow afternoon and I'll show you
round the place, and stop and have tea with us."

I accepted his invitation. His mount, now dancing
frenziedly, as though energy were an electric accumula-
tion forcing an outlet, tingling and shaking from every
muscle, bounded away like a wave at the slackening
of the rein, thunder in her heels. Twice she kicked
up, to the right and to the left, and shook her head
intolerantly. But he sat her as easily as a surf-perched
gull; gave her one up the ribs, then another as they
came to the fence. They went cleanly over, his right
arm swinging back, and then only his head was visible
bobbing away into the distance.

III

ONCE, about a year before, I had happened to be passing along the road when I saw Mr. Colville standing beside a wood on one of the fields of his father's farm nearest in this direction, and with him a bearded old man. We waved to each other, being out of earshot, and afterwards he asked, " Did you know who I had with me there ? " " No," I answered. " It was old Mr. Jarvis," he said. It appeared that he had called to see Mr. Jarvis in the course of his walk. " I'm just going to have a look at my father's sheep. Are you coming, Mr. Jarvis ? " he had said ; and Mr. Jarvis had replied, " Yes, I think I will." I saw nothing startling in that reply, but Mr. Colville said to me, " I was never so done in my life ; you could have knocked me down with a feather." For it appeared that Mr. Jarvis had become such a lover of solitude that none had seen him outside his farm boundary for years. Rather it appeared to be that age had evaporated the belief that there was anything greater to be seen without than within it. His usual reply to a friend who had walked over his land and was inviting him beyond it as they stood at the last gate was, " No, I don't think I'll come any farther," and the quiet tone gave the reason : the simple one of no motive. For I have since tried to lure him over to my land and failed.

So it was all the more remarkable that on that day a year previously he had been surprised by some gleam of sun or song of bird into the belief that there was something over the hedge worth seeing, and had gone with Mr. Colville.

"Yes, that's who it was with me," he repeated. And the implication was that it was a sight I was not likely to see again.

Enquiring further of Mr. Colville, I had gathered that age, combined with deafness, had wrapped old Mr. Jarvis in silence and mystery. A man of knowledge, they said : and because he could hark back so far, farther than any living thereabout, it was as though he could hark back into remotest time. There were some books, "rare big books," over which his silver head was found bowed by callers most evenings and wet days. "I don't reckon any could understand what they were about except he," said the people of Benfield. I asked about them. "I reckon they're Greek," one said.

So I was rather interested to meet this old man, when his son Alfred and I, having walked over the farm, approached the house for tea.

He was sitting in an elbow chair ; a square old man, square-headed, square-handed, square-booted. His hand was one of the horniest I have ever held in greeting. He had a mass of untamed hair and beard.

I feared it was no good saying anything to him unless I shouted, and I was shy of raising my voice to that extent in a strange house, particularly with Alfred's sister, Emily, looking on. Alfred, however, who was never afraid of making himself heard, shouted : "He's been with Mr. Colville at Farley Hall, father, for a year, and now he's just taken Silver Ley."

" Eh ? " said his father, putting his hand to his ear.

Alfred drew a breath, preparing to thunder it again, but his sister interposed, and, stepping lightly over to the old man and putting her lips close to his ear, said in quite an ordinary voice, " He's taken Silver Ley ; he's been staying with Mr. Colville."

Her father, far-gazing, nodded. " Ah, yes, so I'd heard," he said.

I found a moment before sitting down to tea to lean over to the bookcase. There were the books behind glass, heavily bound in leather, with deeply-embedded, difficult dim gold lettering. *History of Agriculture in Great Brit—* I managed to read before turning to a remark of Miss Jarvis's. And after tea the old man unlocked the case and drew out a book and sat reading it close under the lamp. I saw that the pages were double-columned and the print very small. It looked of venerable import. That and his attitude over it, magnifying-glass to eye, had been enough, I gathered, for the picturesque rural mind to make a mystery of, without enquiring more closely. So that was his Greek ! At any rate, he looked a Socrates.

Son and daughter were curiously dissimilar in appearance. He was florid ; she was pale. He looked like growing from broad to portly ; she from slender to thin.

Emily Jarvis, whom I had met once or twice at tea parties at Farley Hall, was a little younger than her brother ; about twenty-one or twenty-two, I gathered. She, I had already discovered, had a taste for reading and music. She, like her father, harked back in her reading, but it was to Courts and Society of the past, not farming. I was surprised to find Creevy and De Retz there, and *Bath under Beau Nash*. Her sadness was betrayed by her smile, and her smile, which was frequent, seemed her pride in not importuning the great world to take her hence.

Her mother was dead and she kept house there. She played the organ in a church on Sundays, snatched an occasional visit to London for a concert. "But I can't leave father for more than a day, of course," she said. I glanced at him, forgetting for a moment that he was deaf, but there he sat, lens and book in his lap, gazing straight in front of him, numbed to the world by his deafness as his hand by its horny layer of skin; oblivious, it seemed, of the ministrations that kept him going.

"Father's wonderful independent," said Alfred to me. "Whatever he wanted done he's always been used to doing himself, so he hates to have to be obliged to anybody for anything, even to-day. He wouldn't ask me to do anything for him for worlds."

But with Emily I gathered it was different. That was a woman's job, to tend the house at home until there came someone who wanted her to be his wife. He was far from realising, I suppose, that he had given birth to someone of a different calibre from a would-be farmer's wife. The turn of the head, the flowing sleeve, the hand's way with the tea-cup, spoke to me of drawing-rooms I had known, and other hostesses.

"You are settling into your little farm?" she asked.

"I am beginning to feel quite at home there," I answered.

"You like it, then?"

I said I liked it very well.

She paused and knit her brows slightly, as though puzzled, and seemed to consider. Then she asked point-blank :

" But why did you come here ? "

" Why, of course, to farm."

" Yes, but I mean why choose to settle right out here ? You came to Farley Hall for your health, I expect."

" Oh, it is not as bad as all that," I laughed.

She flushed. " I didn't mean to suggest that you were ill, only that . . ."

" I don't look ill, do I ? "

" No, not now. I think your year with Mr. Colville has done you a great deal of good. Only now . . ."

" Now the natural thing for me to do is to return to town, you mean ? "

" Well, you have your life ; it's not as though you were middle-aged and retiring."

" Far from that. But is it odd to want to make farming one's life ? "

" Not for some people."

" But for me ? "

" Well, you are . . . clever."

" Far from it ; I never got beyond the fifth form at school, and I was bottom in everything to do with figures. Where could you have got that idea from ? "

" Well, your father is a literary man and your home is in Chelsea ; what wonderful associations it has. I should love to have lived there ! "

" Its associations are all right, but nowadays you meet ladies who wear trousers there, or very short skirts—and one forgets the associations."

34

Emily was wearing a long skirt herself, old-fashioned then, which her hand involuntarily stretched a little nearer to her ankle as she sat cross-legged. Her brother had gone out with a lantern to tend a horse. It was now quite dark outside. Her father had resumed his reading.

"Ah, London," said Emily softly, fire-gazing, as though all desire was ended in that word. Then she looked at me, still doubting, it seemed, that anyone could forsake Chelsea for Benfield for no other reason than that they wanted to.

"You paint, don't you?"

"Not I."

"Then you write."

"Letters occasionally, when they are overdue."

"I mean, poetry."

I shook my head. "Not now."

"But you have done?" She pursued the sudden clue.

"It was rubbish and a waste of time."

"I believe you have had poetry published."

I became specific. "The whole of my published works amounts to one sonnet in the *Westminster Gazette*."

"I should like to see it," she said.

"I have lost it," I lied.

"So now you want to be a farmer."

"I am a farmer . . . or don't you think I shall be very good at it?"

"I'm sure you'll do very well. But I can't help feeling it's a pity, if you've a brain for other things. People are usually farmers because they haven't been brought up to anything else."

"I assure you it takes all the brain I've got. And I'm sure I don't know what else I could be."

"You are too modest."

"Not at all. Why, only yesterday I went to start a bit of hedging and I found I'd gone and bought a left-handed bill-hook. I admit the difference is only a matter of which side the blade is ground, but still, after a year's apprenticeship, and with both eyes open . . . Such things don't give one too high an opinion of oneself."

She laughed at that, and there was silence for a minute.

"I am afraid you don't believe I shall stay farming for long."

She smiled. "Well, we have seen London people come and go before."

"And you can see nothing to show that I shall be an exception to the rule?"

She shook her head. "You will feel lonely, and return to your friends and London."

"London is the loneliest place in the world. Either that or there are so many people dropping in that you can't call your life your own."

"But the concerts, the art-galleries, the plays . . ."

"One can have too much art. One gets so that one longs to see something that isn't spun out of somebody's brain ; a field of mangolds, or dawn that an artist daren't paint because it would be called sentimental. Art is in a curious state," I added—this was a matter on which I felt strongly, and probably wrongly—"when a man isn't allowed to paint a sunset because it is too beautiful." But I don't think she quite saw what I was driving at, and I reconsidered,

Why should I disturb the tranquillity of the fireside with the snarl of controversy? and desisted, saying only : " One gets a keener pleasure from these things for seeing them the less frequently and living in the fields meanwhile. In fact," I added, " it would be a greater pleasure to me to hear you play a little Chopin in the drawing-room here than to be confronted by the whole orchestra of the Queen's Hall. Will you ? "

" Oh, my music is only a pastime," she said, " but if you like I will. I'll go and light the lamp in the drawing-room."

She rose and went out, leaving me alone with her father. He had laid down his reading again and might be watching, for all I could tell, his own reflection in the glass of the bookcase or engaged upon a vision of his own farm in the year eighteen-something-or-other. But I determined to wake the old man to the fact that he had a daughter of note, if lungs could do it.

" Miss Jarvis is very clever," I cried ; " she plays the piano beautifully."

I detected a movement in the hedge-like brows ; they seemed to knit together.

" Miss Jarvis plays the . . ." I began again, but he interrupted me, saying quietly, " Yes, I like to hear her play."

I stared a moment. " But can you hear her ? " I was surprised into ejaculating.

" I can hear music better than I can hear talk, mostly," he said.

I was never able to discover exactly how much that old man could or couldn't hear. His daughter seemed the one person in easy communication with him.

37

His son Alfred entered. Water glistened in his hair. "Raining again," he said (it had been a wet week). "The blooming mud's as bad as though it were January instead of October. Damn the old heavy-land!" he cried. "Give me the grass country—Market Harboro'." He lingered over the name. "God's own country, that is," he added. "Post-and-rails country; you can jump everything flying. Clean going. Horses are up to their hocks in mud all the time here. I've got a cousin near Market Harboro'. Goes like steam. He's got a grassland farm. He wanted me to join him, but father was getting old and couldn't see after things here. He'd never shift. Otherwise I shouldn't stay about here long."

His father, who had sat half-turned away this while, now for the first time addressed a remark to me of his own accord.

"You've bought that place, I believe."

"Yes," I answered.

He shook his head. "I shouldn't have bought just now."

"Why not?" I asked, forgetting to shout it. He did not hear. "Why not?" I repeated loudly. He did not look up from his book. But he had so much the air of a prophet speaking the fruits of experience (aided by his turbulent hair), and there was such a bass-note undertone of foreboding in his voice, that I couldn't rest without knowing the grievousness of my error.

"Why not buy?" I cried, wanting to take him by the shoulder. His eye remained glued to his lens. Alfred, however, did tap him on the shoulder:

"He says, 'Why not buy now?'"

Mr. Jarvis lifted his head, and seemed to go back in his mind as though the question had occurred fifty years ago.

"I remember after the Russian War land kept going down for seven years, and it will do the same after the last war," he said.

"But the Corn Production Act," I objected.

"The Corn Production Act"—Alfred passed it on.

"Corn Production Act . . . ?" The old man repeated the words half strangely. He shook his head. He had no faith in Corn Production Acts.

Emily then opened the door, and we followed her into the drawing-room. It was a cold-coloured rather frilly apartment, and our intrusion seemed to startle it out of a trance that could bear only the tinkle of tea-cups on Sunday afternoons. The fire burned with a tidiness that indicated recent lighting, and still crackled. The coals as yet seemed to sit on the flames rather than minister to them. I hoped inwardly that I had not caused untoward domestic activity by my simple request for a tune. The mantel-shelf contained some of those feathery or parchment-like things in vases which were the stiff ghosts of forgotten summers. The chairs were carefully anti-macassared. In fact, it was a perfect Victorian room, just now derided and in time to become, perhaps, the delight of connoisseurs.

"It's as mother left it," said Emily. "Father wouldn't like it altered"—as though sensing that I thought the room out-of-date. But so was she, though she didn't know it.

Father sat himself down near the piano; Alfred and I sat on a sofa, and when the music superseded

conversation he buried himself in a copy of the
Sporting and Dramatic News. Emily had lighted
the candles at the piano, whose effulgence enhanced
the old ivory of the keyboard and by its particular
steadfast and gentle tone seemed to enshrine that
within its small radius into itself; sequestering her
from us as into an altar-region. She touched music
into being, which took the mind afloat on its stream
and drifted it so far that to one's still-gazing eyes she
herself was but a grace of dark hair, neck, and shoulder.

A nudge from Alfred, and I found a page of the
Sporting and Dramatic before me. "Now, however
did that chap get back into the saddle from that
position?" he muttered *sotto voce*. The picture was of
a steeplechase jump: horses with legs like flung
clothes-props going over, one nearly on its nose and
rider all awry. "He didn't come off, it says." He
read, "Pecked badly, but recovered and won by a
head."

I could not suggest how, and Alfred continued to
gaze at the picture awhile. "Damn marvellous, I
call it!" he muttered, as he turned over.

It had been Chopin first, because I had said Chopin,
whom to this day I unblushingly enjoy. Then there
was Brahms, which, though more difficult, she played
with equal accomplishment, I thought. She had
clearly gone beyond the convention of art as an expression of femininity. But then I could see she had
gone far beyond those drawing-room symbols of
refinement, that obeisance to the ideal of ladyhood
which yeomen's daughters usually made, and then,
marrying, rolled up their sleeves to the dairying or
went out, gum-booted, to the poultry yard light of

40

heart. Perhaps inadvisably beyond, with her De Retz and her dreams, even to the verge of reality and of knowing herself an exile.

The page Alfred had now before him portrayed a lady sitting on a rock drying herself after bathing. The towel was slight enough to reveal romanticised breast and hip and knee. His expression bore a critical aloofness. The next page, though, contained a photograph of people lying about on a Continental beach, which gave a different version of the feminine figure. But there were no more horses, and the light was dim, so he pushed the magazine aside. Indeed, the lamp which hung from the ceiling consisted of the ramifications on an iron vine, in the midst of which lived a gleam almost religiously small and still. It was gemmed with ruby glass around, and put me in mind of lamps which hung above the altar of a church I used to be taken to as a child by an aunt who thought my religious education had been neglected, the which had fascinated me by their small treasures of flames, at which I gazed through my fingers when I ought to have been praying, trying to grasp the wonder of that divine light, for it never occurred to me to doubt that God kept them burning, and when I discovered that he withheld even that small miracle from this mysterious and fragrant service, and that they required oil and wick-trimming just as those in my aunt's pantry, I began to suspect that the business was rather a hoax.

Perhaps it was Schubert's " Cradle Song," which Emily was then playing, which recalled to me my childhood. Her father leaned closer, his hand to his ear. As the last note died away, he said, " Yes, I like that bit of music best." Emily rose from the piano then, and closed the lid. "That's one of the first bits you used to play," he added. She nodded and smiled at him. His attitude of attention relaxed, and he retired into himself again and became stony-visaged. "He always likes me to play that," Emily said to me. "And always says exactly the same thing after it," put in Alfred.

I thanked her for playing. "You must practise a great deal," I said.

"Well, a fair amount," she admitted. "You see, I really love music."

The fire was burning ruddily now. We gathered round it, and a maid brought in refreshments.

IV

On Fridays in the village of Benfield St. George there
was a Bank. A brass plate, teased by a late rose on a
long briar, said so. It was open from two till four
p.m. It was at the house of Mr. Raliffe, a Georgian
house with four steps and two white pillars. Or
rather, it was Georgian-fronted. Behind the square
façade lay three soft-red mountain ranges of Tudor
roof, plaster walls, and overpeering eaves. Doubtless
someone living there long ago, and being something
of a gentleman (for it was a fair-sized house), had had
his serenity shattered by the sudden misgiving that
his house was becoming old-fashioned, and that the
gentry were living now in houses that were square and
high. So he had spent a considerable amount of
money in putting a new face on it, which tried to
pretend that it had a whole house in the same style
behind, and not a gable or leaded window or anything
in the nature of cottage architecture. But he and his
sons were in their graves, and the conglomerate
house, looking like a squire who had married his
dairy-maid, was but a piece of social history, both the
front and the rear being now old and their difference
only a matter of degree.

Mr. Raliffe, who lived there, was the income-tax
and rate collector of the district, but, despite his
thankless task, made the more so as times got worse,
he was a good friend to the farmers, guiding them
through the intricacies of the hundred and one official
forms that successive Governments required them to

fill in and return " within fourteen days," footnoted with heavily underlined penalties for non-compliance. Year after year these things came at them in increasing numbers like flies about the flanks of cattle, and with the same effect, particularly as they felt that those who sent them understood little and cared less about their case. Why, they argued, is the Government so anxious to have an exact report of agricultural stock and crops, and at the same time shows no concern as to whether the business falls into ruin or not ?

Mr. Raliffe soothed their exasperations, all but guiding their hands over the paper ; advised, and urged their case with those stony-hearted ones above him, pleading for patience in the matter of payments. There was eternal summer in his face, ripeness of complexion and golden glint of hair, but an anxious " Ah . . . ! " and a puckering of the brow and distant gaze over the fields when one discussed the future with him. He entered my gate one morning, saying cheerfully : " I am afraid I am not a very welcome visitor, as a rule," and brought a demand for land tax from his pocket.

But on Fridays he was a Bank manager, and sat at home in the " Office." One of the Banks had a branch establishment there for the convenience of farmers. A baize cloth on the table, a framed advertisement of the Dominion Fire Insurance Society and a safe, gave something of an official appearance to the room, which a blazing fire and a loudly ticking clock contradicted. In the depths of winter, those that had come far would stand by the fire saying to others : " No, you be served first ; I'm in no hurry," as they warmed their toes.

I had deposited two hundred pounds with Mr. Raliffe, and opened an account at his Bank, on coming to my farm, and it was an October afternoon, full of the soft glamour of hardly dispelled mist, on which I went to draw my first cheque for wages. There is an air of fulfilment and rest in the landscape and brooding weather of October. It is like a ghost of summer evening all the time; the faint spears of shadow, the sun's shield tarnished and hanging low, and under the trees, instead of shade, pools of their fallen colours. The fields, being mostly stubble, have still the straw-gold light of summer, but the ploughs move there, as in the very afterglow of harvest, and the earth is gradually revealed again that has not been seen since spring. Other men are at work cementing and closing in the gains of the year against the weather turning enemy. The thatcher mounts his ladder many times with his burden of straw, roofing the corn built to be its own storehouse : over the hedge, the spade of the man earthing up the root-clamp is visible at moments ; with regular rhythm it appears suddenly, slaps a slab of grey clay upon the straw, and vanishes for another, till the long hump is a fort against frost, neatly moated, too, where the earth has been cut out. The hedger is there also, defeating the hedge in its summer attempt to usurp a yard of the field all round ; it is still warm enough for shirt-sleeves, working, and he is a summer figure yet. The farmer, with his gun and dog, is walking the stubble for partridges before they get too wild, to prove to himself that he has not lost his aim since January last, nor his dog her nose. As to the city man his tennis-racquet as he takes it down on a summer's evening, his business done, so to the farmer his gun in the evening glow of autumn. He goes out with it, but for survey of his fields as much as to shoot. He never closes both eyes to his job. The eye he doesn't aim with is seeing that another harrowing is necessary here for wheat.

All harvest the men have been working as one gang in the fields, but now they are apart at different jobs again, working alone all day, many of them, observing different meal-times; labourers having dinner at one, ploughmen at two-thirty; the cheerful fellowship of the summer is over, and its many voices. No coloured pinafores in the fields either, fluttering like blown petals, for the children have gone back to school. There the youngster of thirteen sits immured, learning to spell, but dreaming of how he drove two horses and a loaded wagon in the hot days, which he considers the only work worthy of a man such as he. His teacher finds him obstinate and dull.

Standing about the door of the Bank that afternoon were a pony and trap, a car, two bicycles, a greyhound, and a retriever whom I recognised as Mr. Colville's. The window was open at the bottom, and on the sill a great potato, golden-clean, rested on a sheet of note-paper. An unusual display for a Bank, I thought.

" Have you ever seen a potato to equal that?" asked Mr. Raliffe as I entered, and stooped again to his work, much as though it were an entertainment provided for his clients to while away the time until their turns came. I joined the group inspecting it, who, having become familiar with the wonder, already assumed something of a proprietary interest in showing it to me.

" What would you say the weight of it was?"

asked Mr. Raliffe, between the counting of the money.

It was the kind of question that I fear. How often have I been faced with something about the value, size, and weight of which I was entirely ignorant on the one hand, and on the other the bright, expectant eyes of my interlocutor bent on springing his little surprise. Marooned in that silence, I have debated uncomfortably with myself as to the kind of guess expected of me. Always my chief fear has been that I should put it too high (for the prodigious nature of the object necessitates an estimate above the average) and so rob the owner of his moment of triumph, which I would not do for the world. This has often led me to say something too low, which also takes the edge off the *dénouement* by betraying my ignorance of the usual weight, size, and value of the thing in question.

The others, I presumed, had all had their guesses about the weight of the potato—reasonable ones, no doubt—leaving Mr. Raliffe a clear margin for his reply. For the smile and gleam of knowledge was on their faces, and they looked to me to provide a collective triumph.

I let the silence mature, then shook my head and appealed to Mr. Raliffe, in the hope that he would give me the figure, at which I could still express wonder with the words : " I was going to say, about so-and-so." But so sure of my being below the mark was he that he would tell me nothing till I had guessed, so the silence was resumed.

" Take it in your hands," he said helpfully.

I did so, and weighed it up and down till my hand

lost its judgment, and one moment it felt heavy and the other light, and there was only a wild vacillation of figures in my brain.

" I should say about a pound," I ventured at last, and put the thing down.

" A pound ! Ha-ha ! He says a pound ! " The figure was passed from mouth to mouth with relish. " Why, that weigh over two pound and a half. Walter, he was nighest ; he said it wanted an ounce or two to two pound and a half."

" Yes, just two pounds ten ounces," Mr. Raliffe confirmed.

" It's quite the biggest I have ever seen," I said, which was not very surprising, seeing that I had only been connected with the soil for about a year. But the others accepted it as a tribute, and we waited for the next comer.

The man next to be served with cash was a farmer I knew only by sight, but Mr. Raliffe was well acquainted with him, for when he handed a blank cheque over the table Mr. Raliffe merely said, " How much ? " " Ten pounds, please," answered the man, and Mr. Raliffe proceeded to write out the cheque. Then he handed it back and the man took it, and, turning it endways, wrote vertically, his tongue held firmly between his teeth, and in such a way that it seemed that his pen was slowly descending an imaginary spiral staircase. He finished with a determined prod, as though he had jumped the last two steps, that caused his pen (which he had rattled in the ink-pot like a spoon in a tea-cup) to leave a little dome of ink for full-stop. Mr. Raliffe leaned over and carefully sucked this up with a corner of blotting-paper. When

the cheque was turned round, the downward hiero-
glyphic was seen to be his name, done in a copper-
plate hand. He repeated this on the back of the cheque
with the same result.

"I ain't much of a scholar," he said to me, "and
some say that's a funny way to write your name, but
I can't do it any other how. My wife taught me."

I met Alfred Jarvis in the Bank. He said to me,
"I forgot to ask you when you came to tea the other
day if you play hockey. Several of us have got up a
mixed team about here, and I should like you to play
for us, if you'd care to."

I said that I had played at school, and would be
pleased to fill a gap at any time. Alfred suggested
Saturday week at two-thirty on Selbridge Green. I
engaged to be there, and that evening sent home one
of those cards of enquiry calculated to start a search
among the dim cupboards and attics of the house,
for my "things."

I met Mr. Colville there also, who said, "I don't
seem to have seen you, hardly, since you bought that
cow. I see your light from Farley Hall, that's about
all. Sometimes it's there when I first look out of the
window before it's light to see what sort of a morning
it is, and I say to myself, 'He's up before me this
morning.' I'll come and have a walk round your
land one day soon, one day when it is fairly clean
getting about." I was pleased at this suggestion,
because I was always glad of his advice but was
diffident of asking it too often, as I knew he was a
busy man and I did not want to make myself a nuisance. I invited him and Mrs. Colville to tea; inadequate as I foresaw that meal must be with my present

furnishings, but nevertheless a gesture of appreciation of the hospitality they had shown me, especially at the time when I was leaving their roof, under which I had stayed a year as pupil, for this first small farm of my own. I made a mental note to get some ornamental receptacle for the jam, that it need not be placed on the table in the jar; something shallow and fluted, possibly. Not that I minded the jar, in private; its label was company for me, with its account of the jam's " Specially selected " ingredients. Also some paper lace-work underneath the cakes would make the table appear more comely to the feminine eye, I considered.

In the Bank before me also was the inventive-minded Jim Crawley, a man worried by affairs in general rather than, as yet, his own in particular. For he had been cushioned against the prick of lean years by the large amount of capital with which his father had launched him into farming, and which was still big enough to muffle the true financial worth of this or that idea he had put into practice. By the magic of his cheque-book, too, he could see some of his dreams become mechanical realities before his eyes. I had seen them; Robot-like " labour-saving " grotesques, and a fair warning against being granted exactly what one thinks one wants. There was all the difference between dream and reality in the reasons why they should have worked and why they didn't.

Yes, those were days in which a farmer might die and leave his sons £10,000 apiece, which was the equivalent to being a millionaire in our little world. Greater means were not imagined, because needs commensurate with them could not be. During the

war years the prosperity of agriculture had been like
a flower opening and spreading to the full. Now
already there was a nip in that air—merchants no
longer came to the stack where one was threshing and
outbid one another for the corn; prices were wavering at their daring height; but nobody gave more
than a jocular grumble, least of all presaged such a
bitter winter as many of those happy men, now old
and penniless, look back on.

But Mr. Crawley, agile of person and hawk-eyed,
having no importuning "how-to-get-a-living" problem, could not abide in his happy state. He had not
the farmer's philosophy, born of the seasons. Only
Nature's restless transitional moods seemed to have
entered into him, not her patient summer, nor her
stoic winter ones. There was no rest in the man, and
his conclusions were like wine poured before its
time.

"I should like you to come over to my place and
see my new tractor system at work," he said, drawing
me into a corner. "I think it will revolutionise
mechanical ploughing. And I'm building pig-sties
of straw bales for the winter. Do you think there'll be
an election next year? This Government should be
turned out; they haven't got any enterprise; we
want somebody at the head of things who isn't
afraid of bold ideas. I tell you what; we want a new
party altogether. If we could get farmers and labourers
into line . . ." He went on to explain to me by an
intricate argument that it would pay England to sell
goods abroad at less than the cost of production, in
order to gain the market. I remonstrated that it
seemed easy enough to gain a market at a loss, but of

little use, against which he put the saving of unemployment pay and an involved account of cheapness by mass production. But at that point Mr. Raliffe said : " Yes, Mr. Crawley, how much would you like this week ? " and Mr. Crawley seated himself at the table and brought out his cheque-book.

It happened that no one had come into the Bank after me, so that when I sat down to write my cheque there was only Mr. Raliffe and myself in the room. When I had done and was about to rise, Mr. Raliffe said : " I wonder if you would mind my mentioning another piece of business, seeing that we happen to be alone at the moment ; it is about the Board of Managers of the Benfield school. There is a vacancy, and we should like you to fill it, if you are willing."

This took me by surprise, for I did not even know that the ragged and chubby throng with angel eyes but acquisitive hands that made a procession of Benfield street morning and evening, dwelt under the shadow of anything so high-sounding as a " Board of Managers." And here was Mr. Raliffe offering me a leg up into that little Olympus. I expressed a proper hesitation. If he thought I was equal to filling the post, of course I should be honoured to give all the assistance in my power.

" Of course, it's an honorary post," said Mr. Raliffe (I like the word, "honorary"), " and the only duties attaching to it are attending our meetings every few months, interviewing and recommending an applicant for the post of mistress when that becomes vacant, and paying an occasional visit to the school and checking the roll."

Accordingly I became one of that body, and Mr.

Raliffe asked me if I could engage to be at the Rectory the following Thursday at six o'clock, "as we must be sure of a quorum to make our business valid," he said. I promised to be there.

V

I WENT to the Rectory at the time appointed for the
meeting. Mr. Colville and his father were there
already, as well as the Rector and his wife. The
Rectory, somehow, took me back to country houses
of my childhood, when I was just as high as the edge
of the table and gained my impressions, Alice-like,
from that viewpoint. It had a flagged hall, with a
pair of antlers such as I had believed were the only
visible portions of a deer which had been entombed
in the wall; an assegai that I had never doubted
poisoned any whom it pricked; and a hairy shield.
There was the remembered sound of servants' voices
" off." The room into which I was shown with the
others was also one which the child in me recognised.
There was a large religious painting in whose glooms
ghosts might glide. That seemed the natural magnifi-
cation of a young eye. There was a red table-cloth on
the table, and a desk with a shuffle of papers on it, and
a pair of spectacles on them. The firelight and the
lamp on the table, with a globe like a full moon, cast
a spell of cosiness.

> Not undelightful is an hour to me
> So spent in parlour twilight.

The more, as it was a boisterous evening without,
as a reminder of which Mr. Raliffe, who arrived last,
brought in a dead soaked leaf upon his coat, and dews
of rain upon his eyebrows.

"Good evening, Mrs. Maglin; good evening, gentlemen!" he cried as he stood in the doorway.

"A blustery night, Mr. Raliffe," said Mr. Colville.

"Yes, a rough night, Mr. Colville."

"But there, we must expect it," said his father, relapsing back upon the sofa, where he sat beside the Rector's wife, folding his hands into his lap as though resigning himself to the laws of change and decay as well as to the weather. He turned his face aside and watched the great oil painting, twiddling his thumbs the while.

"Why, Mr. Raliffe, if you haven't brought part of my garden in with you!" cried Mrs. Maglin, which caused Mr. Raliffe an alarmed glance at his boots, thinking she referred to mud; a matter in which he was always scrupulous not to offend. But she was speaking, of course, of the leaf on his shoulder, and, going to him, she plucked it off. He laughed as she showed him what it was, and, as the fire consumed it with a slight hiss, "Ah, well, it's a sign of the season," he said.

Mr. Maglin, the Rector, meanwhile was stooping in a dark corner, and there moved a ruby gleam. He came back into the light with a decanter of port in one hand and the glasses, held by their stems between his knuckles, chiming softly together as he carried them.

"You'll have a glass of port?" he asked us, and we did not say no, the strong gust shuddering past the window giving point to our acceptance. We mutually wished ourselves well over our glasses, and Mr. Raliffe, who was always one to add an extra polish to life's little civilities, made special inclination to Mrs. Maglin, thanking her "for providing us with so agreeable a place of business." For, strictly speaking, the meeting-place of the Board of Managers was the school, but it offered so chill a prospect, especially at that hour, that Mrs. Maglin gave us the hospitality of her house instead.

The port warmed us into further chit-chat of the village and villagers' doings and keepings, each contributing news from that quarter of the parish in which he lived, till to my sense as I sat there it seemed to expand into a small republic, helped by the large-sounding names that occurred in it—good examples of how things became magnified by close and long association. Many of the farmhouses were "halls"; an incline of its merely undulating country was called a hill—the most marked was named Mount Pleasant; a certain stretch of water was called "the canal"; brooks were "rivers"; there were "swamps," "wastes," "dykes," and a certain cluster of houses was known collectively as "The Garrison."

We seemed to be a party of benevolent autocrats sitting there in a half-circle before the fire, with Mrs. Maglin's large cat motionless as a church buttress in the centre. Mr. Colville amused us with a tale of how some bullocks he had bought at Stambury Market had caused a local bus full of village women to get into the ditch when they were being driven home in the twilight, an accident from which the passengers took no harm except hysterics. (As it happened, Mr. Colville's was a modified parlour version of a story I had heard from the bullock-drover's own lips. "The chap what was driving the bus, he came round the corner too fast, when he see the bullocks he couldn't stop hisself: his back wheel went into the grass and the edge of the ditch gave way and let him in, but slowly-like. When they felt theirselves a-goin' they old women wholly started a-hollerin'. That wheel never went in more than a foot and a half, and there the bus set, just on the lean. But they old women were that scared, they didn't seem to try to get out, but just stayed in there hollerin', like a lot of pigs in a cart.")

During this story, Mr. Raliffe was shuffling his papers in his lap. "And now to business, gentlemen, if you please," he smiled, rising at its conclusion.

We seated ourselves round the table, our glasses of port, refilled (despite our protests), making an inner circle round the central lamp.

First Mr. Raliffe read the "minutes of the last meeting," following this, a letter of resignation from a member departed the district, and a kind of formal account of how it was agreed that I should be invited to fill the vacancy, and how Mr. Raliffe, on behalf of the Board, made that invitation, and how I accepted it. Then Mr. Maglin, as chairman, made me welcome, seconded by a murmur of approval from the others.

I was glad when this part of the business was over and I could sit back comfortably in my chair again.

"Now there is the matter of faggots for the lighting of the school fire," said Mr. Raliffe. He turned to Mr. Colville's father. "Will you supply them as usual, Mr. Colville?"

This old Mr. Colville agreed to do, and made a note, "One score faggots to school," on a piece of paper.

"The price as last year?"

"Yes," he agreed; "ten shillings, I believe it was."

Mr. Raliffe found that it was so, and entered up that piece of business.

"Now here is a small account from Jennings [the local builder] for two new tiles and rectifying the guttering after that gale in the spring." He passed it round; it was like a complete diary entry for one day, "copied fair"; the deliberate upward and downward sweeps of the letters as an army's close packed ranks surging on; the regularity of it gave an idea of the intense concentration of the proceeding, the curbing of those hands that had been dealing with tiles and gutterings all day, to give an account of their labour. Every action, almost, in its sequence, every nail, every dash of red lead, was set down with a bewildering absence of punctuation and the weighty monotony of a litany. The net cost, when that important goal was finally reached, was 18s. 9d., which I thought was surprisingly little for so much writing. We all looked at the bill, Mr. Maglin saying : " H'm ! Eighteen and ninepence. I expect that's about right, Mr. Raliffe ? "

"Yes, Mr. Maglin, quite reasonable, I think," he replied. It was obvious that Mr. Raliffe was the business head of the assembly : in fact, I was coming to regard him as Prime Minister, and the rest of us as a kind of figurehead oligarchy whom he consulted as a matter of form only. But the next item on the agenda (I think that is the correct phrase) proved that we had decided opinions. The trade bill being back in Mr. Raliffe's hands, he asked, " We are all agreed that this should be paid ? " A murmur of assent went round the table. " Carried unanimously. Then I will settle with Jennings, Mr. Maglin." " Thank you,

Mr. Raliffe." Mr. Raliffe recorded on an official-looking form that we had authorised 18s. 9d. to be paid to Mr. Jennings. While he was doing this, in fact whenever he bent down to record a decision, we slipped back into parish chat and a sip of port, escaping from his supervision. Looking up again, he too would join in for a minute, but gently lead us back to the business in hand.

Mrs. Maglin, at her sewing on the sofa, I think was the cause of this; she was chatty by nature and watched the opportunity for her word.

"I am afraid the wages you pay that man Flinders who works for you, Mr. Colville, don't get much nearer his home than the public house," she remarked to the old man, who shook his head.

"I am afraid that's so. And yet he's as good a man to work when he's a mind to it that I couldn't wish for a better. But seems as though he can't get past the Cock if he's a sixpence in his pocket. It's a bad job when it gets hold of a man like that."

"Dr. Bennet told me," she continued, "that when he went to attend his wife when her fourth baby was born the other day, one basin was the only utensil they had in the house. It's terrible; what those poor children live on I don't know, nor how they look so well."

Said John Colville: "Yes, and I've seen them in the field at the back of the house these frosty mornings without shoes or stockings—eating mangolds. I reckon that's how they live; anything they can get. But they look well."

We all agreed. They were rosy, round-faced, cherubic: that was the mystery.

"Yes. I . . . er . . . called there the other day,"
said Mr. Maglin, looking into his port, " and it was,
as you say, very . . . er . . . unsatisfactory."

Mr. Raliffe, having finished writing, looked up.
" Yes, I have had trouble with the man," he said.
" His house has been condemned, but he refuses to
vacate it. I interviewed him one evening. I think he
had been to the inn ; he was distinctly pugnacious."

But, cutting us short in our surmise as to what form
the pugnacity took, " and now, gentlemen, I have here
a request from the schoolmistress for a new hearth-
brush and shovel," he added.

(Had Mr. Raliffe had to leap Flinders' gate, I wondered ; and was it against that kind of contingency
that he wore a chain to his pince-nez ?)

" Hearth-brush *and* coal-shovel ? " said Mr. Colville
in the surprised tone of a guardian of the public
purse. His tone keyed us up to a sense that here was
our responsibility, and the murmur that followed
indicated that we needed satisfying that they were a
real need and no mere whim of the school-mistress's.

" Er . . . are those in present use worn out, Mr.
Raliffe ? " asked Mr. Maglin. It was Mr. Raliffe's
business, apparently, to know everything ; nor did
he fail to do so.

" The mistress showed them to me. Yes, I must say
that the hearth-brush *is* worn out, Mr. Maglin. It
has been in use for . . . er . . . " he consulted his
papers, " for three years."

" And the coal-shovel ? " we asked in chorus.

But here Mr. Raliffe hesitated. " Well, it shows
signs of wear, certainly. It has a wooden handle, and
that is loose."

"It could be tightened, I dare say," put in Mr. Colville.

"And the mistress pointed out a small hole in the shovel itself. But, as I told her, that does not really affect its usefulness ; it just lets a little dust through."

"Which makes more work for the hearth-brush," I put in.

"True," cried Mrs. Maglin from the sofa, and beamed on me for my domestic insight.

Her expert confirmation carried some weight and was reflected a little on me, I think.

"They will brush the bars when the fire's alight and burn the bristles ; that's the mischief," said Mr. Colville, not to be outdone in fireside knowledge. We seemed to be harking back to the hearth-brush, but Mr. Raliffe kept us to the point.

"I told her to take the lumps and then shoot the dust on the fire from the scuttle," he said.

"Then if the handle was tightened you consider the shovel would do for a while ? " Mr. Maglin asked him.

"For some months, anyhow," he replied.

Seeking for some means of leaving them with a definite impression that the new member was pulling his weight, it occurred to me to wonder whether coal-shovels followed the practice of coals of being dearer. because more in demand, in the winter. But I kept silent, not being sure if that were a possible question.

So we voted the school a new hearth-brush, but not a new coal-shovel.

Next, a question was raised which I gathered had been discussed at previous meetings also, namely the provision of garden plots for the children. It appeared

that for some time it had been in the air amongst the
" authorities " that, though spelling and arithmetic
were good enough in their way, something might be
done towards giving a more strictly technical bias to
the education of these countrymen-to-be. It was
proposed that they should be instructed in the mysteries of the soil to which their lives were to be so
closely bound. An excellent idea—on paper and to
somebody sitting in London, probably. The schools'
managers had been acquainted with it and encouraged to proceed. Mr. Colville reiterated this
evening his willingness to let to the school whatever
amount of ground they might require of a field of his
adjoining. But the previous decision had been to wait
and see how it worked with a neighbouring parish
which had started right away with the garden plots.
Mr. Raliffe gave his report.

" I am afraid it is not very popular with the teachers,
Mr. Maglin, because, when it came to the point, they
found that the pupils knew a good deal more about
gardening than they did themselves, which has proved
subversive to discipline. Not to mention the discomfort of standing about in the cold as against
being in the class-room. No, their opinion is de-
cidedly unfavourable."

Ours was, also, and Mr. Raliffe made an entry to
that effect.

The only other business was to choose the member
in the rota who should be officer for the period; that
is to say, whose duty it should be to visit the school
once a fortnight or so and check the roll. I was
chosen for this; a compliment which I accepted
smilingly but with some inward misgiving, as I am

never at my best when faced with a number of children
of the impudent age.

And so, after further chit-chat, we parted; Mr.
Raliffe on his three-speed pedal cycle; I on my
motor one; Mr. Colville and his father jingling away
wedged into a tub-cart: with flicker and flash of our
lamps on the wet, tumbling leaves, and Mr. Maglin
standing framed in the glowing doorway. It was the
first of many evenings of the kind; sometimes with
summer sunlight hovering between flower and foliage
into the Rectory windows, sometimes, as on this
occasion, with drawn curtains just quivering as at the
thought of the autumn blast outside. Sometimes
we have walked out into a crystal trance of frost,
with a pheasant's call distant yet loud in the silence.
Pleasant evenings to remember, in the days when
corn still fetched its price and the little valley had
nothing to fear.

One day before the lapse of the fortnight (but not
far from it), duty led me to push open the school gate
and cross the empty playground. It was about ten
in the morning. I paused a moment in the porch, for
there seemed to be the silence of the grave beyond the
shut door, and I was struck by the sudden thought
that it might be prayer-time, and what if I should
stride in and find them all on their knees? The
totally unforeseen like that so often occurs to trip one
up. But of course they had all seen me through the
windows crossing the playground, the effect of which
had been immediately paralytic, as any sudden appearance is in the country. When I opened the door,
the schoolmistress was already standing on the other
side of it, and so close at hand that I nearly walked

into her. I introduced myself, and she half turned to the class, who immediately rose to its feet as one child and chorused " Good morning." They stood devouring me with their eyes, delighted at the interruption.

" Good morning," I answered, summoning a jolly voice, and smiled upon them. Still they stood there fixedly, and I wondered if anything further was expected of me. But the mistress led the way towards her desk at the end of the room, and I followed along the aisle between the ranks of standing children, like some high ecclesiastic. It seemed a little incongruous that I should spend the rest of the day hacking at a hedge with a bill-hook.

I found a moment to notice that the hearth-brush hanging by the mantelshelf was indeed almost bald. Then I turned to the desk to call the roll.

" You may sit down, children," called the mistress, and they sat. As I called their names, they rose to their feet and answered them. As there were only about half a dozen surnames in the whole parish it was necessary to call their Christian names as well.

" Walter Barlow." " Here, sir."

" Jack Barlow." " Here, sir."

" Richard Dundle." " Here, sir."

" Rosamund Barlow." " Here, sir."

" Ethel Dundle." " Here, sir."

" Esther Barlow." No answer.

" She has a cold," said the schoolmistress. " She got wet going home the other day. She lives rather a long way off—about two miles."

" Isn't it a long way for some of them to walk ? " I asked, for it was a scattered parish.

" It *is* a long way for some of the little ones, especially in the winter, here and back," said the mistress, with a betrayal of real feeling in her tone.

I signed my name in the book and thought I had done ; but there was another mistress waiting for me at another door—a middle-aged woman. The head mistress I had just left was quite young—in fact, little more than a girl—but a strict disciplinarian, I gathered.

In the next room I found myself facing the real tots—little girls mostly—or they gave the impression of being little girls, being at that (to a man) indeterminate age. All the same, they rose to their feet as I entered, as the others had done and, what was more, curtseyed to me as they gave a concerted whisper of " Good morning," that was like a gust in a small tree.

I liked these children instinctively—they were shy but not self-conscious. They were those that one met walking hand-in-hand, or in couples with arms about each other's waists, haunting the hedgerows in summer, and peeping among them while their seniors fought for cigarette cards under a wall, or assailed the weaker. I had noticed in these infants that there was a certain age up to which they seemed to love one another; and then there came a sudden dividing-line, and thereafter they scrambled and fought.

I called their names from the register : there was a Margaret, a Betty, a Daisy, a Rose, a Lucy, two or three Ethels, Marys, and Violets. Their replies were breaths more than voices. The last of all, the youngest and newest member of the school, I thought at first was absent, hearing nothing, till the mistress urged encouragingly, " Say, ' Here, sir,' Lily." I looked up, and she sat there, her hands full of pinafore, —shining on me without reservation, but not uttering a word.

"Here, Lily?" I encouraged. But she refused to say whether she were a vision or no, sitting alone by the mysterious wellsprings of her benediction. I only wished I were the marvel her eyes believed.

The teacher was one of those middle-aged women with whom a man is on easier terms because they have ceased wondering whether they are fair or not. The younger mistress had shot a glance at herself in the wall glass; her hands now and then gave a moulding touch to her hair as we stood and spoke. All young women seem to do these things unconsciously.

I spoke to the elder woman about the occupations of the children; she took me round the room, showing me their paintings. One little girl who had just dipped her brush in scarlet when I entered, and had held the brilliant blot poised all this while, could no longer refrain from applying it to the paper, and drew it, pressed out fan-shaped, trailing across, despite the shadow of my presence. But then she paused. "Go on," I encouraged, but she would do no more. She was painting the picture of a doll—it was the sash she had just coloured. "Now the dress," I suggested; "what about a pink dress?" She shook her head. "Don't you like pink?" I asked. "Betty's has a pink dress," she replied, which appeared to disqualify the colour.

My movements were of great interest to the class. There were some coloured chalks by the blackboard. I had been very fond of crayon drawing as a boy, and could not resist putting some ripe fruit on the tree

which the mistress had been sketching there when
I entered.

" I hope you don't mind ? " I asked. She smiled
indulgently.

" There," I said to the class as I put the finishing
touches. " Do you know what that is ? "

" A tree," some whispered, while others, bolder and
more specific, said " Apple-tree " or " Plum."

I then drew a cow under it, relying chiefly upon the
horns for clue ; and " Cow " they said, save one, who
said " Daisy." Daisy looked at her, but I discovered
that she was referring to a cow of her father's known
by that name. My pig (identification—a curly tail),
being a large one, was designated " sow." I found
that they knew things less by general terms than by
specific names that they had heard their elders use.
Finally in the tree I drew something roughly spherical,
and paused while they puzzled. One said " Stone,"
one " Apple." Then I drew a few broken lines across
it and they gaped the more. Then I put a head and
beak poking out. That brought down the house.

I rubbed it out—apologised to the teacher—and
went back to my bill-hook in the hedge.

VI

THOSE first months were a buoyant time. My twenty-first birthday was just past; I was a man and my own householder. My work was about me; my fields were as private to me as my garden. My work was arduous, but my mind was easy. My hours were long, but I was master of them and did not have to live as a city man, tethered to nine-thirty a.m. like a goat to a tree. I had no reproach to fear save the silent one of my neighbour's fields should they make a better showing than mine when the time came. I had got the first taste of that fierce and stubborn independence of the farmer which is both the wonder of others and their parrot cry against him when his trade is adverse. The hare crouching in my stubble, the pheasant breaking from my hedge, were mine to kill or let live as I cared. Even the sky, with its clouds as they passed over my land, seemed mine, in which my eyes had their minute's pleasure-dream as I rested on my plough. I lived with the pleasures of hope; and on Sundays it was my recreation to walk about my place planning small improvements here and there, to be done in the future which seemed then so vast. "When I got time," I should do this and that; nor did I doubt the mirage of days to spare. Vain dream of acquisition! Time has become like a bare income, swallowed up by our present needs; they swarm round us like a panic of creditors, and we can but pay them moments on account.

But for a man the air of mastery is his natural element, even though the reality is doubtful. It is an elixir under whose influence he will do double a slave's work and still whistle and sing. Or, if you like, it is a drug which, having once tasted, he finds it hard to be without. And just as a man will endure every privation and still cling to his tobacco, so I have found men that were their own masters, and especially the masters of acres, employ every shift and live in the most wretched way that they might remain so. I began to understand what had at first seemed incomprehensible —why the smallholder was to be seen bent over his task in the fields, evenings and Saturday afternoons, as the hired labourers of the large farmers went cycling by to the cinema, cricket, and football. All the light hours they spent in that earnest attitude, something between wrestling and praying, it seemed, for their mere sustenance ; but from no human master. Oh, the ferocious independence of those men ! It was an obsession, and their minds were crabbed with it, and the tax-collector reaped the brunt of their fury. Harmless Mr. Raliffe cycling noiselessly into their yards ; doing, had they but cared to realise it, his very utmost for them with those that sat in offices afar at tables littered with official papers, as if they were goats that made a diet of them. One smallholder not far from me used regularly to put the clergyman and the Government to the trouble of taking one of his horses or a cart and selling it to obtain their due.

Long shall I remember even the lights and shadows of that first autumn on my farm, the trances of frost, the air before dawn as one watched the earth being unveiled again from the night, the darkness seeming to draw off across the sky like a curtain, leaving the moon, so recently gleaming, faint as a cloud. One wondered what kind of a day the sunrise would portend, and watched for the first birth of colour in the grey.

Nor did I lack companions of my own age. Through Alfred Jarvis I grew acquainted with a circle I had but just touched upon during my year's apprenticeship to Mr. Colville at Farley Hall. They corresponded in these after-the-war days to those who had been the " bright young people " of his own youth before the century reached its 'teens ; those who had driven to dances many miles in four-wheelers and gigs, who had played a less fierce but more sociable tennis, a ceremonial and heroic cricket with his father a veteran captain, the last of the round-arm bowlers, and quite as fierce hockey and all-night cards among the men.

The basis of this upper-yeoman class was three or four intermingling families long settled in the district, with a shifting leaven of those from outside or even risen from below by fortune or perseverance.

Mr. Colville's generation, having reached that seething high-water mark of youth, had a while since downed their hockey-sticks, laid aside their dancing-shoes, and married and gone away in pairs.

And now, with hardly a pause, a new generation stood in their place, laughing and dancing and thinking only of the game. But Mr. Colville would not admit that it was the same ; not by any means. " They don't seem to enjoy themselves as we used," he said. " Why, a fellow will dance with the same girl nearly all the evening : where's the fun of that ? We used to get up to some tricks, I can tell you. It's a wonder we

weren't all locked up. When we took old Sam
Higgins's pony out of his trap and put a donkey in
one night after the Quarter Sessions, and he'd had a
drop to drink . . . he never knew anything about it
until he came to himself miles from home just as it
was getting light. We were a sporty crowd when we
were young; didn't care what we did: we could
have shown these young ones of to-day a thing or
two ! "

How wild that past must have been my imagination
conjectured, building it on his tales; and yet the
surviving photographs in attic corners seemed orderly
enough, yea, even a little sheepish and apologetic in
their melancholy and faded sunlight. Poor glazed
ghosts : one felt it was a treat to them even to have
one stirring their cardboard bones and puffing off
their veil of dust in the creaky attic, and it needed all
Mr. Colville's voice and kindling eyes to make the
smile live on their lips again. How many of those
young men standing daringly arm-in-arm with the
girls of their photograph had been trampled into
French mud, or rotted away unburied. That, perhaps,
came between us and their sun; it was so often
" Poor so-and-So " and " Poor So-and-So."

At any rate, the post-war " young set " seemed
quite bright to me who had not known " the old days."

I turned up for the hockey match on the day appointed. The ground was on a field on the hill above
the model village of Selbridge. Over and beyond it
across the village stood a tall chimney, with a pennon
of pale smoke idling from it. That was the standard
of the Willingtons, a family of agricultural machine
makers, whose great-grandfather had built up the

business from a blacksmith's shop after inventing a new plough. The grandfather had rebuilt the village into nearly a town, his model houses for the workers bearing the monogram " H. W." over their doors. The father had further strengthened the foundations of the business by cultivating the export trade.

The eldest son was just getting out of his car and coming across to where Alfred Jarvis and I and a few others were standing clammy-cold in hockey shorts waiting for the opposing team to arrive. Fair, tall, smiling, he waved to this friend and that as he came along. " Cheerio, everybody ! " he called to us. " Haven't those other blighters turned up yet ? " I learned that our opponents were a team notorious for their late appearances, and someone had formed a theory that the idea was to sap the spirit of the home team by letting them wait in the cold.

After Rodney Willington came his two sisters, lithe girls with bobbed hair, which they swung about when they turned their heads as though they enjoyed the feel of it, and his young brother of eighteen. It was a mixed hockey match, and our team was all present ; the girls ageless in their gymnastic costumes, reminiscent of the schoolroom, and the men putting up quite a creditable show of knees, mine, maybe, being the only ones that bore any likeness to the sunken temples of an old horse. I was to play forward, a place apparently always reserved for new members of a team, and on my outside wing the vicar's daughter. The Willingtons' father was the referee to-day. He strolled about swinging his whistle on his forefinger as he would swing his pince-nez by their ribbon when deliberating. He was a man of fair height and the bulk that goes naturally with fifty-five years of age. He had eyes that seemed to watch for the humour of things, and lips that were ready the moment it was perceived. He gave the impression of being well fortified within himself, and one able to smile quietly at the several methods of life's assaults, because he had already prepared methodically for every one beforehand; a mixture of awareness and imperturbability.

" Just one drop," he was saying ; " just one drop of vinegar on the centre of a mushroom when it is fried; that makes it perfect. Two drops spoil it." He was reputed to be a connoisseur of good living.

" I should think it would be horrid," chattered the vicar's daughter, screwing up her bright child-face.

Mr. Willington grinned slowly and shook his head in time with the swing of the whistle. " Lovely," he said.

" Who've you brought in your car, Alfred ? " asked Joan, the seemingly elder of the Willington girl twins.

" My sister," he answered.

She looked at him with mock seriousness, followed by a small explosion of laughter. " From Market Harboro' ? " she asked. Evidently there was a joke of a mysterious affair in that, his garden of Eden.

" No, really my sister," he said.

The Willington girls screwed up their eyes towards the lone figure in the car over on the other side.

" But she never comes to watch us play hockey."

Alfred shrugged. " She thought she'd like to to-day."

Barbara Willington turned to me. " I expect you

know Alfred's sister; she's awfully high-brow: much too clever for us. How did you manage such a clever sister, Alfred?" She tapped his head with her hockey-stick resoundingly. "I suppose it was to make up for the omission there." She turned to me again:

"But perhaps you are high-brow?"

"That I'm not," said I.

"I seem to remember somebody saying that you had gone to stay at the Colvilles' for your health and to paint or something."

So the fantastic rumours circulated even here.

"It must be nice to be clever," she went on, "only one must find so very few people worth talking to."

I said, "You wouldn't find my cottage very high-brow."

"What's it like?"

"Oh, nice and cosy. I have a picture of the death of Nelson and an engraving of Jerusalem from the north-west, or it may be the north-east. I have rome *Nash's Magazines, How to Use a Gun*, Mrs. Somebody-or-other (in leg-of-mutton sleeves) on *Hackneys and Hunters*: and—let me see—and oh, yes, Cowper's *Poems* (that's rather damning, I admit, but I bought it for the pretty pictures) and the *Little Girl's Cookery Book* because I have to make my own breakfast."

"I should love to see you," said one or two of the girls.

"Quite efficient," I replied; "no comical accidents any longer. You should have come in the beginning, when I first tried to make porridge."

"What happened?"

"Well, the book said four handfuls of oatmeal:

but it looked simply ridiculous in so much water; I gathered that must be a misprint, and half filled the pot. I cooked it at night, letting it simmer till the fire went out; when I came down in the morning, the stuff was pouring out all over the stove. Apparently it swells."

However, I didn't tell them of the morning when my breakfast and frying-pan were ruined by bubbles of lead appearing instead of bubbles of fat, owing to the bacon being too lean to fry itself in its own juice.

" Why didn't you invite us to the house-warming ?" asked Joan.

" There hasn't been one."

" Well, let's have one, and we'll all come."

" Er . . . of course, that would be a great idea . . . but . . ."

Just then the vicar's daughter cried, " Oh, here they are ! " The opposing team had arrived and cut short the proposal. I was just hesitating about the fact that I had only crockery enough for two.

We all got into position, the captains having tossed. Altogether the field made a good show of youth, as we stood awaiting the whistle on that already reddening afternoon among the yellow hedges; sinewy men and nimble girls with unsophisticated complexions, and quite a sprinkling of the Colville generation come to watch the usurpers of their stage and play. I thought surely we didn't make too bad a showing, even against memory's sunset glamour of the great days of yore.

The whistle blew, and we stood tense while the hockey-sticks cracked together thrice over the ball; then a fourth collision, this time for possession of it, and the game got going, all of us swaying to the right, whither the ball had been hit. My memories of hockey were that the knuckles were the hardest done by, but I discovered that the hockey of public schoolboys at the barbarian age was nothing to the mixed hockey matches of after-life. The girls were viragos at it, saying never a word, but scuttling round the men like rabbits; neatly acquisitive to the extent of flicking the ball from one's very feet with the points of their sticks. I was rather reminded of the bees and the drones at the time the latter are expelled. The men were best at a good straight knock or run, but for twisting, eluding, finessing, and turning on their tracks, the girls were bewilderingly swift and exact. The men would lumber about crying, " Oh, well done ! Take it yourself ! Bad luck, sir ! Centre, Jimmy ! " but the girls, with pressed lips and intent eyes, were silent, and as lightning to their thunder.

Mr. Willington, Senior, trundled to and fro, the whistle pouting from his lips. There was something of Mr. Colville in his make-up, the same inspiring quiet. He never seemed to hurry, yet was always there.

I had never played mixed hockey before, and at first could not efface the tradition of *noblesse oblige* and forget the sex of an opponent. I felt rather like those old photographs of policemen being attacked by suffragettes, but, being diddled of the ball once or twice, I soon gave up that courtly attitude and it became more of a marriage-dispute : often she got her way, but sometimes I did, and she was after me like a hornet. But, without tempting fortune too far, I got the ball away to the elfin vicar's daughter on the wing, and she was a match for anybody. Several determined rushes we made together, but somehow the ball got too far ahead as we centred it and their full-back made for it for a clear swipe. Then, indeed, it was the manly thing to do to charge full tilt at it also, and this duty fell to me without exception. I accomplished it with a show of spirit, though, indeed, it was as hopeless of success almost as the charge of Balaclava, and gave me the uncomfortable feeling inside that those fellows might well have had, seeing that the ball was lying almost at the opponent's feet and I was merely a target for the cannon-force with which his stick, raised to the utmost permissible, was about to drive it. And once it did as I feared—rose and came hurtling at my face. Up went my hand in self-defence; it knocked my thumb, rattled against my cheek-bone, and fell a little to my right. Immediately there was uproar; cries of, " Shoot ! Pass ! Take it yourself ! " mingled in my ears. My actions to me at that moment seemed to me very slow, and time to lengthen out as in a dream, when consciousness of urgency is its own impediment. I got the ball, then for a dreadful moment fumbled with it in the mud. The full-back was upon me; I had a sense of my elfin ally hovering near; flicked it to her just across his feet. Now we were past him, going clear towards the goal. There stood a hefty damsel. The other back crossed and tackled the vicar's daughter; she passed to me; I steadied the ball and shot. It thudded against the goalkeeper's pads. But she was no elf: I was on her before she had recovered from her surprise that she had stopped a goal. Her stick gave a sudden desperate, mechanical swing, as though actuated by a lever in a pier-machine, and rattled on my shins. Mine put the ball into the goal. That was the first score, and came of the luck of getting a bang on the thumb and face which I had been praying to avoid. Well, *res severa est verum gaudium*, as was written up in our school gymnasium in letters of gold—unconvincingly enough to those who sweated there at "double mark time; knees up . . . up! . . . UP!" My knocks did not hurt me at the moment, for the heat of the battle is numbing, as I found in my first fight with a boy at school. But my thumb was bleeding somewhat; my handkerchief was in my coat in the side-car of my motor-cycle, which was some way off. I started to run towards it. But as I passed a car, a handkerchief was fluttered at me. It was Emily Jarvis. She had noted my crimsoned hand and guessed my need.

"But I shall mess it up horribly," I said.

"No, you won't. It doesn't matter . . . is it hurt much?"

"No, it's just the blood. Oh, thanks. It's awfully good of you"; for she had already grasped it and was tying the handkerchief round, scalloped edges, monogram, and all. She got a gold safety-pin from somewhere between her blouse and her skirt (women seem to be a mine of such things) and fastened it all in a moment. I returned to the field.

"Good effort," said Joan Willington.

"Yes," I said, holding up the expert bandage: but she was referring to the goal.

It acted as a spur to the other side, and just before half-time they had scored once against us. During the interval, I went up and spoke to Emily Jarvis in her car. Her face nested in the collar of her fur coat. "Aren't you getting cold?" I asked.

"I believe so," she said, "but I shan't feel it till I have to uncringe and move. Watching the game makes one forget about it."

"You don't play hockey?" I enquired, though her appearance alone seemed to answer that question. She had somehow the aloofness of fragility, of one whose "health would not allow her," though I never heard it put into words, and nobody, least of all herself, ever said she was delicate; in fact, I knew she did a good deal at home, only somehow one never caught her at it. Wherever found, she always had the air of having been waiting there quite a long while; and of not running out to meet life, like the Willington twins, with their springing hair, but sitting and letting life come to her.

She hardly shook her head at my enquiry. "Or watch it?" I added.

"How do you know?" she asked. "This is the first time you have played hockey here, isn't it?"

"I think I heard somebody say so, seeing you here."

She replied, after a pause, "It's not always easy to get away. Father, you see."

"Yes, of course. It's a pity you can't get out more often. It would do you good," I added foolishly.

"Oh, I'm all right; but dull, you mean."

"No, no; just that . . ." Of course she was all right. "You have other interests, of course."

"In a way, perhaps. There's always lots to do."

"And the books you are fond of."

"Yes."

"And music."

" But that's different."

" Yes," I agreed, as we surveyed the field, the players, the tattered trees, and the low pale sun of late autumn.

" It must be rather nice to be a man," she said ; " but how is your thumb ? You've got a bruise on your cheek, too."

" My thumb's all right ; it's your handkerchief. Are you sure you don't . . . ? "

But the whistle sounded for play to begin again and saved me from a clumsy question.

In the second half we pressed our opponents. But they were strong in the defence. Time and again Rodney Willington, our captain and centre-forward, bombarded their goal, but could not pass the large lady goalkeeper, bulked out as she was with pads and sweater. It was as though Paris were sending a very homely apple to Minerva as a facetious consolation prize, which that goddess emphatically returned. Once, however, he got it past her, and we finished up two goals to one.

Tea at Selbridge Hall, the large family house of the Willingtons, in a room hung with photographs of groups of bearded men with top-hats and folded arms, or interior ones of them holding books or chairs ; Willington ancestors, building committees, etc. ; probably the whole history of modern Selbridge and the works could have been told in them. Their ponderous solemnity would have been great fun to the London circle I had known, but the present company took them for granted.

I found myself next to Joan Willington at tea. We sat round the great dining-table, and there were auxiliary tables for the overflow. I had not been in such a chattering, spirited throng since I left school.

Joan cried to her immediate neighbours : " He has just taken a house, and he has invited us all to the house-warming." (The Willington twins were what Mr. Colville called " Real tom-boys.")

" A cottage," I corrected her, and hoped the house-warming news would not spread to the entire room.

The comments of the circle I had forsaken would have been something like : " Has it a thatched roof and quaint beams ? " and " How nice to escape from the rush of modern life ! " but here thatch was connected with earwigs, beams were not " quaint," and it was the rush of life that was wanted.

" The only thing is," I said, " I don't know what you are going to feed out of, unless we all eat out of a pig-trough and have beer and coffee in buckets."

" Everyone must bring their own," said Barbara. Then another idea struck her. " Let's make it a firework party, and have it on November the fifth. Will you invite us on November the fifth ? "

Their father, who was circumambulating like a benevolent butler with plates of scones and toast, paused at this little vortex of enthusiasm.

" Well, there, you girls are always getting up to something," he said, and passed on, smiling. He was proud of his daughters.

I had washed the blood from my hand before tea and bound my thumb with my own handkerchief. Joan noticed this, and said she hoped I hadn't lost Emily Jarvis's handkerchief. " No," I said, " I have got it in my pocket."

" Are you going to wash it for her ? "

" Well, I'll send it to the laundry."

" What a lovely scandal there'll be ; lady's hand-kerchief going to the laundry from a bachelor's house."

" Or I can get the village woman who looks after me to wash it."

" She's sure to gossip. I'll send it to the laundry among my things, if you like, and bring it you on November the fifth, and you can give it back to her with a bow and make a little speech. She'd like that," she added, knowing that she wouldn't.

" You're sure you haven't lost it ? " Barbara enquired, after a pause.

I put my hand down to my pocket. The handker-chief was not there, and the pocket gaped open in a tell-tale way.

" You've taken it." She widened her eyes at the accusation, but would answer me neither yes nor no.

Whether Miss Jarvis, sitting at a little distance, heard or deduced what we were talking of, I cannot say, but when we rose from the table and happened to be near together, she remarked that I had got my own handkerchief on my thumb now.

" I'll have yours washed and ironed before I return it to you," I said. " Thank you very much for the use of it."

" Not at all," she said. " Give it me as it is."

I expostulated that I couldn't do that, as it was in a horrible mess that would make her ill to see.

" Oh, nonsense ! " she exclaimed and waited for me to give it her.

" No, I simply couldn't," I said ; nor could I, seeing that Joan had filched it. Through her practical joking, that dainty yet gory relic of the game had attained an undue prominence (as a slight thing jested about sometimes will), and I began to wish I had not made use of it. People came between me and Miss Jarvis; Mr. Willington was leading those of his generation who had been onlookers of the match into another room, where, as the door swung open, glasses could be seen on a table, and a beverage that warmed by a different agency.

" Yes, yes, just a drop," he was urging one, with a hand on his shoulder; " it was chilly standing about there to-day . . . we old fellows must look after ourselves. Not too many of us left, you know ! " His friend yielded as they strolled on. " Remember that match when . . . "

Miss Jarvis was no longer beside me.

" Come and have a look at Rod's new hunter," said Alfred, putting his hand on my arm as they passed. I went along with them. As we walked out of the room, I saw Joan and Miss Jarvis facing each other in a friendly dispute; Joan was laughing, Emily Jarvis was smiling—just.

We went round past the garage, with its two cars and the young brother's motor-cycle, to the immaculate stables, where the hunter stood revealed when Rodney switched on the electric light. Alfred stooped about it, felt its legs, looked in its mouth, observed it standing back and observed it close to.

" I thought there was something wrong with one eye at first, but I don't think there is," said Rodney. " I've only got him on approval."

" From Finch ? "

" Yes."

" Oh, he's all right, I expect. It isn't like buying

out of the district. Which eye did you think?"
They tested the eyes, shading one and waving a hand
before the other to make it flinch. I, considering it
foolish to pretend to a knowledge which I hadn't,
contented myself with patting the animal's neck.

"Come to my room and have a smoke," said Rodney
as we returned to the house.

"Lucky devil! I wish I could afford a horse like
that," murmured Alfred to me as Rodney went ahead
up the stairs. His room reminded me of an undergraduate's at the university. I looked out of the
window into the garden, with its great sycamore, its
tennis-courts, its box-edged walks. A gardener was
sweeping up leaves; a bonfire's sleeve of smoke reached
up over the wall. Within, there were photographs on
the mantelpiece, two girls silver-framed on a table,
two hunters' photographs on the wall, pipes, a cricket-
bat, the *Sporting and Dramatic*, leather lounge chairs,
gun, stuffed white pheasant . . .

"Coming to the dance?" Rodney asked, as we
went down, and "See you at the dance!" cried Joan
from the porch, where the last of the hockey tea were
dispersing. There was a dance at the village hall that
night, a hall built by Grandfather Willington.

"Or come in and have coffee with us first," said
Mrs. Willington, "unless you would care to rush and
change and get back here for dinner."

I thanked them, and said I'd call in for coffee, so I
returned to my cottage, which seemed as humble as a
mouse after the square manor of the Willingtons.
For probably the first time its walls, whose beams were
as bent as oldest inhabitants' legs, observed a man in
twentieth-century evening dress, trying to see himself

84

whole in a head-and-shoulders mirror. The ceiling
seemed to have grown even lower and the walls to
have crowded in. My sleek black and starched linen
had lifted me temporarily out of the surroundings with
which I had grown so in accord, and made me a stranger
to them. I felt as though I were the direct cause of
Nelson's collapse in the oleograph.

I mustered my lamp and all the candles I had sticks
for, but still found I was fumbling with shadows
instead of the creases of my tie. One does not realise
how dim the old lights are compared to the new till
one sets about dressing for the evening by them.

When I got back to the Willingtons', the younger
members of the family were all changed, and having
coffee in the drawing-room, excepting Rodney, who
was descending the stairs. A young lord of life he
seemed, the one to carry on the Willington works and
tradition to even greater prestige, I surmised. But
straws show which way the wind blows. As I was
taking off my coat, I heard his father call from his
study door, "Is that you, Rodney?" He opened it
and looked out. "Did you get that quotation off for
Monday's mail this morning?" "No, father."
Then, after a pause, "But I'll do it in the morning."

His father's brows contracted. "No, you won't;
you know you'll be fast asleep till ten o'clock."

"Well, I . . ."

"Oh, never mind, I'll do it. Go on to your dance."
The old man turned back into his study.

Rodney gazed for a moment at the closing door;
then turned and walked on through the hall, biting
his lip; but, seeing me, he brightened immediately,
and was laughing as we entered the drawing-room.

The dance was lively, with refreshments at half-time, all done by the Willingtons and their friends. A chattering group at the supper-table asked of each other : " Is Ethel here ? Has anybody seen her ? " And they shook their heads and said, " Nobody sees anything of her since she has got married. She never goes anywhere now." On which the vicar's daughter, my partner at the moment, commented, " I can't understand why as soon as people get married they seem to give up everything. I shan't. I shall go on just the same."

I agreed, feeling at that moment that gaiety need never cease.

" See you at the meet to-morrow ? " That was the question that flew about towards the end of the dance. For the next morning was the first day's hunting proper after the short cubbing season. And these people liked to fix the next appointment before parting from the present. There was another grand excuse for getting together. Some would be there in cars, some on horses, and they would make another cheery open-air day of it.

Should I be there ? I wavered. There was something magnetic about their jollity that made the vision of Mr. Willington turning back into his study seem irrelevant and unreal. And the music thrumming us on, floating us over the glistening floor with its gusts of rhythm . . . yes, I should be there, I told the face laughing up into mine. The music ceased. I should be there—probably.

" God Save the King."

The sleeping village windows were being bombarded with headlights. Now the church tower was steeped in light, now a leafless fruit-tree, like a skeleton transfixed in a grotesque salaam.

But, reaching my farm, feeling the horses' warm, enquiring breath upon me as I passed by the yard on my way from the motor-shed, sitting again in my awry easy chair among the bending beams, I remembered I was a farmer with another field of wheat waiting to be sown, the ground in perfect order and the seed all ready. To-morrow—to-day, in four hours. For the first time, I felt lonely.

VII

PERHAPS some may consider the last chapter a digression, with no real place in the kind of story this should be—the whim of a dawdler in the courts of memory. Yet, though they should think they detect the breath that stirs the scene and betrays it to be but scenery, and see my farming as a pretty background for me as I act my " good time," with a parental cheque ever available to cushion me from the bare bones of life, nevertheless I am sitting here in the back room of my farm holding the mirror truly and fairly to that period of my existence. It was the same that presented itself to any young Suffolk farmer in 1921.

No, if I seem to give undue prominence to a side of life which should not so much concern me, it is that several communities form the life of a country district, and I touched the fringe of most of them. I tell of them only as they remain in memory, for times of friendship and vivacity which are our lives (or the ornaments of our lives) stand out disproportionately to their short duration, till they seem to become the measure of our past ; while the days of work, eyes to the ground, that go between, are much less easily or coherently recalled. Those are a speechless recollection ; they are distilled into an emotion. A whiff of smoke, a plumy tree, a horse's mane wind-ruffled (yes, even in London), and such slight chances alone summon the humdrum days from sleep to surge into the mind with all their slow-learned certainties.

One thing further before I continue to those events which were about to break into, and end for a while, my life alone. It is that while in the city the conveniences of modernity are common to all, in the country at this time not very large differences of income made widely different showings, from the oil lamps, bedroom candles of the farmers, to the electric light, central heating, and bathrooms of the Willingtons. Yet the farmers' forebears had ridden horses to great-grandfather Willington's forge. And the Mr. Willington of this day was still unashamedly one of them, despite his wife's strict enforcement of seven-thirty dinner in place of his father's six o'clock tea. He and the Colvilles had been schoolfellows, and still enjoyed many a shooting-party together.

Varied though they may seem, the people who formed my world were only variations on the yeoman scale; there was farming in it somewhere, whether it was guiding or making the plough.

Such were my first days as an owner-farmer. Fifty acres was not a large acreage, but it kept me busy. The locality would not think otherwise than that it was the queer hobby of one who might easily have been living a life of pleasure, with my father as a reservoir of wealth in the great city. Chance words heard in the twilight struck the note—" Him? why he's poisoned o' money."

But I knew how mild a dose of that poison ran in our veins, and I was in earnest. I did not go hunting on the morning following the dance. At six a.m. I and Walter who was untroubled by joyous alternatives, were swinging sacks of seed corn into a cart, and the first sunbeams lit on me walking behind the machine

89

which sowed it, watching the grains drip—drip—
drip from the revolving cups into the hoppers, or,
armed with a kind of pike, spearing away dead weeds
that caught and clogged them.

The hounds, as it happened, ran in our direction in
the afternoon. They passed full cry within a field of
where we were working. The cars of those who were
not riding went by on the road, gliding as though they
conferred the freedom of life on the occupants—at
least it seemed so to one who trudged five acres of
soft earth all day. They waved—wondered maybe—
and were gone. Walter, who had been holding the
horses' heads during this distraction, returned to the
drill-handles. The horses ceased to whinny and quiver
—the thunder of hoofs died. Rooks settled back on
the field, and we started to cross it again.

VIII

It was in the early spring. At the end of a dry March the wind grew suddenly timid, and there came some days of such weather as breathed a warmth into one's bones and not a chill when one stood for a little while to stare at anything. So that farmers paused, greeting one another over hedges, and said, " Yes, there's getting some power in the sun now," and went about in great haste trying to get all their spring cultivation and sowing done at once, as though summer were almost upon us—all except one old wiseacre, who took it as an opportunity for his yearly practice of digging a hole and putting in his hand in the presence of one or two friends. After a thoughtful silence, he withdrew it and shook his head. " No, there's no warmth in the dirt yet " ; adding, " Nothing will grow till there is, so it might as well lie in your barn as in there."

The wheat I had sown in the autumn began to cover the ground, and I looked at it secretly pleased, using my judgment to assure myself that it would cover a hare, as the old proverb says it should in March. The hedges I had cut were already sprouting again, and the delight of small flowers awaited one where one rested and looked aside. Nor was I sorry that the hedges were shooting again, particularly on account of the first one I had cut down, for I had made a poor hash of it, which I hoped the new growth would soon mask. Even the children whose roll I had called in the school knew enough to have made mock of that piece of handiwork had they come upon it. It had really been due to the villain in the ironmongery shop at Stambury allowing me all unwittingly to buy a left-handed bill-hook. I remember to this day the curious smile upon his face, which I couldn't understand. The blade, being ground on the wrong side, glanced away from the work at every stroke, instead of biting into it, so the stems were all hack-marked and split and not cut off nearly close enough to the ground. Mr. Colville, walking over one morning, had paused to watch me, and by his silence I had begun to feel that something must be wrong, which only made me the more confusedly energetic. Then suddenly he exclaimed, "Why, if you haven't got a left-handed bill! I was wondering what was making it cut so badly."

These days of early sun also woke the old men who had been hibernating all winter, and brought them peering and creeping out of their cottage doors in greatcoats, and collecting together and discussing the new world; thus tasting of death and resurrection before their time. The oldest of all, one Charlie, called facetiously "the boy," was the first abroad, wheezing and hummering and leaning agape on his gnarled staff at the cross-roads waiting to catch some-one to whom he might start once more to recount the epic of his life. As he was ninety-seven, it took a long time, and few could stay for more than a chapter.

The birds and the old men and everything that had life were stirring; and, if they had speech or song, speaking or singing. The dark, broken ploughlands of winter were giving place to fields laid level with the harrows and dried to a light brown dusty colour, and

the odour of turned earth was in the air. The rib-
rollers that had rested all winter shone like silver
again, and the harrow teeth shone, and implements
stood in the fields of an evening, shafts shooting up at
the sky, earth crumbly on their wheels, bearing all the
signs of only a few hours' rest from use; so different
from the few skeleton derelicts of winter. These
things are the signs of spring to the countryman
where he passes, the robust toilsome signs, as also
the shining cast shoe and the trampled flowers of the
field's edge where the horses have turned. The
Underground does not advertise these.

But in London, too, the air had a message, and the
bosom of earth must have heaved a little under its
strait-waistcoat of paving-stones, and its load of
London. At any rate, sparrows were fluttering on the
copings and cornices, and there were some blades of
grass, looking very newly-painted, sprouting up in the
precious earth of the window-boxes. This I saw from
the window one morning during a week-end at home.
And I found that they were more poignant there, those
few striplings and a flutter of a wing, than all the
multitude of the fields that one had left. Almost
dangerously poignant, I considered, to anyone who
could not get out of four walls when everything was
leaping up and stretching its limbs. For the country
wasn't like that really. It wasn't an escape, as I had
thought at first; it was a wonderful grappling influence, like love in its depths and darkness. It
wasn't delicate; it didn't tremble; it was like a
blundering, uncouth mother with lovely children, one
of whom by luck might survive.

I had been home several times to London for short

week-ends since I had taken the farm, and had given them full accounts there of all I did, so that it had become like a serial story. As soon as I arrived, it was : " Have you weaned the calf, yet ? " or " How many of those pigs lived that were born just before you came last time ? " My sister, who knew what pigs looked like when they were young, bore me out as to their fascinating silkiness. I brought always a brace of pheasants, partridges, or a hare. I brought cream, skimmed off the milk that morning ; I brought at Christmas a Suffolk ham.

A curious restlessness came over the family. My father evolved a theory that my desire to farm was an instinct of the family, after generations of town-dwelling, towards recuperation and self-preservation. I took my brother of thirteen back with me in the side-car to spend a week of his holidays there. It became a fortnight. He shot some rabbits, got bitten by a ferret, spoilt a pair of shoes and two pairs of stockings, and on having to return to school used oaths which would have satisfied a golfer of fifty.

My mother, ever aware, though never fearful, of the possibility of fortune turning its back on us, remarked that she felt that, whatever happened, we had a shelter to fall back on in the farm.

My mother spent a week out there ; my father a week-end. He liked the solitude of the fields in which to walk and the guaranteed immunity from meeting round the corner somebody who would slap him on the back and swear to having worked with him in '95 but whose name and face he couldn't for the life of him remember. My mother was continually discovering fresh antique details ; curly hinges, latches, brass handles painted over. She even found in a lumber-heap an old black kettle which proved to be copper, and spent hours scraping and polishing it till it shone like a new penny. She carried it back to town with her for our ingenious maid to mend with a patent appliance called something like "Fixit," in the use of which she was expert.

My mother, though, did not consider my domestic arrangements quite as satisfactory as I did. Though the crockery was clean enough, it appeared that a daily help who came in for two hours or so each day had not time for such refinements as dusting and cobweb-hunting. I murmured vaguely about getting a housekeeper, but did not relish the idea of sitting of an evening with a middle-aged lady, like a young man who had married for money, for I could not condemn anyone to the kitchen, which was an annexe. My mother was also a little apprehensive of my breakfast mechanics whereby everything cooked itself while I made the coffee.

"That frying-pan is sure to upset," she said.

"No, it won't," I answered, "because I've balanced it like that every morning since I've been here."

However, on that particular morning it did happen to give a sudden lurch for some reason. It just goes to show how inanimate things can try to make one look a fool. For the rest of the week my mother took over these matters.

It was a fortnight after this that I was spending from Saturday night to Monday morning in Chelsea. It was that day I spoke of when the impulsive season gave little hints of the wildness of nature even in a London square.

"It's a beautiful day," said my father, standing gazing out of the window after breakfast.

"Glorious," the others echoed sighingly.

There followed a silence. Suddenly:

"We must give up this house," my father said, without turning round. We looked at each other with a wild surmise.

"Why . . . how do you mean?" my mother faltered.

"We can't afford to have two houses; one here and one in the country," he replied.

"But you . . . your work?"

(Now I am convinced that my father was merely the spokesman and justifier of something that was in everybody's mind all the time. For a long while I believe the window of that room had to their imagination commanded a view much wider than that of a Chelsea square, and this conversation was but the admission of it to one another.)

"I can stay with William" (his brother living in London). "You and the children must go into the country and live on the farm: I will come out at week-ends."

My brother and sister, just home for the holidays, looked at each other in ecstasy. My mother kept calm.

"You're sure it's . . . it's necessary?" she asked, seeking material justification for indulging in the vision.

"My dear, I know the state of affairs," said my father with enigmatic precision. "My income has not risen with the cost of living."

"Oh, yes, do let's!" cried the children.

96

I confess that this was a bombshell to me at the time. I had gathered that since their visits they had begun rather to envy me the country, but never dreamed that a family migration was in anybody's mind.

But soon all were agog with the scheme. Out came pencil and paper, and in no time a sheet was covered with figures showing how much it was going to save us per annum. The time-table was consulted for fares, and by estimation the price of a week-end ticket for my father was arrived at and added to the " cons." " We must reckon it all out sensibly," said my mother. Still, there was, on paper, a big saving. It was such a beautiful day outside after such a trying winter. The sparrows fluttered and chirruped, and snow-white clouds followed one another through the blue sky like a fleet *en fête*.

" But the house," I expostulated. " It won't hold us."

" Let me see : how many rooms are there ? " my mother asked me and her memory.

A new sheet of paper was taken, plans drawn, rooms allotted, furniture placed or discarded with a thought. But there followed a silence. With the best will in the world, it was impossible to make it seem anything but ludicrously cramped.

" Perhaps a room could be built on," my father suggested. " Or a shed or barn turned into a library, where I could have my piano." (I had a disturbing vision of the domestication of the chaff-barn.) " I have always wanted a room quite apart where one could play without being heard. My life has been spent with too many people gyrating around me."

97

" I must go down there again and look at the house with this view," said my mother. " We can't decide anything till then."

So they left it for the moment, undecided and yet in a sense decided. Our servant, a retainer, was told of the project, and she, too, became excited about it. The clearing away and washing-up went with a merry clatter. The others did not quite know what to do with themselves, being in a state of suspended action. During the day the household would collect at odd corners of the house, and discuss, and laugh and go into distant and speculative details. Then my mother would exclaim : " Well, we must get on ; all the jobs are behindhand already, and we'll never get anything done to-day ! " and they would disperse, only to gather again somewhere else in an hour's time.

My father, now that the ball was set rolling and was gathering to itself every moment more of the cloudy texture of expectation, improved on the occasion by moralising on the vagaries of Fortune and how she is continually jerking our arm as we hold the rudder. " I must say Fate plays some curious tricks," he mused. He analogised profusely and ingeniously. Now life was like a game of chess in which a move apparently dictated by necessity is so altered in its effect by subsequent ones that good may come out of peril, or vice versa. Now it was a great painting or tapestry, the whole of time, across which we crawled like flies, able to see only that spot on which we stood, and so unable to observe the pattern of the whole, and that it was already complete.

He went on to demonstrate that there could be no such thing as Chance as we conceived it, since a chain of coincidences must have been going on since the beginning of time to bring us to our present moment of imminent change. He even went so far as to assert by incontestable logic that our proposed move might, and, in fact, must, in some small way alter the course of history.

I am afraid my mother respected the logic of words but little, and adjured him to stick to the point.

" Ah, but what is the point ? " he asked triumphantly. " Truth can be viewed from so many angles ; each one right in itself. That is what makes it so confusing."

To which my mother replied, " You really can't wear that suit any more, not even on Sundays ; the trousers are scorched by your standing with your back to the fire."

On Monday, my mother returned with me to the farm in the side-car of my motor-cycle. The children had cried, Couldn't they squeeze in too ? But it had been explained to them that this was purely a business, and not a pleasure, visit.

The visit merely confirmed the fear that the house was too small for us.

" Of course, if it was absolutely necessary we could crowd in here, I suppose."

" That's it ; but how necessary is it, exactly ? " I asked.

" Well, of course, he knows best," she replied, " but as far as I can gather the buying of this place took all our actual reserve of cash, so that to carry on as we are would mean selling out those very good South American shares . . ."

It was all rather involved and vague, but such a

romantic spice had been given to the future by the idea of life on a farm as gathered in the glimpses of a few visits, that none questioned the necessity as deeply as they might have done had prison or exile been the prospect. Maxims quite foreign to the true character of the family were repeated : " Nothing venture, nothing have," and others of the kind.

The house was a real check, though. But Mr. Colville, who was never without a way out of a difficulty, for himself or for others, suggested, " Why don't you go and live in the house of Groveside Farm just down the road? My father could easily put the foreman into a cottage, and would be pleased to let it to you." We looked over Groveside, and my mother was delighted with it. It had large rooms and a fine square hall ; was considerably more commodious than the Chelsea house, in fact.

Less was heard now of the financial saving of the proposed step, which was going to involve our owning or renting a farm, another farmhouse, and two rooms of a flat in London. To tell the truth, the family wanted a change, and to go back on the idea now would have made that life intolerably drab which till this green thought had been injected had seemed quite usual and unburdensome. Perhaps I was somewhat to blame in my accounts of the life of the fields ever since I had started as a pupil of Mr. Colville's ; London surroundings leading me on to enthusiasm in the telling. Why, was the unspoken question, should we not share this wonderful new thing that the eldest son has found ?

However, Rome was not built in a day, nor was the Chelsea house sold, Groveside vacated, leased,

redecorated, and made ready for habitation as easily as
the wish and the imagination accomplished it.

Friends were amazed. " We always regarded you
as a Londoner through and through " ; " My dear,
you are an absolute town-bird ; you couldn't possibly
stand it for long," were remarks addressed to my
mother. Some plainly thought there were matri-
monial differences—" Separation, ha ! "—and put
their noses in the air, scenting some trouble. However, it was nothing like that, but as I have said.

Luckily it was a time when houses were in great
demand, and the Chelsea one sold without difficulty
at a good price. I, in the country, supervised the
painting of Groveside, trying to interpret to the
village firm of decorators with their usual " range "
of tints and papers my mother's artistic colour-
dreams, and many a time the master pushed back his
cap and scratched his head on being faced with the
pieces of pasteboard my mother had covered with
carefully mixed water-colour of the required tone.
Would this do ? The man showed me the nearest
tinned colour he had, which was about as like as tinned
salmon is to fresh, and I had to shake my head and
temporise without telling him that she would have
designated it mud. Three special messages had to be
sent to me before the decorator could really be
assured that the ceilings were to be tinted a paler
shade of the colours of the walls.

" Well, I can do it," he said, " but I don't know
that you'll like it."

I did not bother to tell him that we had been living
in a house with tinted ceilings for the past twenty
years.

He implored me to have a new grate in a room from which, for some reason or other, the former grate had been removed. My mother was, of course, for a hearth-fire, but the decorator, who was used to a clientèle of farmers and not countryesque Londoners, could not understand that. And the village lady who came in to scrub remarked, " Of course it spoils the room, doesn't it ? "

Meanwhile, I continued at my cottage of Silver Ley, leading the life I have indicated in the preceding chapters. There were some shooting-parties with the Colvilles in the winter and I *did* have some hunting, on a horse Mr. Colville lent me. Spring became summer, and I cut and carted my first corn crop, but with some difficulty, owing to a wet harvest. My attitude towards the impending family migration was passive and non-committal. It would be nice to have them down there, I thought, and supposed it would be more convenient to live at Groveside with them, as they expected I should. I was even looking forward to seeing how they would react to country life (remember, we were eight miles from any town), and secretly wondering how long they would stick it.

It was late autumn before everything was ready. Mr. Colville advised, " I should get them to wait till the spring if I were you : this is the wrong time to move into the country from London. It's enough to put them off altogether to have to spend a winter here straight away ; not being used to the mud or anything." But it was too late ; the new owner was taking possession of the Chelsea house in the middle of November ; moving, as it happened, *from* the country. The new owner in course of conversation, hearing they were bound for the country, remarked, "Well, I'm glad it's you and not me." On being asked why, he shook his head with a wry smile. "Never again; I've been bitten once."

Now, the reader may think he foresees exactly the story of high hope and total disillusionment that seems bound to follow. However, though all the signs for a while continue to point to it, this rocket flight of country impulse did not fizzle out so tamely; in fact, it soared quite a fair height and has a burst of a kind of radiance in retrospect. There follows a curious if not remarkable period in the history of a family, telling of how it was uprooted from friends and ways of life it had been accustomed to for generations, and transported into surroundings and among people who were as foreign to it as dry land to fish, and what a lasting effect that had upon the lives of all its members, not to mention the entertainments of misunderstanding by the way, and how far it managed to shave off its corners to fit the round hole into which it had so squarely planted itself.

IX

I HAD locked up the barn, hen-house, and granary,
hung up the keys, extinguished my hurricane lantern,
lit my lamp, poked up the fire, and was now sitting
down to my tea and glad to be in, for the evening was
raw and misty, as it had been all day. The day was
the one originally fixed for the removal of all our goods
from Chelsea to Groveside, and, had there not been
an impenetrable fog, I was to have expected them
early in the afternoon. But of course they did not
appear, and I took it for granted they had abandoned
the attempt for that day.

I was glad of it, for it was no weather for shifting
furniture about bare apartments, with all doors wide
open and the chill driving through : no, the fireside
of one's settled home was the only place one had heart
for, and no more generous communication with outer
darkness than sealed doors and windows admitted
through their chinks, where alone a sly air hovered.
I was congratulating myself on this—in fact, was just
knifing the crown off my egg—when the air gradually
grew alive with a deep murmur which increased to a
rude clatter. I paused in horrid premonition, my
eyes fixed on the clock, which said ten to six. Surely
not at this hour ? But only too surely it was. The
hoped-for diminuendo of that clatter did not take
place ; it was obvious that a heavy motor vehicle
had paused outside. I rose, opened the front door,
and went to the gate. There were lights in the

fog, and a man's voice called out, " Are we near Benfield ? "

" Why, yes," I answered. " Where are you making for ? "

But before he could reply, I heard my mother's voice call my name, and cry, " Is that you ? "

Then I went closer, and saw her sitting up there beside the driver of the van, wrapped to the chin and looking small and wan with cold. Behind her peered out the gaunt, Wellington-nosed visage of our servant from between tarpaulin curtains as she sat somewhere among the furniture piled within.

" But why on earth——? " I began. " I never dreamed for a moment you'd come to-day—not at this hour."

" We have been travelling since ten o'clock this morning," said my mother. " It's been an awful journey, and we're frozen."

" But why ever did you start ? "

" They are so full up with removals, they said if they didn't go to-day they didn't know when they could fit it in. But I'm so glad we've found you."

" Well, come inside. I've got a fire and some tea."

" But we can't," she almost wailed. " The men have got to start unloading at once. They've got to get back to another job to-morrow."

" Unload to-night ? " I shouted violently above the noise of the engine. But then, seeing the futility of further parley there in the fog, with everyone's nerves on edge, I resigned myself. " All right, I'll be down there with the key of the house in a moment."

The van moved off down the road, and a second one behind it. I relit my hurricane lantern, and

followed on foot with the key of Groveside. " Grave-
side " I felt like calling it as I tramped along, furious
with events which had led to my mother's prolonged
exposure. It was so like her to deny herself even a
cup of tea and a warm fire to expedite matters on others'
account. I would willingly have had the whole
caravan struck by lightning and consumed utterly
—furniture, removal men, servant, and all—that it
might have left her free to come and sit comfortably
with me in my cottage. It was a moment of real
bitterness, and being inclined to extravagant vehem-
ence when roused, I then heartily cursed the whole
scheme, its originators, seconders, and all persons and
things that hindered her from sitting in peace.

However, I had now arrived at Groveside, which
was but half a mile down the road from Silver Ley,
past the Jarvis's farm, and put vain lamentations out
of my mind. The first van was stretched across the
narrow road in an attempt to back itself through
the gate up to the house. The house stood about
fifty yards from the road, and the space between,
though once and in living memory it had been laid
out in a well-kept drive and pleasure-garden, was now
totally overgrown with grass, on which the wheels
could gain no hold, but churned it into mud while the
vehicle groaned aloud and slithered from side to side
like some animal in the obstinacy of terror. The
reader may object that, according to my account of it,
the night was too dark for one to see what was happening, but the scene was lit by the lanterns of the small
crowd that had collected already about the gate.
Never have I known that miracle of the English countryside to fail, that, wherever you journey and have

mischance, even but the upsetting of a pig, in a few minutes the scene—deserted before—is animated by persons converging to view the event, just as though every tree had been an ambush. The sight of anything upside down, or moving when it ought not, or not moving when it ought, is always a wonder, though aeroplanes going over in droves have in these few years lost the power of attracting an upward glance.

There was nothing for it but to unload the van where it was and carry everything across the fifty yards of grass and mud to the house.

So the business proceeded. For illumination there was nothing but candles stuck about the house in bottles and on ledges, which alone needed one person's entire attention to see that the house wasn't burnt down. I managed to coax a fire into being with some damp sticks in one of the rooms, but my mother could not be by it for more than a moment, but stationed herself in the hall, to be confronted by each man as he brought in a piece, and to tell him to which room it belonged. For, though ordinarily the furniture was familiar enough, much of it had been packed in parts, and she alone could say to what piece of furniture a slab or a rail belonged when she saw it. Though even she hesitated at times, and the servant and I were called to hurried consultation there in the windy candlelight, one voting that it had to do with the bedrooms, another that it belonged in the kitchen. Such is the material as well as the mental disintegration of domestic migration.

Besides this there were certain delicate pieces, much prized, about which she was apprehensive, and if I did persuade her to warm herself for a minute by the fire, it was only on condition that I mounted guard and gave the alarm when a treasure was being brought in, that her anxious eyes might escort it past the perils of doorways and crooked stairs.

Yes, it was a nightmare; the gloom, the damp and cold, and the hurrying to and fro and bumping, heaving, grunting all over the house, and all around the black far-stretching acres. Meeting with familiar bits of the London home in this place, trailing so-phisticated memories, by the light of a candle in a bottle, added an inconsequential jumble of dream. It lives with me yet, whenever I pass that gate.

The least mischance was the bringing to naught of all the village woman's careful scrubbing, for by the end of the evening the floors were not just soiled; the mud lay about them in chunks; flaps of it stuck from the treads of the stairs in a way that those who have experienced only ordinary removals may find hard to imagine.

Hearing of their arrival, Alfred Jarvis, good fellow that he was, came along with his sister to offer that they sleep the night at their house; in any case to go back with them there and then and partake of supper. The latter I managed to persuade my mother to do, and she returned, saying what a nice girl Miss Jarvis seemed and how glad she was we were to have them for neighbours. I gathered that she had caught sight of some of those books of memoirs which happened to be a favourite kind of reading of hers too, and had spoken of the subject. I found that this was so, and our disjointed discussion of her and her tastes was the only gleam of amenity in our present barbarous state of mere encampment, with fragments of what was

" home " lying about like bits of a broken kaleidoscope.

At about midnight the first van was emptied. The
second was to be left till the early morning. Then my
mother and her maid set about preparing food and
drink for the men. I had previously got in a case of
beer, and in a little while there was hot tea also ; but
bless me if one of the men desired neither, but asked
if he might just have a glass of water, which was the
one thing we hadn't got—only a kettleful which I had
brought along with me from Silver Ley—because for
some reason yet to be discovered the pump wouldn't
work. It just gave a kind of wheezy death-rattle and
for all our endeavours would bring up nothing.
This caused further blank looks among us.

Water would certainly be needed for to-morrow,
and as I had in any case to return that night and lock
up Silver Ley (I was sleeping at Groveside, as they
didn't care to be alone in the house with strange men),
I took a pail and went off there and then to bring some
water back with me from its well.

I drew the water and set it by the gate. Then I went
into the house by the back door, and made it fast
from within. But I paused on the threshold of the
living-room, for the lamp was still alight on the table
and my tea set round it basking in its beam just as I had
left it—years ago, it seemed ; even the top of the egg
remained not severed, but hinged back as at the
moment my knife had paused. The fire dozed in the
grate, and the furniture grouped round in its familiar
way expressed an untroubled patience, as of a dog not
doubting his master's soon return. It was a picture
so at variance with the cold, dark scene at Groveside

that I seemed to be seeing it afresh, as one returned from a long journey. Ill-furnished as it was, I loved the place, even to the flowers on the clumsy china. It had been the scene of content and of hope to me during the past year. One thing I had overlooked in the family move was that it meant the end of this home of my own. It was a thought that made me lean against the lintel with a sudden sadness that the room witnessed for the first time in me, though I had sat there dog-tired many a night.

But I roused myself, extinguished the fire with the contents of the teapot, turned out the lamp, locked the door, and returned to Groveside with the water.

X

" AND still I haven't found the brass rod belonging to
the back of the sideboard," said my mother. " The
removal men must have forgotten it."

But it was found by my man Walter embedded in
the mud that was our garden after that night of
trampling, which single example may be an indication
of the confusion that reigned, and the indiscriminate
heaps of " outdoor effects " lying dumped about the
door, to which were relegated any bit of iron or wood
not immediately identifiable in the light of a motor-
lamp by the men. Numbers of things were discovered
in these heaps after rain-washed days, which caused my
mother hours of polishing to restore to their interior
shine.

This particular rod was lifted by Walter out of the
mire as he was clearing the ground for a load of bush-
faggots he had brought down from Silver Ley, seeing
that there was not even anything with which to start
a fire at Groveside.

" That's a handy bit," Walter was ruminating.
" I've been looking for something like that to stop
that old sow jumping over out of the sty—wild as a
cat she is."

He was putting it into the empty cart when from
the house our servant shouted emphatically, " Hi ! "
and came quickly out and seized it out of his hands
with such determination that the abashed man

retreated a step or two with wincing alacrity, as though fearing she were going to drub him with it.

" Why, that belongs to a piece of furniture that cost a hundred pounds—the missus has been looking for it all over the place," she cried, which still further frightened the unwitting Walter, as though with the possibility of apprehension for theft. All he could say was, " Well I never ! "

Then my mother appeared and took the brass rod. Whereupon Walter intervened with a handful of straw, saying " Let me clean the slud [i.e. mud] off it first, ma'am."

While he was doing so, my mother chaffed him about his intended use of it—a way she had of putting all strangers, high or low, immediately at ease. Walter smiled and scratched his head.

" Whatever would you have said, ma'am, if you'd come and see that tied on to the old sow's place ? "

Then he addressed himself to the maid (whose name, by the way, was Sarah), my mother having returned indoors with the rod.

" I've brought you some kindling," he said.

" What ! " she cried. " Some kidneys ? "

" Some kindling," he repeated, and pointed to the faggots. " Faggots."

" Faggots ? " she repeated blankly, her mind still in the butcher's shop.

" Some wood to light the fire," he explained.

" Oh, I see—how big they are ! " she added, surveying the brushwood and thinking of the fire-starters that used to be bought from the oilshop.

She was about to return indoors, but paused on the threshold. She picked up the mat.

" Did ever you see anything like that ? " she exclaimed. " Whatever's going to be done with it, I don't know."

It was an ordinary good-sized fibre doormat, such as had seemed in London a boot-wiper adequate for the dirtiest weather. But already it was to the eye just a slab of mud.

Walter shook his head.

" Ah ! Them ain't a mite o' use hereabout," he said. " We get some mud here in the winter. The only thing is to have some old bags down by the door, and a scraper."

He washed the mat in the pond and hung it on the wall ; found an old chaff-bag and laid it by the back door ; and after a little further looking about found a piece of iron from an abandoned implement, which he fixed to two stakes and drove into the ground.

Besides the mats there was also an implement my mother had bought from a big London stores especially for the country—a very neat and efficient-looking (in London) arrangement of fixed brushes, one below and one on each side, but equally clogged and impracticable after the first day here.

The Sunday after the removal my father came for the week-end. He was in high humour as I drove him from the station, and immediately set about arranging his books, which had all been dumped on the floor of the room intended for the library, where they stood almost covering it four feet thick.

Like Dr. Johnson, he was often to be found in his library on a Sunday afternoon, with a pair of old leather gloves on, " buffeting " among his books.

Asking my mother why she was so earnestly

attending to the newly lit dining-room fire, he was answered, " I'm trying to see why it is smoking."

" Smoking ? Is it ? " he said, as a great cloud puffed from the chimney. " Ah, yes, a little. I was going to ask, have you any idea where my old gloves are ? "

" They'll be in the hall table drawer—where you usually keep them, I expect."

He went, but soon returned. " But where is the hall table ? "

" Oh, I forgot ; it got taken into the little back room by mistake."

He departed again, repeating, " Back room " to himself. He returned.

" But the table drawer isn't in the table ! "

" Oh, dear, no, of course not ! The drawers were all taken up to the bedroom on the right of the stairs. It's on the left-hand side."

My mother and I were both squinting up the chimney with streaming eyes for signs of any obstruction, when we heard his voice again.

" There's only one drawer there, and that contains mostly hairpins."

She went upstairs with him this time. " Here are the gloves." She brought them from the bedroom.

" But you told me that bedroom." He pointed to the opposite doorway.

" No, that's my room ; you've been looking in the dressing-table drawer. I said, on the left-hand side of the room on the right of the stairs."

" Oh, I thought you said on the right-hand side of the room on the left of the stairs," he said, pulling on the gloves and returning into the book-room.

Later, on questioning the foreman who had lived at Groveside, I discovered he had not used the room we had made the dining-room, as the fire never would go properly. It was only by nailing a sheet of tin across the front of it that I was able to keep the smoke within bounds, and then only if the door remained ajar. The strokes of my hammer had just ceased. As though it were the magnified echo of the final one, a great clatter sounded from the next room.

"Whatever is that?" we asked each other, and rushed in.

My father was lying full length in the books, with several breaking in a white foam of open pages over him.

"Don't be alarmed, my dear," he said, picking himself up and readjusting his spectacles. "I am not hurt."

It appeared that he had climbed to the top of the library steps with an armful of books; had placed some in the shelves, and then indulged in a habit which always made his arranging of books a process stretching lengthily out from week-end to week-end —I mean opening a book and falling into a meditation over a passage.

This he had done standing on the top step. At length, closing the book, he had attempted to put it in the shelf, but found it and the rest in his arms were too large for that particular one, so would have stepped down again with them—would have, had there been a step there where he trod. For he had forgotten, in repeating to himself, maybe, the line:

"The iniquity of oblivion blindly scattereth her poppy,"

that he had not turned on the steps, and so descended on that side where there were none.

"I was surprised for a moment," he commented.

"It's a wonder you weren't killed," said my mother.

I will not detain the reader with further anecdotes of the kind, for there were mishaps enough those first days at Groveside to fill the rest of this book. There was, however, the matter of the pump, which has already been mentioned. Seeing that it would give forth nothing but a hollow gurgle, despite propitiatory jugs-full poured down the top, the local builder was called in. He dismantled it, fitted new parts where needed, till the apparatus was mechanically perfect. Still it wouldn't work, so then he suggested looking at the well. When he did so, he found that there was a bare foot of water there, and that had been the reason of the pump's not working all the time. It had not occurred to him, he said, that the well was dry. It was only twelve feet deep. The drought of the summer had depleted the water, and the scrubbing-woman had accounted for the rest. But after several deluges it filled up again, and it was no longer necessary to cart water from Silver Ley.

Old Mr. Colville, going the round of the farms, called one day at the back door, and seeing my mother in the kitchen, remarked, "It's handy having a pump at the sink, isn't it?"

She, all her life until a week ago, having been used to taps hot and cold over it, thought the old man had that in mind and was speaking sarcastically. Her reply was an ironical laugh. But in truth he was perfectly serious, comparing it with the more extreme inconvenience of having to wind up a bucket from a well in the garden or even fetch water from a land-drain. Which only shows that convenience is comparative, and what you haven't had you don't miss. Happy old Mr. Colville, and lucky never to have experienced a town water-supply in that it had allowed him pleasure in the sight of a pump at the sink. Which seems to show that civilisation, instead of increasing our contents, merely augments the possibilities of discontents.

The first weeks at Groveside were a period of complete bewilderment for my mother and Sarah, the maid. Till then the idea of living in the country had been little more than that fields were to be seen from the windows instead of houses, and birds whistled in the mornings instead of errand-boys. The result of the lack of everything that had been considered a necessity was that our former gentility was impossible without an army of retainers, which was out of the question to-day. Now I, in my cottage at Silver Ley, had accepted life rough-hewn within as without. My furniture had been of the simplest. But Groveside was—how shall I put it?—the shell of our artistic London house, while we that lived there—my mother particularly, whose clothes had always been of the smartest and notable for that *je ne sais quoi*, that elusive slight " difference" which is known as *chic*—came to regard clothes in no other way than as protectors. As the weather grew colder, old trunks were ransacked for shapeless and long-outmoded woollens. In fact, the whole history of feminine fashions for the past ten years was re-enacted in a winter at Groveside.

For a while a brave attempt at compromise endured.

Change in the evening, etc. But who would go up
with pleasure into an icy bedroom and change from
warm clothes into chill ones? What a shameful
waste of body-heat! That died out. Dinner gave
place to late tea. High tea in our august dining-room,
adorned with copies from old masters in gilt frames,
done by my mother in her student days! Hobnail
boots treading the pile carpets! I felt out of place
in my own home.

Somehow my cottage had been cosier than this, ill-
furnished as it was. The rooms were low and small
and soon warmed; the rooms of Groveside were
square and airy, and habitable in the winter up to a
radius of three yards from their fires. There was
always a shiver in that house, haunting it like a restless ghost, and squeezing itself into our circle as we
sat round the fire of an evening.

But Silver Ley Cottage was now occupied by Walter
and his wife and children. I had got him to move
there when I left, for it was unwise to leave a yardful
of animals all night with no one to hear if anything
went wrong. And he was glad enough to do so, for
it was a much better habitation than the one from
which he moved.

So the family gradually settled to its new centre of
gravity and entrenched itself among country ways, but
still not without a sense of blankness and being at a
loss, and silently wondering but not voicing the question why exactly all this upheaval had taken place,
and what had been the precise necessity. For on the
first of January the decorator's bill arrived, and the
pump-expert's, and a few other people's, and the rent
was paid, and of course there had been the sixty odd

pounds for removal. We did not continue to congratulate ourselves on the financial wisdom of the step—nor did my father volunteer any details.

Not that the family was miserable—it was just at a loss, having been a London family for generations. Excepting my brother and sister, whose Christmas holiday was one long exploration, and scouting of rabbits and wild-fowl, and tumbling among the chaff in the barn. The world was very wonderful to them that winter.

It was indeed a family Christmas. The desolation without made us gather the more closely within. After dinner we sat in a half-circle round a log fire, growing a little silent at the sound of the wind whistling to us over the acres, and watching the embers.

XI

You would think that the family, at least as to its adult
members, on finding itself in surroundings so unfamiliar as to amount to hostility, though wrapped in the
lovely guise of Nature (I speak of the elements, not
humanity), would have occupied itself exclusively in
making life tolerable within the walls, and let the
vision of the farming life my enthusiasm had raised,
and which had lured them hither, remain a romantic
view from the windows of a fire-lit room. It was only
natural that they should have been persuaded by recent
experience that it was no more.

But not so my mother, leader of the family, and
Sarah, her able lieutenant. Instead of allowing herself
to be besieged into patient endurance, she turned
defence into attack.

Now, with the expenditure of a little more money
in the house a tolerable imitation of modern convenience might have been arrived at. Instead of
which my mother, hitherto a beautifier of drawing-
rooms, with all her zest went in for life as it had been.
All the antique and inconvenient things with which
we were surrounded, even those whose use had been
abandoned by the country-folk themselves, she ob-
tained knowledge of and put into operation, making
them the source of new pleasures and hitherto un-
dreamed-of experiences, that to one less supple to life
might have served but to point bitter comparisons with
the existence so impetuously abandoned. In short,

having come into the country, my mother resolved to do the thing thoroughly.

Thus, on Christmas morning, when they might have sat chilly and complaining of draughts and cold stone floors (a bitter day it was), she set all to assist in the great enterprise of cooking the dinner in the brick oven. She had got the blacksmith to make her a baker's peel, and while she and Sarah prepared the different viands on the kitchen table, I was commissioned to bring in a faggot, my father to help me chop it, and the two children to carry the sticks in armfuls to the oven.

The brick oven is just a cave of bricks hollowed out of the wall. When this was full of the chopped faggot, a match was put to it, and in less time than it takes to tell the thing was a furnace. The kitchen was as ample as a barn, but the light from the oven on that dark winter's day tinged all the whitewashed walls with rose. The sudden roar and ferocity of it compelled the attention of us all, and we stood idle for some minutes round that Moloch-mouth from which every now and then a tongue of flame lashed into the room.

But swiftly it died down, and my mother, looking in, remarked that the brick had turned white, as Walter's wife had instructed her, and that therefore the oven was hot enough to receive the turkey and his accompaniments. Accordingly I took the old spade placed ready for the purpose and scraped out the hot embers. My mother and Sarah filled it with the dishes—those that took the longest to cook being farthest in, and those done the quickest nearest the door. Every little while one or other of us would peep in and gaze on the turkey and all adjuncts to the feast, enshrined in their glowing alcove.

Actually and in theory this is the ideal method of cooking—in a slowly diminishing heat; and I have often had cause to observe how many old and primitive-looking methods are scientifically the best ones. So much so, that in the heart of civilisation—the best hotels of London—wood-fires are installed for grilling; and it is also a curious sidelight on progress that these old methods are nowadays prohibitively expensive, and only for the wealthy. The rest of us have to be content with the inventions of the age.

At any rate, our Christmas dinner was a triumph, and what with our labours of wood-chopping and tending the oven, we all had glowing cheeks and good appetites. To my mother belongs the honour of turning what might have been a rather forlorn occasion into a great game by her experimenting with the mediæval. It was one of the most animated dinners we had had, and as for the flavour of the food cooked thus, we were astonished that we had remained so long in ignorance of the real lusty taste of things.

On the evening of Boxing Day we attended one of the gatherings of all the Colvilles in their family home at Benfield. We felt honoured in that, as otherwise it was entirely a family affair.

These things were the first gleam of a possible new life after the sheer bewilderment of the first month or two.

From this gathering my mother, who had now begun to seek on every occasion the society of farmers' wives to get domestic information, carried away a recipe for the sweet-pickling of hams and bacon. The next event was, therefore, that we killed a pig. For this we needed the services of none other than Stebling, the carrier whom I had met at an inn the day after I first arrived in Suffolk as pupil to Mr. Colville, for pig-killing was a sideline of his, so my man Walter told me.

Accordingly, on the day appointed, Stebling arrived in his faded wagonette, wearing the same old bowler hat, fungoid about the crown, dented in the same place, and the same tartan neckcloth as when I had first set eyes on him. In his carriage he had a tub and several curious implements, and a sheathed knife hung from a girdle at his waist.

The pig was in a pen by itself. Stebling sharpened his knife over the unsuspecting creature, at which moment my father, happening to pass by on a walk, likened the pig to Humanity and Stebling to Destiny, but did not stop to witness the action of the one upon the other. Stebling appraised the creature and the farm generally to the accompaniment of the whetting of his blade. Walter and I stood by, to give our assistance when needed. Stebling was a bubbling well-spring of small-talk, which escaped from him as uninterruptedly as patter from the lips of a conjuror.

" Policeman, he comes to me just as I was coming along the road to you, sir. He says, ' Stebling, there was somebody about after Squire Hargrave's pheasants last night ; did you see anybody about the fields as you came home from Stambury ? ' ' No,' says I, ' I never saw a sight of anybody ! ' No, sir," he confided to me, " I never see anybody on the road, and I don't know nothing about anything if I'm asked. I don't say I mightn't have seen some funny things travelling the road after dark if I'd cared to look. But if there's anyone in a field on the one side of me I look on the other side. So I never see nothing. It don't do, sir, travelling the roads alone after dark like I do, to know anything about what goes on aside of them. Because there's some as might think you knew too much, if it got to Squire's ears, and very likely they'd stop you on the road and let you know pretty quick that they thought so. Yes, sir, nice little place you've got here; rare good warm places for stock to lie in o' nights. I remember old Billy Edgecumbe what had this place when I was a boy having a hundred fat hogs in that yard. Yes, sir, a hundred. You never see such a sight in your life. Billy got regular afeard to feed them in the end; he was only a little-sized chap and they used to rush at him so when he went in with buckets of meal they almost had him down.

"Once the Reverend Jowley saved his life. He happened to be passing and what should he see but Billy's legs sticking up out of a swill tub. Dashed if he hadn't fallen in head first and couldn't recover himself; that were such thick meal; and reckon he'd a' bin squaggled to death if parson hadn't pulled him out by the legs. Rare mess he were in. He went to church every Sunday for a year after that. Rare huntin' man Reverend Jowley was. Sought the Lord on Sundays and the fox on weekdays. How he loved horses! True as to God, my father remembers him driving to church tandem and blowing one of them long coaching horns instead of having the bells ringing to let the people know 'twas time to begin. Well, now, we'd better have the pig-rack into the place. Has your missus got the water boiling, Walter?"

We were having the pig killed at Silver Ley and then brought down to Groveside to be cut up. As soon as killed, it was to be plunged into a tubful of boiling water, which Walter's wife was heating in the copper. The rack on which the pig was to be killed was set firmly in the straw of the pen. Still the pig was unperturbed at the preparation, standing in a corner and envying his brothers in the next pen a repletion which had caused them to leave a little food in the trough, and gazing hungrily at it ; for he, being doomed, had not been fed that morning. But those had been driven elsewhere that they should not see him die.

Suddenly Stebling grasped his tail. Immediately he bellowed in panic and would have fled, dragging Stebling with him, had there been anywhere to flee to. Walter and I caught him by the ears. For a minute he struggled against the three of us with super-porcine convulsions that were almost a match for us ; then we jerked him off his feet and dragged him sideways on the rack. Losing the use of his legs, he lost also his power. I was given his hind-legs to hold, Walter his fore-legs. Stebling, with his back to me, bent over his head with his knife. Ceasing his struggles, he had ceased also his hullabaloo, and lay with a pathetic quiescence. No further complaint did he make, and his life passed from him as softly as a breath and with no other sound but the outpouring of his blood. His hind-legs which I held gave a quiver or two, and then I became aware that the firm grasp of my hands was needless, for it was but dead flesh they held. He lay in that attitude of abandonment to lassitude as in sleep, save for a red stain across his white throat.

We dragged him, a sagging sack of flesh, from the rack into the tub which Walter had half filled with the boiling water. He went in with a wallop, and sat back on his hams with water up to his neck, a gruesome travesty of an old gentleman gone to sleep in his bath. But Stebling lost no time in setting to work scraping him, scrubbing him, and shaving him with his thin keen knife, till he was as pink and hairless as a new-born babe.

Then he was taken down to Groveside and carved up—a process which my brother and sister watched from a distance, feeling that something rather awful was afoot, but also very interesting. But when Stebling lifted the head and pointed it at them through sheer bonhomie, my sister fled. My brother, though, taking it as a challenge, came reluctantly nearer and watched the rest of the proceedings at closer quarters. When Stebling lifted a ham and suggested he should take it indoors, he paled, but nevertheless received it in his arms and hastened off with it, not returning.

The kitchen was permeated with the rank, cold smell of raw pork, the joints being laid out on the table. The hams and breasts were to be pickled ; the rest was disposed of in different ways—a joint for ourselves for roasting, and one to Walter's wife for her trouble with the boiling water, etc. Walter also begged the bladder that he might make a balloon of it for his children. The intestinal tube was the perquisite of the butcher (old custom entering even into the killing of a pig)—the " small bellies," as Stebling called it as he wound it up as though it were a plough-cord and put it in his basket. Then there was a heap of oddments that were to be made into sausages (my mother had a recipe from a farmer's wife). Also there was that medley of the creature's digestive system known as "pig's fry," a favourite breakfast dish among the country-folk. This was fried for breakfast the next morning, but my brother and sister showed little appetite for it, while my father refused point-blank even to look at it, demanding a boiled egg, and that pig's fry, if brought on the table, should be in a covered dish, and the cover replaced as soon as anyone had helped themselves.

"Pooh!" said my mother. "You don't know what's good, you people," and ate hers with relish. But she always had a taste for unusual foods, from winkles to haggis. It was not very long after this that she made a pie of some moorhens.

The charge for the killing of the pig was five shillings.

There followed mornings when my mother and I shared the duty of rubbing with salt those parts of the pig that were to be pickled. Pork was cold handling at 7 a.m. in January, and if one had a scratch on one's hand anywhere, the salt made one painfully aware of it. After that, for three weeks the pork was steeped in a pickling mixture of old ale, vinegar, and brown sugar, turned every morning and rubbed with it; also a chilly proceeding. Then it was sent to Stambury done up in canvas bags to be smoked in oak sawdust, then hung up in our kitchen to mature.

Previous to the killing of the pig my mother had bought a sausage machine—a very similar machine to a mincing machine—and after the pig had been jointed, and the joints set aside for different purposes, there was still quite a heap of oddments of pork—for when in doubt about any piece we had said, " Oh, we'll make sausages of that." But we soon found we were going to have many more sausages than we could possibly consume ; the machine kept pushing them out like the salt-mill in the story of *Why the Sea is Salt* that went on grinding for ever. We had literally yards of them.

But my mother was not long at a loss. She did them up in parcels of a pound and two pounds, and sent them to all our London friends as a triumphant sign of accomplished family metamorphosis.

How one thing leads to another ! There came in a very few days a number of enthusiastic letters. Our friends had never, they said, tasted such sausages in their lives before. They had caused quite a domestic friction in some households, it seemed, husbands being provoked by them to wonder with some acrimony why they could not always have sausages like that, with a suggestion that their wives did not know where to buy.

" Oh," said these wives, " if only you would send or bring us some every week, and other country produce as well ! "

The result of this was a scheme formulated in a night, whereby I found myself returning to the family's former haunts with a side-car loaded with eggs, butter, poultry, lard, etc.

Groveside was a house structurally in two halves. A door on the opposite side of the square hall to the front door, when closed, cut off the front from the back. Cut off, that is, those rooms where the furniture and pile-carpets still gave a reflection of our polite London life from the brick-floored barn-sized kitchen and the also brick-floored, rough-and-ready back breakfast-room. I mention this as it corresponds with the division of the family's life there. More and more the back of the house tended to become the headquarters, and the front rooms to be left cold and forsaken, as busy-ness encroached upon the whole of the day. At first we used only to breakfast in the little back room, but later we took to having lunch there, and then tea.

For when you start a ball rolling, who knows where it is going to stop? From that first chance remark of Mrs. So-and-So's that she always pickled her own hams, and the acquiring of the recipe and killing a pig of our own, the family suddenly found itself involved in extensive undertakings, including egg production, dairying, chicken-fattening, and retail marketing.

I forgot to mention that in hiring Groveside we hired also a six-acre meadow beside it. My mother invested in poultry and poultry-houses and set them down on it. My mother was that kind of person whose native enthusiasm does makers of poultry appliances good to see. Travellers for patent poultry food called daily, seeing new scientific huts in the field, and not those converted out of old wagons and threshing-drums, that canny farmers use.

Besides this, another cow was purchased. And now the local manufacturer, who had failed to impose a churn and separator on me when I had first come to Silver Ley, tried again and was successful. These were installed in the dairy of Groveside, and the cows were moved down there and milked in a barn on a corner of the meadow.

All the apparatus of butter-making was bought

—thermometers, rollers, pats, boards, pails; not omitting a wooden stamp with a design of serenely sailing swans upon it, a progress which was to prove not altogether symbolic of our own. But that happened to be a hopeful day at Stambury, an afternoon of holiday after lunch at the chief inn; and the choosing of a pretty thing is always a light-hearted occasion. That particular one served as a focus for our pleasure in the outing.

My mother went to Mrs. Colville and learned how to make butter. Mr. Colville expressed justifiable doubts at the schemes the family had on foot, after having been in the country only a few months. Though without the slightest wish to interfere, he did very wisely hint to the effect that it was best not to try to run before one could walk.

Now, at the beginning there had been no suggestion that the family should do anything in the country but live there with me. Agriculture was my business alone. But I found that after first putting one toe over the threshold they also were drawn into the web; and to such an extent that very soon my mother was considering her part of the business quite as important as my own, and, furthermore, would criticise my procedure in some respects. Nor did she realise that if I lay in bed till seven-thirty owing to work being at a standstill after a night of deluge, it wasn't a sign of lethargy and disgust at farming as a career. I had grown used to being my own master at Silver Ley, and resented any suggested resumption of the parental sway. Especially as I, too, had experienced that work-fever of the beginner on taking over Silver Ley to the extent of utilising Sunday for lime-washing pig-sties.

I was warned by a farmer's wife that I should never prosper if I worked on Sundays. And she was more nearly right than you may think, though not for a religious reason. The point is this : you cannot paint a large picture by always having your nose to the canvas ; you must stand back and see it as a whole from a distance. That is what the farmer does on Sunday. He walks round, thinks things over, considers what has to be done and what is still to do. I have never yet seen a furious start send anybody full-speed to fortune. The established farmers have now for a long time been my model ; they are like the stars in the sky ; meteors and thunderbolts arrive suddenly in their midst, and go rushing past them with great display, which, however, soon burn themselves up and are gone, while the others continue to shine in their places and move with the orderly year.

But I am wandering. The family, after its first bewilderment and disappointment, suddenly brightened with a breeze of enthusiasm, and that enthusiasm was its life, though it had to puff a little to keep up with the rate of things in which it involved itself. Early and late, candlelight lit the great kitchen like a last sunray—and there was I counting eggs into boxes, Sarah trussing chickens, my mother patting up butter into rolls, my sister putting her finger on the knot when she was told, and my brother jotting at my dictation in a note-book ; while distantly as a remembrance of other days, came the sound of Bach from the front of the house, where my father sat alone in the twilight and played the piano.

Every Saturday at dawn I set forth, all weathers, on the motor-cycle and side-car loaded for London, spent all day delivering the goods and taking orders for next week, and in the evening motored the sixty miles home again. People were delighted with the things, and friends avowed their intention of visiting us in the summer to observe my mother's incredible adaptability. Friends told their friends, and in a little while we did not know how to cope with the orders, and the side-car groaned and swayed till I feared to load it any further. Yet we would not say no to anybody; though the eggs and poultry we produced were inadequate, our neighbours supplied us with theirs. Also, we bought a van. It was delivered on a Thursday. I went once up and down the road with the man who brought it, and that was all the tuition in driving a car I had. A driving licence was given me for five shillings for the asking, and on the Saturday I took a load of goods to London. I got into the ditch not ten miles from home in trying to avoid a hen, but a passing lorry pulled me out and I was able to continue. I nearly knocked a woman down in Piccadilly Circus; her umbrella rattled against the spokes of the wheel as a man snatched her, shrieking, aside. Only Providence saved me from serious damage to myself and others. I was certainly a public danger.

I look back on this period as one of rashness and importunity, the quiet methods of my former farming overset, that part of it that had been my whole occupation left more and more to Walter, while I and the family wrestled with affairs of which we knew little.

Still the high-water mark of our activity had not been reached. Our commitments became like a machine which enslaved our energies—and one gathering speed at that. It allowed us no time to turn round ; that was the real trouble. No sooner was one obstacle surmounted than another presented itself : we were so held down to the immediate and urgent that we were never able to stand back and observe things quietly as a whole, and review our position. At times I was visited by that uncomfortable feeling of one holding taut reins that his horse was becoming a runaway—and sometimes, at some difficult moment, such silent glances passed among us as hinted that the idea was general. And now and again in the course of that year we noticed that the stairs were still uncarpeted for want of time to spare—which seemed to emphasise the kind of mill-race into which we had been swept. And all the time our kind friends in London were telling their friends, who in turn told their friends.

Did it pay ? That, of course, was the test. But it was a question not so easy to answer as would at first sight appear, despite the many note- and account-books filled with my rather erratic writing for that purpose. " Strict accounts " had been the firm-lipped resolution at the beginning, and the result was a mass of details in which the would-be amateur auditor could maze himself within ten minutes of coming to the attack. In theory it should have paid hugely (" Cutting out the middle-man," etc., etc.). Actually on paper it paid fairly (remember, our " turnover " was only the margin between wholesale and retail prices—for we could have got wholesale prices at home at our own door), and in reality one could not avoid the suspicion that Mr. Colville's doubts were not, after all, disproved, for while engaged in this enterprise I could not attend to the old farming round, had to employ another man there, and both men and fields lacked proper supervision. How to weigh that in the balance-sheet? Wear and tear and depreciation of van, etc.? Should we have had a motor but for the enterprise? There were a hundred cloudy considerations that would not be distilled into mathematics, and made me understand the cry I had heard from more than one farmer: " Accounts? I don't keep no accounts: my bank-book shows me well enough how I'm doing."

But we went on month after month, confusing, perhaps, busy-ness with progress, and money-handling with money-making.

XII

Autumn, being the end and the beginning of the farmer's year, brings with it a host of changes. One important one occurred about the time the family came into the country. It concerned my former instructor, my friend and now my neighbour, Mr. Colville. Farley Hall, of which he was the tenant, was sold. It was there I had lived with him and learned of agriculture and country life. The proceedings were for a while wrapped in that secrecy wherewith, I cannot help thinking, men like boyishly to magnify the business in which they are engaged. One day, as I strolled into the yard of Farley Hall (it was but a short distance across the fields), a party of men were getting out of a motor-car by all four doors. They surrounded Mr. Colville in a confidential way, who stood among them, his stick in his hand and his retriever at his side. I saw that they were strangers to the district and intended private conversation with him. As I had only come to borrow an implement he had already given me the offer of, I saw his yard-man Midden about it, who stood in the cowshed doorway gaping, as also did one or two other workmen occupied about the yard. A paralysing sense of the deep significance of a strange arrival had them all by the throat, so that even I too was caught up in it, and stood staring.

Particularly this was so on account of rumours that had been circulating in the district—and the difference between rural district rumours and national rumours is that the former are nearly always right. It was as though the very veiled and confidential attitude of the strangers confirmed what the men of Farley Hall had been thinking. It was that the farm had been sold by the local landowner to a syndicate of boot-manufacturers from the North, who were in their turn intending to blandish the farmers into buying the farms of which they were tenants at a profit to the syndicate. This caused much uneasiness among the men at Farley Hall, for the last thing they desired was another master. Not that Mr. Colville paid higher wages or demanded less than other masters : in fact, he was strict to see that " a fair day's work was done." I can only put it that he was a born leader, and was worked for as others have been followed into battle. This sense of leadership in people is unmistakable but undefinable. Often have I been with Mr. Colville in crowded places—restaurants, race-meetings, railway stations, hotels. Not another seat, not another room was to be had, or the queue was half a mile long, and an hour's wait seemed inevitable. Yet, a few words with somebody in authority and it was, " You come along with me, sir —I'll get you in." Among twenty people clamouring for attention in some matter, he, standing quietly stroking his upper lip, has been the one attended to. Even cars dared not go wrong with him. He had one for six years—and the back axle broke the day after he had relinquished it.

" The men are as uneasy as the devil," said Mr. Colville to me one day. " They know there's something in the wind."

"Will you buy the place?" I asked.

"They'll have to come down in price a lot first," he replied, without mentioning figures.

The men's suspense and their attempts to weight the balance on the right side were betrayed by remarks flung out in the course of the day's work, as though at random, they being presumed to have no inkling.

"Best farm in Benfield, sir," the old barn-man said, as Mr. Colville commented with satisfaction on some newly threshed corn lying there; and then after a pause, more daringly, "You'd never get another farm as good as this, Master."

But Master kept his own counsel.

The syndicate's tactics were: Having come about the farmer in an ingratiating way and metaphorically patted him and said, "Good dog—there, there," to remark that, so far from wishing to upset the farmer or disturb him in his occupation, they had come to him first and, yes, in strict confidence on account of eager rumour-evoked enquiries—"Is Farley Hall for sale?" In fact, they daren't let it be known or it would be snapped up before they could turn round, and that would be most unfair to the present occupier. For they liked to deal squarely with a man; no hole-and-corner business of selling over unsuspecting tenants' heads for them!

Of course, they knew it was worth more to him than to anyone else, but they had not taken advantage of that—no, they offered it to him at really a bargain price. And why did they do that? Of course there's no philanthropy in business—a little confidential laugh there—even a farmer would know that. The reason is, sir, we are Busy Men. It is not to our ADVANTAGE to remain here negotiating for the real market value of a splendid farm like this ; we should be merely losing money at home. All they desired was to wind up this affair as quickly as possible and get back to their—metaphorical—lasts.

There was in time to be a certain ironical truth attached to that remark. For the local landowner had been a man of riper judgment than these fair-weather gentlemen from the North turned amateur dealers in estate. He, like old Jarvis, was old enough to know what happened to agriculture after wars.

Mr. Colville particularly had the advantage of them in that his lease had yet two years to run, and he let them depart without showing that he appreciated the offer of the confidential bargain, inviting them rather —nay, even in a fatherly way advising them—to publish the news immediately abroad and close with the first man to offer their price for possession in two years time.

" But if," said Mr. Colville finally, " someone should offer that for immediate possession, I don't say that I wouldn't be prepared to take a consideration to get out at Michaelmas."

So the affair remained on tenterhooks for a time, and every so often they would turn up at Farley Hall to try some new inducement. Nor did this car-load have much success elsewhere, and in the end auction sales were proclaimed, catalogues prepared with the names of the chief lots in Old English lettering, and till half-way through the winter they sat in draughty halls, trying by an elaborate technique to panic the stolid throng into the belief that their holdings were being briskly bid for. As sale after sale resulted in only a few odd acres being sold each time, like the mountain that gave birth to the mouse, they grew despondent, and then despairing. Many of the farmers did buy their farms in the end, but at an average of £2 an acre less than the syndicate had paid the landowner.

As for Mr. Colville, he did not want to leave Farley Hall, where he had lived many years, but he said, " I don't like the idea of locking a lot of money up in land, with the future so uncertain."

Then another person appeared at Farley Hall—a short, wiry little man in an impressively large car. At length it came about that the price he offered for immediate possession, plus the compensation Mr. Colville was prepared to accept, was a little more than the figure at which Mr. Colville himself was prepared to buy.

On the day when this deal was concluded, I happened to be talking to Mrs. Colville in her dairy. Mr. Colville, the new owner—a Mr. James—and the spokesman of the syndicate, Mr. Bland, stood together in the yard, visible through the slats. The rest of the syndicate had gone (and stayed at) home ; only Mr. Bland now came to and fro on this heavy business of disposal at a loss, as he, it was rumoured, had the largest commitments in the matter. He was facing the dairy, an altered man from the buoyant one who had first stepped out of a car in that yard. His face looked thin and worried, I thought, and he was muffled and cold-looking. Mr. James departed, as Mrs. Colville and I talked over poultry matters to the pit-pat of her butter-shaping. Then, as the other two turned to come towards the house, I saw Mr. Bland falter a moment. He recovered, continued, then suddenly swayed over, his hand to his heart, and would have fallen had not Mr. Colville caught him.

I ran out to lend my aid, and between us we helped him, gasping distressfully, to the house. He was laid on a sofa in the dining-room, and while Mrs. Colville tucked a rug about him Mr. Colville applied brandy to his empurpled lips. This revived him, and after a while he ceased to gasp, and murmuring, " Thank you, thank you," lay quietly with a distant restful look in his eyes, as though mere existence at ease were a benison to be enjoyed. We stood watching him, feeling almost the same physical relief in his quiescence after the strain of his struggling back from the brink of oblivion into which he had almost slipped.

He raised himself on his elbow.

" It's very kind of you, Mr. Colville—I have these attacks sometimes—lately especially. It's standing about in the cold in farmyards, talking, and the wind cutting into you. I've done little else for months." He paused and sank back again. Mrs. Colville stole from the room ; I lingered unnoticed on the threshold. " I wish I'd never touched this land, Mr. Colville," he muttered hoarsely. " We all wish we'd never touched an acre of it."

Mr. Colville sat bending over the man, more like a family doctor than a victor.

In the following autumn Mr. Colville moved. When I had asked him how he was going to find another farm at such short notice, he just said, " Oh, I've been looking around quietly for some time, just in case." Indeed, those recesses of his mind wherein time stood disarmed by his forethought, and which were the bulwarks of his imperturbability, had a prepared answer to this contingency. A farm just three miles farther from Benfield was so ready to be his that it required little more than the stroke of his pen to make it so.

(In this was the exciting whisper of a story which could be a novel in itself. A hint at the climax must suffice—a horse that should have won didn't, and, in a style only found in fiction nowadays, all had depended on that.)

The accumulations of upwards of twenty years at Farley Hall caused it to be more like a migration than a removal—as, in a sense, is any large farmer's change of habitation. Those who inhabit just a house know what a quantity of the flotsam and jetsam of life is found to lie stranded in attics and cellars when it comes to a turn-out. Imagine, then, how it is with the farmer, whose "furniture" includes every tool of his trade, as well as things broken but not past mending, obsolete things which "might come in handy," and all those that seem to creep away of their own accord and huddle into corners. The cart-sheds, barns, stables, granaries—all these are spaces for the siftings of Time, besides the ample house. Even in the twilight of the cobweb-bannered roofs, so high and inaccessibly crannied, stack-cloths, sacks, etc. hung, hoisted to be away from rats.

Every morning of that early October a procession crept by in the mist while I worked in one of my roadside fields, pulling up mangolds. One saw little more than its outline, the piled shape of loaded wagons, each with some lank machine in tow, a horse's head nodding as it toiled uphill, a man sitting on the shafts. Four or five, there would be, and behind them a flock of sheep perhaps, pattering and bleating, followed by a single figure with a staff, and a dog at his heels.

Whenever I visited Farley Hall, there was Mr. Colville with the pitched-out contents of buildings around him, and more boys than ever in attendance. Now that there was no doubt about his departure, the men had come to making the best of it; they enjoyed the actual occasion as schoolboys the last day of term. All this exploration of lofts and places, and turning out of dark corners with lanterns. Old driving-coats that had hung on the same hooks for years were taken down, stiff and dusty, shaken, looked at this way and that, and brought out to Mr. Colville.

" What shall I do with this, master ? " was the slow but hopeful question.

One glance was enough. " You can have that, Simmons—it'll do for you to go to church in ! "

" Thank 'ee, sir." And he carried it off and stored it where he kept his dinner-basket, showing it to a friend as he did so, saying, " It's only got a rent or two in it as my missus can mend up."

Innumerable things and parts of things were unearthed, and occasional conclaves of identification held over them as the dust was stroked away. Possible further uses were suggested for them by the rustic brain ingenious in primitive mechanics.

In the midst of the yards, as I say, stood Mr. Colville, conducting the whole operation with the eloquent and imperative motions of his stick. Now it would be plunged deep into some skeleton of a machine which lurched under its thorough probing; next moment it would be answering the enquiry of a man with a horse with a wide sweep, as though gesturing him to the horizon. Then again it would be flung aside as Mr. Colville climbed into a wagon himself and loaded some awkward-shaped thing in the way he saw it would best fit. Meanwhile the group of boys clustered about the heaps of the " rejected," sorting them again after the men had had their pick, or scattered on different errands for Mr. Colville. It was rubbish indeed that reached the bonfire that smouldered day and night on the near-by fallow !

Mr. Colville's new farm was as far on the one side of my own farm as Farley Hall was on the other, so I was no farther from him actually than before, though his old mother lamented his departure from the parish of Benfield as though he were going to a foreign land.

A few men he took with him to Park Farm, Sarrow —Midden, his foreman, of course, and two others— but the rest awaited Farley Hall's new owner, not without misgiving. Words he had spoken and rumours of his intentions as to work and wages were exchanged in the Cock Inn. Said Bob, the chief ploughman, " As long as he treat me civil I'll work for him, but not if he don't—not for nobody."

Bob, it was known, was a valued man. He had refused Mr. Colville's offer to go with him to Park Farm, as it would have meant leaving the house where he had lived from childhood, and his father before him; but an ignorant or overbearing master he would not endure. It is the man who knows least who is usually the most insistent. The *trained* farm-worker dislikes working for an ignorant master, even though he be lax and over-generous. The man who contents him is the one who makes himself feared, in the old sense of the word—for his personality and not for his threats. Mr. Colville's parting advice to Mr. James, the new owner, was, " I shouldn't fall out with Bob over an extra shilling or two wages ; he knows every field of this farm, and he's nimbler than his own sons."

But Mr. James, swerving into the yard and coming to a stop with skidding wheels, was not one to pause for advice in his dash for success.

Visiting Mr. Colville one morning before breakfast, I found him, axe in hand, beaming and perspiring beside a rocking apple-tree. A whole orchard stood between Park Farm and the road ; this he was laying low.

" I cut one down every day before breakfast," he said, pointing to the fallen trunks strewn around. " It gives me an appetite ! "

Before the long, low house was nothing but tangled branches and trampled earth, but Mr. Colville knew what he was going to do.

" I hate a place housed about so that you can't see what's going on in the yards from the windows," he said, " and they were mostly old trees in any case. I shall make a tennis lawn in front here, and we'll have some more parties in the summer, as we used to have at Farley Hall."

One evening, just after he had finally moved in, I stood talking to him at his gate.

" How is the new man getting on at Farley Hall ? " I asked, having by this time become as interested in my neighbours' doings as any countryman.

"I reckon he's taken too big a bite," he answered after a thoughtful pause. "You see."

"It's more than he can afford, you mean?"

He nodded. "He's sacked half the men to start with."

"What?" I gasped. "When?"

"This morning. That doesn't look very flourishing, does it?"

"But how does he think he's going to do a farm of that size if he doesn't keep the men on——?" I asked.

"He says we are behind the times, paying a lot away in wages. He has engines and a couple of tractors; he's going to do all the cultivation with them, he thinks—but it won't suit this heavy land. He'll find out if he goes plouncing about there with them in wet weather. Why, man, it'll be mud up to your neck in no time."

We smoked in silence for a while, meditating these changes. It is a pleasant and not vacant pastime leaning over a gate at the end of day with one of a mind with yourself, as all know who have done a day's bodily work—especially overlooking the valley which contains the village that is one's home, and exchanging news of the doings on farms on the slopes around.

Occasionally a vehicle went by on the road. I had also acquired the countryman's habit of making that an interesting interlude—of listening, too, for far sounds in the still air. How they are conceived in the womb of quiet, from the first seeming make-believe of the ears approaching into undoubted being, and then into debatable, and then certain individuality.

A murmur broke our silence before I did.

" Is that a ploughing tackle ? " I asked.

It was just dark, and we were turning to go in. Mr. Colville paused.

" That's James moving into Farley Hall, I shouldn't be surprised. His traction engines have been past here all hours of the day and night for the last week, shifting his stuff."

We waited, and heard them come furiously panting up the hill. They clattered by, wagons hitched behind, fountains of sparks shooting out of the chimneys at every puff. For a long while the ground shook with their thunderous make-believe of speed, and after they had gone their dragonish spurtings were still visible in the night.

Their passing seemed somehow characteristic of Mr. James's methods.

" It's all very well—but it doesn't do to go bald-headed at things like that," said Mr. Colville as we walked down through the yard.

Those few moments (after our conversation in the long unbroken stillness) as of a disruptive force invading the land, stand out in my mind's eye as a portent of the beginning of the decline of Farley Hall, known as " the best farm in Benfield," and for many years trim, weedless, and rich-yielding under Mr. Colville. How this came about, and its effect on the men and their families who had worked there, remains to be told. Nor does the tale concern Farley Hall alone. It came upon the whole valley in the end, till even the best farmers had to allow tangled hedges behind which the harvest sheaves could not dry after rain, while the men had to load them wearing gloves

146

on account of the thistles which the farmers had been unable to afford to hoe out.

But this is a foreshadowing. At present no one worried seriously, and as for our family, the enthusiasm of the amateur still roused us early from our beds to face discomforts which we would have considered unbearable without it.

XIII

THEORETICALLY our London trade should have paid, and was paying, yet actually we did not seem to be any richer. Incidentally I gained an insight into the function of the middle-man, and saw that all was not beer and skittles with him, as the producer and consumer seemed to cry to one another across the gulf he bridges between them. I began to realise, also, how much of the money which the consumer says he gives so plentifully, and of which the producer says he receives so sparingly, fell through the hole in the middle-man's pocket into the gulf of wastage and wear-and-tear. What Mrs. Binks of Surbiton doesn't realise is that for the privilege of going out at any moment and buying a chicken ready for the oven, she has to help pay for all those other times when the chicken is waiting for her and she doesn't want it.

Then there were friends, the friends I had left, and returned to as a purveyor. It was, " Stay here the night and go back to-morrow." So then, the day's work over, a bath in a bathroom so paved and tiled that it seemed like a chamber out of the Book of Revelation, and as far from the trampled soil as that dream, and one's naked body a thing of ivory in a casket of alabaster, even the same that had laboured in mud and dirt.

And so I arose, shaved and changed, delicate-skinned as a prince of smiling languors. I inhabited again for an hour the heaven-on-earth of body-comfort. A small select drink, a meal in which the food was dwarfed by the appointments of it; then the electric fireworks of Piccadilly Circus; the theatre; rustling banks of people in the twilit auditorium all coming to a focus in June the dancer, clad petal-perfect on a rose-bright stage. The dream-pleasure of it might have turned like Cinderella's robe of a night into bitter discontent with the resumption of the old clothes of the morrow, but that I had been through all that before—it had been fight swaying me to and fro all my first year of agriculture at Mr. Colville's—and the truth had won that such flower-like moments are rooted like flowers themselves in mud, rare and brief holiday-dress of the toiling seasons. To feast, first fast. And on account of the rigorous country days I sat back and took nothing for granted here. The lowering of the lights was excitement, the striking up of music enthusiasm, and the rhythms of the chorus all trance to me.

In the bar during the interval I learned that my companions on the whole considered that the thing was a bit of a hoax by So-and-So (not present), who had said it was good. But I absolved myself from any critical responsibility.

"I can't judge, because I enjoy all these things nowadays," I said.

But these escapes into the modern world may have unwittingly had something to do with the difference between the theoretical and actual profits of our venture. In the country, at any rate, one cannot spend; at least not ephemerally. The price of a dinner would have represented quite a large order at the village grocer's—a week's provisions.

But enough of that. I had been through a winter

of it, and as I paused in a survey of the young corn on one of the fields of the farm I heard the hunting-horn ring out, long-drawn and wistful in the near-evening.

"That's the end, then," said Walter beside me; "the last day of the season."

So then I knew that spring was fully here and summer on the way. The air seemed both warm and cool at the same time; it was scented with young verdure and broken earth.

The Willington girls came riding across the next field on their way homeward. That, too, was of young barley, and though by rights they should have gone round the edge, the temptation to cut across was too great, it being a long but narrow field. When they were half-way across, I showed myself through the hedge and waved at them in mock indignation, and shouted, "Ho, there! riding over my corn! How d'ye think we farmers are going to live?"

They turned with a start, but, seeing it was me, they laughed and turned their horses' heads.

"Sorry, squire!" cried Joan, coming near.

"Squire to you," I answered. "Look at the shape of my leggings."

"They don't seem to have got any," said Barbara.

"That's just it."

My leggings were even a small joke among the Colvilles. "Rare pair of buskins you've got there," Arnold had cried, and being himself in trade, had added, "What did you pay for them?" Actually I had unearthed them at a sale at a certain London stores which I will not name lest it should deem itself libelled, but which I always feel is the complete country gentleman's shopping centre. They were a very low price owing to their antique cut—I think they belonged to the '90's, and for once Arnold was unable to say, " I can do them cheaper than that." So he made a virtue of the fact that he couldn't do them at all—" they're quite out of date." Their antiquity consisted in the fact that they ignored the shape of the lower leg, being completely straight in line : they even expanded a bit about the ankle on account of the boot, and altogether gave one's legs the sturdiness of tree-trunks—which I thought suited the business very well.

" Do you remember, grandfather used to wear leggings like that ? " said Joan to her sister, and they both laughed.

" Haven't seen you for ages," said the sisters. " Is it true that your people have all come to live down here too ? "

" Yes."

" And don't you live by yourself in your cottage any longer ? "

" No."

" Doesn't your mother allow you out at night, or what is it ? "

" I've been trying to make farming pay."

" But nobody does these days. They say it's no use trying, so they just enjoy themselves instead. Are you coming to our hockey dance on Friday ? It'll be about the last : summer will soon be here. I've just got a new tennis-racquet. Father's already talking about the flower show."

" Will you treat me to a ride on the roundabouts ? " asked Joan. " I'll ride pillion on your horse."

" Side-saddle ? "

" I prefer astride."

I shook my head. " A real lady rides side-saddle."

" But astride is safer—side-saddle I should have to cling to you to keep on."

" What of that ? " I said.

" Isn't that like a man ! " cried Barbara.

" Is it a bargain ? " I held out my hand, as farmers do when they hope to clinch a deal.

" You're coming to the dance ? "

" Provided that the supper-dance is with you."

" You've become a complete farmer—you bargain over everything. All right." They continued on their way.

I watched them till they passed from view behind the hedge. It was long since I had seen them and their friends. Joan's lively face, with the light gold hair whisking from under her hat, recalled to me as I walked through my fields on that spring evening the first phase of my life here when I lived alone in my cottage. Somehow, since the coming of the family, life seemed to have lost its proportion. The removal, the family's discomfort and bewilderments, and then this helter-skelter of enthusiasm which had rushed us into the retail business, had completely severed me from that youthful company. Not for a year had I drunk of their fountain of high spirits. There is something in the air of spring much more than the mere calendar date of January the first, which makes one take a perspective view of life. The zest was dying from me ; the impulse to toil had become a grim mechanical one on account of the mental distraction of having too many irons in the fire.

I met Mr. Colville's father on the way home. A
party of young men went cycling past in their best
clothes.

"People are always out and about nowadays," he
complained, "never at home seeing after their
business. You see that row of cottages of mine?"

"Yes," I said. They stood only a few hundred
yards off. He took me past them.

"Now, look at those gardens."

They were large gardens, but only one out of the
four was wholly cultivated; the others had small
patches dug up; the rest was sprouting weeds and
grass.

"Before the war the men that lived there got a
quarter of the wages they do to-day. I often
had occasion to go into one or other of them.
The gardens were all cultivated, and there was always
plenty on their tables. Now many of them spend all
their money over the week-end, and the rest of the
week they've got hardly anything to eat—and look
at the gardens." He shook his head. "What's coming over men?" he asked me. "I'm an old man:
I don't understand. It's the same with farming," he
added; "we're in for bad times as plain as can be,
and nobody takes any notice. Everybody's buying
cars. Five hundred pounds for a car—farmers can't
afford it. Stay at home and don't spend anything—
same as we used when times were bad in the old days
—that's the only way to come through."

After a brief talk, the old man continued on his
way, in his lonely out-moded prudence daily
watchful of all his acres. I was grateful to him for
being one of the few people who recognised that

farming was to be my living, not my hobby. I respected his advice always, but that of this evening most especially, as to be allowed to stay at home and labour simply in my fields instead of rushing about in a van with eggs like a higgler, would have appeared as a reprieve. I haven't the curve of nose necessary for such things. The sunset of that day made me sigh for my former way of life.

"Dance?" exclaimed my mother, vigorously patting up butter, in a tone that made me feel as though my talk with Joan had been a guilty conspiracy, though I could see no reason why I should have felt so. In fact, I did not dance enough for my age, that was the trouble; for when one loses one's jollity one is half-way to losing the battle of life. But we had become so taken up by this never-time-to-turn-round existence that I feared my mother's impatience of any frivolity. She was thorough to the ultimate degree—not till the last drop of water had been squeezed from the butter or the last stub-quill plucked from the fowl, would she let them pass.

However, summer brought release. The demand for pork naturally subsided during the hot weather; butter became difficult to handle; eggs were needed for sitting. Our customers went out of Town for holidays. So we called a halt provisionally " until the autumn."

But now, deprived of the arduous labour of plucking and drawing fowls, my mother insisted on helping me with the milking. It started at hay-time, so that I could get to the field earlier. Any of those bright mornings she was to be seen walking down the road to the barn where we milked, in a kind of smock and pink flapping sunbonnet. She had stated her intention to Mr. Colville. Mrs. Colville had cried, "Well, I never—and to think you've lived all your life in London!"

Mr. Colville said politely, "Well, really, in a way it's a woman's job," not seeing my dissuading gestures in time.

As she liked to attempt always the most difficult form of anything she desired to master, a cow with particularly small teats was her choice. She had heard that cows are persuaded into a ready yield by song. Singing had been one of the accomplishments of her youth, so now Gounod's "Serenade" trilled through the old barn, while morning sunlight shafted through its holes and crannies like a breaking in of glory. It even came to the ears of the nonagenarian Charlie who lived near by, so that one morning I found him statuesque at a corner outside, listening mouth apart and head cocked on one side like a hen's.

One day I met Charlie in a sunken lane, standing staring at the trunk of a tree that grew upon the bank. He turned slowly as I approached.

"Yes, sir," he cried, lifting his stick, "that's where young Joe Ridley met his death, right against that oak-tree." I had no idea who young Ridley was, nor in what year he met his end, but without pausing the old man continued, "That were a terrible business. It were evening time, just about dark. I was just finishing off a bit of hedging up yonder when I heard farmer Wilson calling for help. Several times he called as I went down to him; and his voice was hollow-sounding because it was a still night.

"I said, 'I'm coming, sir, what's amiss?' and he

said, 'There's a cart tipped over in the lane and the chap's underneath it, and I do believe he's dead.'

"I came to where it was. The cart filled the lane up so that I couldn't get by.

"Mr. Wilson said, 'We must get the horse out first.' I said, 'I'll be round in a minute,' and I climbed up the bank into the field and round that way to where the horse was. The horse had one shaft on his back and the other right between his legs.

"I said, 'You hold his head, Mr. Wilson, while I undo the traces,' and he did, and we got him out. Then we laid hold of the cart.

"'It's young Ridley's cart,' said Mr. Wilson. 'And I reckon it's young Ridley underneath.'

"I could see a chap's feet stick out from underneath, but they never moved.

"'I do believe he's dead,' said Mr. Wilson again as we lifted the cart off. Well, there he lay, sir, and never moved. The moon were just rising; I remember seeing the shadow of the trees come over him. It was the nave of the wheel done it. It had caught him right across the head. There was a gash just there, right beside his eye. Oh, so deep you could nigh see his brains, poor fellow. He must have tipped the cart up against the bank in the dark. Yet there was a light on the cart still shining. The keeper what looked there next morning said he could see the mark where the wheel went, right up on the bank.

"Then young Ridley's father came up. He'd been on his way to meet his father at the station; he'd been to Christmas market at Stambury, and as his son weren't at the station his father had walked on. When he came near he cried, 'What's amiss there?' as though he was a-feared of something.

"Mr. Wilson was leaning down over the boy, and his father knelt down by him too and searched all over him with his hands. 'Feel all over him,' he said, 'to see if there's a bit of move in him anywhere at all.' But there weren't a stir in him nowhere. 'Oh, he's dead, he's dead,' he cried.

"It made me feel bad to look at him, sir, with his head crushed in so, but his father he never faltered looking at him, and said, 'Joe, my poor boy.' Well, I went for the doctor, but I might as well have gone for the parson, for all the help that mortal man could be to him then. And the policeman come. But I went off home, as I couldn't do no good there, and sat down afore the fire. And my missis said, 'Ain't you going to have your tea?' And I said, 'No, I don't feel in the mind for tea to-night, and nor would you if you'd seen what I seen,' and I told her.

"That were a terrible end to come to, sir, and him a young man."

Life became easier for us with the warm weather. Sometimes my mother and Sarah would come into the field in the afternoon, and we would have tea together in the hay, Walter included, for whom a bottle of beer was provided.

"Ah!" I heard him say one afternoon, after scrambling down by the rope from the loaded wagon (a piece of rural gymnastics that amused my mother) as Sarah handed him the beer. "If I weren't married already I'd hang my hat up to you."

But Sarah assured him that he would quickly take

it down again. She was an odd person, never gracious, ever faithful. She had come to us from the slums of Islington. She had become under-nurse when we were all children, then just nurse, and finally, as we grew up, general servant. She read exclusively the novels of Dickens, which she liked to bring into the harvest field; knew every character and every phrase almost. She was something like a Cruikshank illustration herself.

At hay-time and harvest there is no privacy in gardens, at least not in undulating Suffolk. At any moment a man may peer in on the Vicar's tea-party from the top of a loaded wagon where he lies regally at ease on the journey to the stack. I personally have tasted few sweeter moments than those snatched lassitudes between loading and unloading. All sense of vehicular progress is lost, despite the clink of harness and driver's voice below. One seems to float on a wind-swayed fragrant cloud just like the old gods, and maybe such moments brought the legends home to ordinary men in olden days.

Journeying thus from a roadside field to the farm, I passed by the Jarvis's garden. Miss Jarvis sat sewing there beside her flowers, and her father, still as an effigy, in a chair under a near tree. I waved to her from my couch of hay, and she lifted her hand in answer. How long, I wondered, was she going to remain tethered to that old man?

XIV

On the day of the flower show I returned to that
youthful circle of which the three young Willingtons
were the centre. It was a day of days in the district,
of interest alike to those who sought pre-eminence
with the potato or with the tennis-racquet, to those
who wished to swell the hospital funds and those who
just wished to dally with their loves. Two local brass
bands attended. It was one of those breathless,
echoing days of summer, and wafts of their deep-
throated music floated even as far as the drowsy hollow
of Benfield.

" Aren't you coming to the show ? " I asked Miss
Jarvis.

She was in her garden, cutting flowers, while her
father sat in his usual rustic seat, dozing or reading,
or just petrifying. She straightened herself and
turned her head. I opened the garden gate and
walked in.

" Hark ! " I said, pausing on the broad turf path.
" Do you hear the music ? I believe—yes—it's
Patience, isn't it ? "

We looked at each other, listening and piecing
together the fragments.

She nodded. " I think so—what a long way it
carries."

" It's—let me see—that thing at the beginning—
oh, you know——" I hummed to the distant
sound.

Twenty love-sick maidens we,
Love-sick all against our will.
Twenty years and we shall be
Twenty love-sick maidens still.

" How still it all seems here. Benfield is forsaken
already."

" Everybody has gone to the show. Sure to be
popular—it's such a perfect day—apart from the
horticultural exhibits."

" I can't say I'm very interested in giant marrows,"
she said, but then the music came again, more insistant
jollier ; and she paused to listen, then looked at her
father—and then at me.

" My side-car is empty," I said.

She shook her head, and stooped again to continue
her flower cutting. Still her fingers paused. " I
couldn't go like this," she said.

" That's all right. I'll wait."

" I couldn't very well leave him. He might fall
down, or anything."

" There's Alfred."

" He's going."

" The maid, then."

" She's gone."

I looked at the motionless mass of beard and hair.
" He'll be all right," I said.

Her eyes were wandering over the flowers. " Here's
a buttonhole for you." She snipped off a small rose
and put it in my coat. When the delicate play of her
fingers had ceased, she still remained for a moment
near. Music summoned again.

" Come on, Emily," I said.

She picked at a thread in her gardening gloves for a minute in silence. "I don't go about much. You see —they think I'm different somehow—odd."

"Well, *be* different," I said. "What does it matter?"

"It would be all right in London, I expect, but here——" She turned away.

I fingered the book laid beside sewing in the chair in which she had been sitting. It was *The Diary of a Lady-in-Waiting*. I heard her scissors start to snip, snip, again. I put it down.

"Well, if you really won't come, I'll be on my way."

I turned as I closed the gate. She stood with idle arms like a picture in her blue frock, scissors in one hand, jumbled flowers in the other.

"Perhaps—later on when Alfred goes—I don't know——" she said. So I left her tending her flowers and her father, with music wafting to her from the holiday world beyond.

The show was held in the grounds of the Willington Manor. The stone lions of the terrace seemed even more startled and staring at the sight of the populace invading the place they guarded. On one part of the great lawn, youths in racing shorts crouched tensely, waiting for the word "Go!" like part of a Greek frieze. On another a tennis tournament was in progress, while along the nut-walks, the avenues, couples strolled or stood gazing into lily-pools. In the rose-garden and beside the flower-beds was to be observed many a strained seat of tight best trousers as the owner peered to spell out some complex name on the grey lead plate. Here the professional and cottage gardeners resorted—grizzled and tuftily whiskered

161

for the most part, with flat collars and bow ties tucked well under. Here, too, strolled lovers, by the magic touch of arm on arm elevated to a different and more day-dreaming pleasure, which seemed to pity those garrulous technicalities which were the only holiday fare of sapless old men.

In this neighbourhood naturally were the flower and vegetable tents; set just beyond the garden at the park's edge, pillared around by the straight trunks of well-tended trees, and themselves pavilioned with the heaped foliage just parting and shifting to breathe small sun-glories through. A romantic English forest setting, which made one hope to find knights arming within, or canopied kings, rather than nests of potatoes bland and pink, formal starch-stiff let-tuces, all seeming ready for heaven, and those gross spherical fruits of the earth which look so insecure and out of place on ledges of the church during Harvest Thanksgiving, compared to the joyous foun-tain sprays of oat and barley sheaves. Perfection does not fascinate me, so I did not spend long in the show tents. I was half-awed, too, by the curious hush they seemed to impose on all who loitered there, which made me feel that I ought to remove my hat.

I walked through the park and found Mr. Colville clay-pigeon shooting, at which sport I took a turn (it looked so easy to smash those discs as they hung in the air), and lost to him, as I expected, three times out of three. I bowled with him for a pig, but in that he did no better than I. " I don't think either of us will increase our stock to-day," he said as we strolled off to seek fresh entertainment. One soon presented itself. A tug-of-war was preparing right before the house. Old Mr. Willington, with quizzical preoccupation, was twining the rope-end round his ample body. He winked at Mr. Colville and patted his corporation.

"I reckon you could work this job even better than me, Colville," he said.

At the other end of the rope was none other than the great Will Westray, a noted farmer of the district, girdling himself and laying hold upon it with his arms while his feet wedged themselves firmly in the turf—a spectacle suggestive of the preliminary to some new labour of Hercules. The rope was manned all along by the brawn of Selbridge and Benfield. Two of the Colville family hung there in that posture of sitting on air, and the blacksmith and the publican of course, while the doctor umpired and Mr. Raliffe organised the team by megaphone. It was the first time I had seen Mr. Raliffe in flannels. He usually wore dark trousers clasped to his ankles with cycle clips, as he was nearly always cycling, and I had come to regard this as the natural shape of him.

At the middle of the rope, Alfred Jarvis and young Rodney Willington faced each other, their respective teams behind them. The Selbridge team had also their manager, who had also a megaphone, and what with the bawled instructions that went on through these instruments right into the ears of the ranged men, and the boasts and pleasantries hurled from one team to another across the chalked line, such an increasing uproar came from this end of the field that by the time all were set for the contest the side-shows were deserted and a mass of spectators had gathered. These also shouted encouragement to their friends at

163

the rope, which made the doctor's aloof and dispassionate attitude seem almost inhuman as he lightly held it at the centre as though feeling a pulse.

At the moment he judged fair he released his hold and gave the sign. The roar increased tenfold. Above it could be heard the rhythmic " Hea-ve, hea-ve ! " through the megaphones, while Mr. Raliffe crouched, urging his men back as though his swaying body could do it. For a moment neither Selbridge nor Benfield yielded an inch : then a mighty convulsion of the Selbridge men made Benfield feet begin to slip. Mr. Raliffe's fist quickened its rhythm ; it was as though he would punch his men back. A counter-pull of singular unanimity checked the movement, and for another minute both sides strained without advantage. If anything, Selbridge wavered a little. Their coach, sensing it, redoubled his efforts. " Now—altogether—HEAVE ! " Suddenly Benfield had slithered a whole foot, then, after a momentary recovery, another foot. " You've got 'em, boys ; now again—HEAVE ! They're coming ! Keep 'em on the go ! HEAVE ! "

Right to the verge of defeat was Benfield brought. Selbridge, having the pull of them, had broken their rhythm. The stone lions seemed about to leap up from their haunches with excitement. The doctor crouched close, calmly and intensely watchful, as at an operation, for the moment when they should be over. Mr. Raliffe danced. " Hold them ! " He held up his hand as though to stay the one-way traffic. With a last effort Benfield stood their ground.

" Steady," Mr. Raliffe commanded, " steady. Now, all together—HEAVE ! "

Nothing happened. Again--not an inch. For the third and, one felt, the last time. Then Selbridge faltered, gave a little ground, gave more. Now we were all in high hope again. I felt my lips mouthing the word " Heave " every time our line strained backward. Alfred Jarvis's complexion was indeed " blackred." I saw Mr. Colville's body swaying with our men—yes, and those of all Benfield's supporters, as though wishing could do wonders. Slowly Selbridge were pulled back to their starting-point. There was no *débâcle* ; they fought every inch of the way. But Benfield were in unison as never before. They drew them on. Will Westray was like a lion at bay. His feet seemed to clamp themselves to the ground ; his head shone rose-pink under a dew of perspiration ; his arms were like gnarled boughs with effort. His body twisted and strove to return, as though everything he loved were in the direction whence he was moving. Even so, by his effort alone, it seemed, there was a moment's pause when he appeared to be holding the whole of the opposing team. The next, a mighty heave pulled the Selbridge men upright, another sent them lurching forward to defeat. The doctor's arm shot up. The rope dropped. Benfield cheered—their men relaxed, reeling and laughing.

Mr. Willington led the teams, Mr. Colville included, towards a private arbour for refreshment.

I wandered away, and came upon the vicar's daughter with whom I had played hockey and danced. She was in charge of a houp-la stall, a moneylosing sport which has fascinated me from earliest days. It has always seemed to me that it should be possible by chance completely to encircle one of the "glittering prizes" so generously displayed. One day perhaps it will happen and my interest then cease. I bought some hoops with about as much hope of success as of winning the Calcutta Sweep, and meditated at what to aim. Some pots of red jam stood up provokingly. I had my fling at them.

"Bad luck," she said.

"No, just luck," I corrected, observing my last one perched like a drunken halo. "In any case," I added, "my interest in provisions isn't what it was, seeing that I no longer do my own housekeeping."

"No, I hear you don't live in your cottage any more."

"I'm afraid not."

"Did you prefer it?"

"I liked my cottage—it was my very own."

"You never gave that party after all."

"I meant to, only things intervened."

"We haven't seen you for such a long time."

"I've been very busy—but I mean to enjoy the summer."

"That's it." She added, "There's another tennis tournament next week."

I saw some interesting play on the courts through the corner of my eye.

"Well——"

"Try your luck again."

"Later, perhaps."

"See you at the fair this evening."

"Yes, rather; and I promised Joan a ride."

I moved on, and came to some seats under trees beside the tennis courts. There I sat and lit a cigarette, pleased enough to sit alone in the shade for a while after the spectatorial exertions of the tug-of-war, with the busy-ness of pleasure going on all around me on these proud swards this summer's day. Pleased enough to return to this life so long forgotten, and taste its opiate hours of ease.

On the court under the tree nearest to which I had sat myself Joan was playing a lightning game. Her hair was like a wave splashed to and fro, gold to the sun's gold, with something of the brilliant effect thatchers make on a sunlit morning when they whisk the bright new straw with their forks till it lies in an airy heap. There was something of the pixie about her, seen from where I sat in the green shade—alert of lip and eye, an incarnation of all the tiptoe moments of the game, awaiting a serve with such challenge as though mischief were the soul of tennis, and a smile that would have been child-like but that it seemed to begin at the corners to curl back upon itself with a suggestion of something else, I knew not quite what, except that it is hidden in every woman, as unsuspected by doltish man and as fatal, when the time comes, as a knife in the garter. Then it was fine to see her tense attitude dazzle suddenly into speed, so that even her small skirt seemed a clumsy laggard, and back shot the ball swift as echo.

The band was playing " Prithee, pretty maiden," with as tripping a measure as brass could imitate, which was rather calf-like ; but the trombone lingered sentimentally over " Willow-willow-waley." The flashing instruments gave something of an architectural flourish to that still, circular wall of men's backs with the conductor's wand dancing fancifully in their midst.

On my left, at a little distance, tea-tables were being prepared in the open air, and ladies who were interested in the proceedings, I felt, from the " good cause " point of view were manipulating urns under an awning with the thoroughness of mechanics, turning taps on and off, screwing up and unscrewing. Occasionally one would grow ghost-faint in a steam-cloud, and emerge bearing a large brown teapot by handle and spout, trailing a shred of vapour.

The crowd, having dispersed from the tug-of-war, had now collected in knots round the different side-shows. The clergymen (of whom there were quite a number in official capacities) were having a great time. To-morrow was Sunday, but for this afternoon they could turn Devil's advocate without a scruple, luring people to skittles, darts, and gambling games of all kinds. They looked as happy as prisoners on parole. One, in particular, somewhere behind me was giving a disquietingly authentic impersonation of a market mountebank. Even I, I felt, would soon be lured by his tone to get up and see what it was all about. No amount of reasoning ever cures me of this ; whenever anyone shouts in the market-place I stand and gape ; I become the gull, the sheep, the goat, hypnotised by his abracadabra, metamorphosed. Magicians abound among us.

Beyond the lawns, in a meadow just beside the park, I observed the striped panoplies and glitter of the fair, waiting its turn with the coming on of night to put a hectic flush to the memory of this seemly holiday, a dash of ancientry, glowing and roaring in the gloom like the passions of the dark ages.

I was able to appreciate also, as I sat under my tree,

by what gracious degrees the manorial homes of England graduate into the countryside. First the house, proud, quiet, and personal, then the lawns and formal gardens, where Nature is but man's carpet and the ornament of his leisure. Then the park, where he allows her half her will; then the meadows and the open countryside, where the power is, if anything, on her side, though she is friendly and generous if he serve her well. And still beyond, by picture and story, impressed on the mind's eye, all the burning and freezing wastes, fierce floods and socky places of the world, as though threatening his precarious Eden. Yet here he strolls, forgetful of Time's siege.

Another thing I saw which had an inviting strangeness. It was the old avenue that used to be the drive leading to the old manor, which a Victorian Willington had pulled down when he built the new one. It led now from nowhere to nowhere, which very fact made me feel I should like to stroll there. Though the trees were in full foliage, there was a slight debris on the ground beneath them, on account of their age probably, which gave a sense of autumn there.

Two village women came and sat on the seat beside me. Said one, " Oh, how my legs do wholly take on. I seem to have been a-walkin' all day."

It was the hot weather, they agreed, and, after discussing the troubles and treatment of legs for a while, moved on.

Then came a little girl, and sold me a bunch of chocolates done up in coloured ribbon. I laid them on the seat, and kept a look-out for another little girl to give them to before they should melt. Then Joan came strolling over from the court, the set over. She looked fresh and cool; her partner, walking towards another group, purple and perspiring.

"Mrs. Williams lent me her husband for the tournament; I've just returned him," she said.

"Not in very good condition, though," I remarked. "You played a jolly good game. Have a chocolate— or chocolates," I said, offering the bunch as she sat down. "I was looking for someone to give them to."

"I saw you buying them from the little girl in pink. You made quite a picture."

"I like little girls," I said. "You'll say I'm sentimental, I suppose."

"I'm not," she replied.

"No. You play tennis too well."

Tea tickets were being sold and the tables beginning to be occupied. Steam was up in the urns. I suggested to Joan that she would like some tea, so we went in that direction. At the entrance to the enclosure I bought two one-shilling tickets of a youth on my left, and yielded them immediately to one on my right, who then admitted us. We were hailed; and there were Barbara and Rodney Willington and the parson's daughter, who had somehow escaped from her stall, and Alfred Jarvis and others, at an already overcrowded table. Two more chairs were brought, and we joined the circle. Tea was poured for us from the apparently inexhaustible teapot; green-whiskered sandwiches passed along; and bread and butter, and cakes whose colour harmony seemed to belong to my glimpse of the fair.

"Did your sister not come?" I asked Alfred as

soon as I could get a private word to him through the general babble.

"Yes—she came, but I don't know where she is now," he replied. "The High Church curate from Sarrow hauled her in to help him run some gambling hell of his over there somewhere. I expect he'll give her tea."

So we chattered and clattered our way through the meal. These people, Joan especially, were a release from man's sober self-communing of every day. The weather, the parked and swarded surroundings, and all of us there made it seem as though the population of Benfield and Sarrow had got through somehow into Elysium; that peasants, yeomen, gentry, were here enjoying a green and golden eternity. The long light hours made it seem as though Time itself stood still. Faint winds wafted us, scented from near fields of blossoming beans and clover, the only reminders of our labour beyond the gates. Here, to-day, it seemed everyone was with his or her favourite dream. Courting couples walked through bowers; children had coloured sweets in plentiful supply, and having escaped supervision, were playing chasing games among the trees. Mrs. Willington, fingering a pair of lorgnettes in a way that left no doubt that she considered them the insignia of the lady, was realising her dream of publicly playing the hostess to the authentic aristocracy whom she had successfully persuaded to her own select party on the terrace. That was holy ground even to-day—her royal carpet —all very fine but for the fact that her husband was visible walking through the park with a group of yeomen with whom he was obviously on the most familiar terms : in fact, the violence of the sudden gust of laughter that swept them gave the impression that his story had been a *risqué* one. They were moving in the direction of his hunters at grass. There they stood, Mr. Colville among them, to whom I knew the perfect horse was equal to the great poem or picture— and then on towards the model farm buildings. They were the " old sports," and these the maturer joys of fête-days for them now. We, or at least the company I was among, were their offspring, the " sports " of to-day.

Tea was over, but that gay mood which spins its delight out of nothing, like the spiral in a wineglass, and makes even the breaking open of a chocolate a diversion, was still mounting. Shades of the prison-house were banished by this sun. The clergymen at the side-shows found us ready. One game of real agri-cultural origin was an attempt to " kill " an artificial rat with a stick as it dived swiftly across a sloping board. The sticks' " bang, bang, bang," was as a drum to our revels, had there been any need further to summon up the blood. After that the dead-quiet affair of trying to drop a penny through a tank of water to cover a shilling on the bottom. It looked simple enough.

" I bet you I do it first go," I cried, ever the im-pulsive dupe, poising my coin. But then it went slithering away slantwise like a thing enchanted, sinking slowly into a far corner, while we watched in suspense. We left many coppers lying in the water. Uneclipsed, the shilling still shone up mockingly like the moon in a well.

On again towards where another clergyman loosened

his throat within the wall of his collar to bawl his
slogan yet again. Our group shifted and changed
within itself; threads of chatter caught and inter-
woven like a cat's-cradle on the finger-tips of Time. A
green glass tank of lemonade stood under a tree, like
an aquarium, lucently expressive of that word " still."
A green thought in a green shade. Barbara had some.
I handed her the glass—it was sticky, authentic. The
bergs of half-lemons resumed their poise after that
slight disturbance.

Our *fête galante* progressed. We paused to cheer a
bicycle race, but the grim faces of the riders never
relaxed. I gathered that many a village boast and bet
hung in the balance; and many a girl should think
more of this one or less of that as the result of it.
What an affair of honour the young peasant makes of
a sportive contest.

The pig was again bowled for. The little chap was
there in a pen for all to see. Someone discovered a
likeness to one of the neighbouring clergy. We
crowded round to adjudge the matter. The pig, of
all that had come together here, was " not amused."
One scratched its back and it lay down mollified. An
old labourer hovered near, as though feeling more at
home in this grand place beside a reminder of his
cottage life.

" Ah ! " he said, " I can call to mind this here show
when Mr. Willington's father first held it in the park.
We had some rare fun with he "—alluding to the pig,
not old Mr. Willington. " Bowlin', that ain't nothin'.
We used to grease 'un and let go in the park, where all
the women and girls would be in one place. We used
to set he loose by them, and the one that catched could

keep 'un. They ran all ways. What with them a-shriekin' and the frit pig a-hollerin' it was rare sport."

But already the golden age was failing us ; the sun was beginning to decline. Then, I remember, not far from the old avenue, we came upon the side-show of the High Church curate of Sarrow. His face was too delicate to be just handsome ; it verged rather upon the beautiful. It was a sheer racecourse device he had, a slowly revolving pointer on a great disc of numbers, blatant as roulette, but blessed by the green trees, by the expression " fête " and " in aid of——" There was a ring of excited faces round this ; the pointer slackened speed slowly ; the curate hovered over it. I expect he had been shouting and spinning it all day, and was tired. At any rate, a lock of hair had fallen across his white brow, and, as I momentarily saw him, it only required that the artist should have put his spidery hand clinging to a glass, a background of tobacco haze and a frisk of skirt, and there would have been the young debauchee. How nervously the balance seems to tremble at moments between our best and worst.

Opposite him, Emily Jarvis, but so caught up in the spirit of the thing also, eyes bright, lips apart—I expected at any moment to hear her cry out, " Rien ne va plus." But I should not have heard, for the band was ending a tune with almost ecclesiastical pomposity near at hand. The pointer ceased ; all the faces suddenly broke into vivid expression. The more odd these looked for that it was all dumb show to me on account of deafening music. Frustration, mock despair, delight, with a cinema sense of over-emphasis. Emily was shouting something to the curate ; she had been surprised out of the quietude of her garden by an afternoon of this, to an almost desperate hilarity. What a pair they made, that moment, who had escaped out of their dutiful lives. Banked fires that had suddenly caught the breeze. Upon the board between them, sun-spots from the shifting foliage danced like gold pieces.

Joan, from the opposite side, was grimacing at me some news. Suddenly I tumbled to it : she had won. We must have reached that stage of hilarity when one does anything on the spur of the moment, without a thought. I snatched the rose from my buttonhole and flung it to her for congratulation. Emily was handing something to the curate. The flower hit her wrist and fell upon the board—the one she had given me. She felt the touch, looked down at it, then at me, then at Joan. The band's last chord ceased. The crowd was dispersing.

" That was for me," Joan laughed.

Emily picked it up and gravely handed it to her.

I was leaning against a tree in the old avenue that now led from nowhere to nowhere. The fête was nearing its end. Some of the side-shows were being packed up ; people were drifting away, some through the gates, but most in the other direction towards the fair, which was just getting up steam. The avenue consisted of some fine old elms, and I had found, and was examining, one of which I had been told, it being full of hooks on which they used to hang the meat for the hounds when a pack had been kept there years ago. The youthful company had gone, or I had gone from them—I forget which. It was pleasant to be alone in the evening light here.

I saw Emily Jarvis coming down between the trees, alternately lit and shadowed as she passed them. The curate distantly was packing up their show.

" You aren't going already ? " I cried as she came opposite.

She started at my voice, for I was half hidden by the tree. I began to go towards her, but she didn't stop.

" Yes," she said as she passed, " I must be getting back."

She hadn't changed her blue, rather old-fashioned frock after all, I noticed.

" But the fun is only beginning," I said ; " the fair, you know."

" No, I must be back," she repeated.

" But——" I had to follow her to be in earshot. " What about a lift ? "

" A friend is taking me. Oh, there she is."

She began to run. I quickened my pace to the point of that, then stopped. Her dress flickered through the dying gleams as she hurried away. At the end of the avenue whence she had come, the fair had begun to glow and glitter and rattle.

But I did not stop for it.

XV

But to business. Since the spring I had returned to my work in the fields again. I worked with zest in the freedom of a pair of flannel trousers and an open-necked shirt, and all the livelier for the heat of the sun. It exhausts some, but to me it has always been the life-giver—not to sit and bake in, but to work in, to perspire with work until even the least breath of a summer's day is a coolness diving to one's body through the unbuttoned shirt-neck. Being thus heated, the sunlight is one's natural element and one is hardly aware of that torridity which is sending gentlemen at garden-parties panting into arbours. But I am no sun-bather. Sun-bathing is eroticism. What creature exposes its flesh to the sun? Say one plucked a fowl alive and let it go all on a summer's day. What a thunderblast from the R.S.P.C.A.! Every beast has its clothes—man only thinks it good to roast himself red. Every beast goes into the shade to lie down; I, too, get me under a tree or into a cool, quiet room.

But it was like holiday to spend whole days in the fields again, and to exchange the hot vapour smell of motoring and that nervy lassitude for meadow fragrances and real fatigue.

So far, so good; but could I make even two pounds a week out of my fifty acres? Two pounds an acre—that was the average profit to be expected in normal times. It may sound like squalor, but it must be remembered that the farmer half-lives out of his farm, and in any case he can control his living expenses to a much greater extent than his town brother. In addition, there are all kinds of little bonuses which cleverness, forethought, and luck may get him. He can hold out against adversity longer than "modernised" man, because his domain is partly provisioned by God. He can always go out and kill something. As long as he is just holding his own there is always the flush of hope in his sky.

Because I had come to know what I wanted in life I was not afraid of the prospect of two pounds a week. I could achieve it with that—home and its patient pleasures. As to knowledge and company, I preferred the poetic pedestrianism of a Gilbert White to the society of the intellectuals of the twenties. Chasing through their conversational mazes became more and more of a strain on the rare occasions I rejoined them. I lumbered heavily in the rear of that whim-winged company, and relapsed with lazy relief to hearkening to the unconscious poetry of rural directions—" You keep right on till you come to them there downfally housen"—and to sporting with Amaryllis—or Joan—nonsensically in the shade. As for living in narrow compass, there are worlds within worlds, and to know thoroughly the whole of a single acre of my land would have taken several lifetimes. Besides all this, the post-war world appeared to me ugly and threatening, overpopulated already with high ambitions, and would-be wresters of power. I only wanted to live in peace and earn my bread.

Trade had been adverse since I had started farming,

but in those precipitous times probably less so than
many other kinds of trade. Farmers pulled long
faces, but they had not yet realised that their wartime
pat on the back nationally was but a panic impulse ;
the Corn Production Act's immediate repeal gave them
a taste of political wriggling, but still they thought it
was but a momentary sinking of the prosperous breeze.
I too, hoped. For had not I, too, listened to the
speeches of 1918 ? " The agriculture of England must
never again be allowed to fall into national neglect."
A youth may be pardoned for thinking that the chief
men of his country are not mountebanks. (And now,
in 1931, the elders are railing at " political apathy " !
Well, never mind, this is not a diatribe.) But I hoped,
and worked for the future.

I engaged an extra man for harvest, and that was
Simmons, who had been Mr. Colville's general handy-
man at Farley Hall—rabbiter, stacker, thatcher, and
carpenter. For he was out of a job, and confirmed
rumours that had reached my ears that things were not
as they used to be at Farley Hall. Simmons had been
turned off at the beginning, though Mr. Colville had
spoken up for his technical abilities. No doubt one
look of the new owner's eye had observed but a
middle-aged man of small physique and pessimistic
expression, and judged him a bad investment in a
moment. But there were eight men only now, I
heard, on the whole five hundred acres. Simmons
had a cottage at the edge of that farm. A little farther
on there was a group of cottages, six or so, which also
accommodated the Farley Hall men, besides others
scattered on and around the land. Eight men at work
where formerly had been twenty.

Was it true, I asked Simmons, that James's men ploughed with tractors up to midnight? Such was the tale in Benfield.

"That's a fact," he answered. "All week he's been on the fields against my house. He has motor-lamps on the tractor, and what with the light shining on the windows, and the noise, there ain't no sleep for any up our corner for half the night."

And other precipitate ways of Mr. James he told me of. Besides this, the roof of his cottage was leaking, he said (life never had been a rosy affair with him), and Mr. James took no steps to repair it; didn't care, it seemed, whether the house stood or fell.

I asked him about the men with whom I had worked while I had been there with Mr. Colville. Some had found employment with neighbouring farmers, others had wandered far afield. One, the eldest, having just gained his old age pension, had enjoyed it for three months, then died. These things made my year at Farley Hall seem already a long way past.

Harvest over, I still employed Simmons for a while. He thatched my little stacks as neatly as he had done Mr. Colville's great ones. He worked there in the sunlight and among the sharp shadows like a pigmy in a street of golden houses, more overbent than ever by his task, with a kind of paralytic nimbleness. He shook up the straw with his fork till it lay puffed as light as air, flung a flash of water on it from a pail, which crushed it like lightning to the ground. Then he drew from the heap with both hands to and fro, rhythmically as a rite, till he had the straws all lying packed side by side like rushes. He bound a bundle, slung it on his back, and went scrambling away up the stack, where he pinned it in place with stakes and twine.

Because of the days I had spent with him on my first coming into the country, holding a post steady for his mallet at Farley Hall, holding nails for him, handing up his hammer—I his mere apprentice then, though now the master—and because of the summer days spent on the narrowing stack passing him the sheaves which he laid in place, mounting us ever higher till we stood together dizzily on a tiny space as on the pinnacle of the temple—because of those days which I liked to remember, and in that he had given me at least the illusion of being some use and not entirely a nincompoop, I liked to have him here. But my small holding could not afford him for long, I knew, and by October go he must. He accepted his notice in silence, without pausing in his work; but his mouth sagged a little more than usual.

Later I threshed some of my corn. Ghosts of frost began to appear on the thatch in early mornings, and the droop and furtive fall of foliage presaged winter.

Mr. Colville, being a large farmer, had his own threshing tackle, but we of lesser acreages employed a man who designated himself "machinist," who had two or three tackles touring the district, being hired by one farmer and another. There peregrinated with each tackle, not employed by the owner but offering themselves for service with it to the farmers, several persons called "odd men." A fitting title, for odd they undoubtedly were. The procession that was heard one twilight morn clanking like a visitant ghost from afar, and which steamed up to my farm gate about the first flush of sunrise, set my black retriever barking furiously. There was a suggestion of something between a modern and a mediæval expedition of a military order, or rather, of the ragged remnant of one. The ponderous elevator looked like a scaling-ladder, and the other machinery like siege engines of one kind or another, while the rabble that followed behind were clothed in the chaffy remains of soldiers' uniforms—this man a tunic with burst elbows, that one with khaki slacks and puttees, another with an officer's hat dragged bonnet-like over one ear and one eye, while he cocked the other at me as he spoke up for his comrades. Nor was their conversation unlike that which Shakespeare puts into the mouths of his comical " godams " in Flanders—in tone, at any rate.

They waited while their spokesman negotiated with me for their employment. The bargain concluded, they immediately set to work, under the captaincy of the engine-driver, to help manœuvre the machinery out of the narrow road which it blocked, through my narrow gate. To the amateur eye it looked like trying to get a grand piano through a cottage door. But by much backing and shoving and wrenching of the mud-wet wheels, and cries of " Lock her round, boys ! " and " Woa ! " the procession entered my yard, the weight of the traction engine making the very gateposts quiver as it passed through. Luckily there was no traffic going by on the road at the time.

It appeared to me to have been a difficult manœuvre, but the remark of the engine-driver, " If we hadn't any worse places to get into than this we shouldn't have much to worry about," gave me a hint as to the difficulties of that kind of life. Indeed,

I have in my time seen these great engines bogged, ditched, and in one case turned completely upside down at the bottom of a pit, or lurching and sliding on the mud with monstrous puffings, but as helpless as though blown about by the wind.

The engine-driver seemed to be the hardest worked, despite his stationary post; he had to turn his steering-wheel round so many times to make the front wheels alter direction either one way or the other. As he could only do it while the engine was in motion, owing to the weight, it was quite distressful even to the onlooker to see him purple in the face with furious turning in order to get the maximum lock in the minimum time. Particularly as the wheel had none of the dignity of a ship's, but resembled in size rather a toy, or that of an early motor-car.

The ragamuffin crew, like most companies of men, had both its leader and its clown. This last was the village idiot, a creature of Shakespearean crudity—Gobbo or whoever you will—only he was known by the name of the village where he lived, a notoriously inbred and loafing community. His face was covered with whiskers half an inch long, and in the midst lips parted apparently in the extreme of laughter. A comical enough sight, until one realised that he had no other expression; that the laugh could not or would not come off that face; and then it seemed rather ghastly. "*L'homme qui rit*" kept suggesting itself to me as I watched him where he worked at the most unpleasant task of the lot, through a haze of dust beating out of the machine. He worked well and tirelessly. That aberration which branded his face with an insensate chuckle thrilled his small limbs with a clockwork energy. He was a marionette on an invisible string. Maybe God Who made him found him amusing.

"Is he really always like that?" I asked one of the men. "Haven't you ever seen him angry or glum?"

"He's always the same," the man remarked. "Once I see him crying, though, when his bird got killed—he had a jackdaw. The tears ran down his face ever so fast. But he was laughing just the same," he added.

It was good corn I threshed that year and took to Stambury market. When I stood in the centre of the group in the Corn Exchange while the merchant poured it to and fro from the bag into his hand, and others crowded round awaiting their turn with their own samples, attempting to forecast the value of theirs from the price quoted for mine, I gathered from a whisper or two behind me that mine was a " useful lot."

But, as I have mentioned, the bottom seemed to have fallen out of the market, and I could get offered no more than a guinea a sack for my barley. In this situation, which had become the sole topic of conversation since harvest, I listened to the opinions of others. The young men who had entered farming from the army had much to say and many schemes, but it was the old men's views I wished to overhear, for they had been through bad times before, while the others had not. But the old men, I found, said the least, and when they spoke it was often in enigmas.

"It's no good going to the barn door," said one at

last, when I felt my questioning was growing impertinent.

I was helped to elucidate this riddle by chance, having fallen into conversation with another in the cattle-market. This one was very deaf, and it was only with exhaustion that I made myself heard. Also, as men grow old, I find, they grow less and less inclined to face a direct question, but a word or two in it will start them full steam ahead along some single-line track of memory, and away they go, nonstop into the distances. Where the broad road of experience used to be, behold a railway track, with main lines, and sidings with buffers. Along these lines only can they go, shiny with years of use ; there is no deviation unless you are clever enough to pull the lever which works the points in time. Their main line, to which all others seem tributary, is comparison of the old labourer with the new. Once being allowed to reach it, they race ahead, and you can give up hope then.

The scene when the first reaper and binder came into the parish, the scene in his father's great barn at the harvest supper by the light of lanterns slung to the beams, the triumph of beating Jim Tulliver's black mare in a twelve mile road race to market, these the old man detailed with sonority, but I was not that day seeking the picturesque, but the practical. There had been bad times before, and this old man had come through them ; they had but paused him in his climb from being a foreman's son to the owner of flocks and herds. Expedients were stored somewhere in his mind.

"Don't buy anything and don't sell," was a

difficult saying that he gave me. The countryman is the foremost in his love of casting his deepest wisdom into the form of riddle, paradox, or aphorism to make it the more portentous.

On the basis of a casual remark of bad times, too, a basket-weaver told me his life-story. The word basket-weaver has come to have an unfortunately mock Wordsworthian and Olde Craftie significance. The man I refer to was one with apron, spectacles, and bristly hair, behind a counter.

"The trouble is," he said, hooking me down a basket I needed and squeezing it testingly, "they won't take their coats off at the job." His *was* off, as it happened, which combined with his apron to give him a neat and busy air.

"They've had a good time, and they've got into a way of living according. They've cars now. They set their men to work in the morning, then they go out and about. How many come to Stambury on business and how many for the day's outing?"

He added, "You may think I'm hard, but I learned my lesson in a hard school." His views on the wages question were interesting. "All the farmers talk about is, 'Wages must come down.' They give a man the minimum wage and then expect him to work well. Why should he? He couldn't earn less. Now, if I were a farmer I should pay my men a few shillings a week extra. The result? Every man would work hard to keep his job, because he'd know that there'd be plenty after it if he got the sack; and the sack to him would then mean earning *less* elsewhere. So I'd have an efficient gang at a few shillings extra a week;

and you know, being a farmer, that a good workman
is worth the price of two bad ones."

At that I had an inkling that perhaps it was the
blight of social standardisation that was falling on
agriculture. The basket-weaver, I could see, had been
hard bitten by life; there was challenge and brusque-
ness even in the flash of his spectacles. His one
æsthetic pleasure seemed to be in feeling the resili-
ence of his baskets, which he squeezed and crushed
all the while he was speaking, till one half-expected
them to squeak or collapse. They never failed to
spring back nimbly into perfect shape.

"My father was in this line of business," he said,
"and I started just like the young chaps to-day.
There didn't seem anything to worry about. I was
out and about a lot enjoying myself. Then, when I
came of age, my father offered me a share in the
business. But I wasn't very keen. I wanted to start
on my own. 'Very well,' he said, 'you shall have
your share and that'll give you a start. Your life's
yours to live as you think best.' I could see he wasn't
pleased, but he was a fair man. And so he started me.
Things went all right for a while; but then times came
a bit slack. I didn't worry, though, not till one day
a wholesale firm I owed money to wouldn't let me
have anything more till I'd paid up to date. I got
angry, and said I'd deal with someone else. Then,
after a bit, I found that people were getting a bit shy
of dealing with me, and one or two that had obliged
me with cash hinted that they wouldn't object to being
paid a little on account. That frightened me a bit,
but I'd been going on in an easy way so long I'd forgotten how to roll my sleeves up at a job. I'd never

denied myself. When I wanted a cigar, I had one, or a whisky and soda. I took to drinking more, so as to put myself off facing up to the real muddle I was in. The worse things got the more I relied on something to turn up, but I knew really what the end would be.

"Then I met my future wife. Not five hundred yards away from this very place, as it happens. It was knowing that I cared for her that really made me see myself and my position. 'I'm bankrupt,' I told her. 'Never mind,' she said, 'you'll make good in the end.' 'What makes you think that?' I asked. 'Because you've got it in you,' she said. 'I've been a damned fool,' I said. 'Maybe everybody's a damn fool once,' she said, 'but only a born fool goes on being.'

"Well, I went bankrupt, and the first thing after that she married me. People thought she was a damn fool or worse, I can tell you. Then I went back to my father.

"'What do you want here?' he asked.

"'A job,' I said.

"'Right, you shall have one. Not because you're my son, but because you know the work and I'm a man short since yesterday.'

"Well, he gave me the worst job of the lot—hamper-making—and payment by result. I had to give up drink and smoking. When the men had left the works, I used to stay on till midnight, and my wife used to come and sit with me and read to me to pass the hours while I wove hampers.

"At the end of four years I'd got fifty pounds saved. Then I saw a chance. I said, 'I'm going to invest that money in planting a bit of land with osiers.'

My friends began calling me a damn fool again; said I was as good as throwing the money away, and what about my wife, etc. Even my wife begged me with tears in her eyes not to do it. That was the hardest. She knew what it had meant to get that little money together. But I felt so sure about this. Mind you, I knew the job—there's ways and ways of planting osiers. I did it—even against her will. In a year or two I'd doubled my money, and for a long time it paid me over and over again. That's how I got started in the end. Of course," he added, " I'm speaking of some time ago. There's nothing in it now."

He hooked down a bunch of baskets. " They can send these over from Holland and Belgium in any old hulk—they can't sink—and cheaper than they can be made in England. The English are the better; but there, people want the cheapest, so I have to stock both."

That was the basket-weaver's story.

As to the abandonment of smoking, it struck me that it would be more difficult for a young man to do that now than then, even with the best intentions. It has grown to be one of the unnoticed adjuncts of life, like tea-drinking or the buying of safety-razor blades. Old Mr. Colville was one of the few men I have known who gave up smoking. When offered a smoke by a stranger, he would shake his head, saying, " When my youngest boy went to the war I shut my cigar-box and said I wouldn't smoke any more till he came back." The stranger, prepared for the worst, would here assume an uncomfortable and funereal face. " And when he did come back, I found I had no inclination to start again," the old man added. Many an awful pause I have witnessed created by those words. Needless to say, the old man was quite unaware of it.

But he did explain to me why one " mustn't go to the barn door," and " not buy anything nor sell anything." The first meant that the farmer must not rely on the mere selling of corn (i.e. in the barn) for his living, but must look to his yards that they are well filled with stock also. As for the second, the economy at the back of that was : don't sell your corn at a poor price ; rather grind it and use it as far as possible for stock-feeding instead of the many kinds of proprietary feeding-stuffs that commercial travellers make their living by persuading you to buy.

The ordinary commercial traveller may complain of his lot as from rebuff to rebuff he goes on, keeping up his self-confidence with a drink and a joke with his colleagues : I certainly envy him none of it. Yet he has at least but to enter and send in his card. What of his brother in an agricultural firm's employ, who has to wade through acres of mire to find his man, to take out his little samples and display them in a rainstorm, and argue and cajole and employ all his optimistic tricks while he stands and freezes ? Then back across the fields probably without success. And still to present a smart, genteel, confident figure to the next man on his round.

The corn market being so bad, I increased my stock (the remedy of several post-war farmers was, " Buy a tractor and sack some men "). Besides pigs and poultry, I added a few calves to those my cows had bred themselves. There was a double object in this. All summer milking had been quite a pleasant

occupation even with a dash of the romantic in it—
for my mother. Meantime the weaned calves capered
on the meadow and gambolled towards my brother
and sister as they came out with pails of gruel to feed
them—which was their holiday duty. For some time
quite a tussle took place as they endeavoured to
restrain the creatures from spilling the lot, as they
punched their heads into the pails just as at the cows'
udders. The calves never seemed to realise that they
had extracted the last drop from the pails, but would
continue wiping their rough tongues round the zinc
indefinitely. My brother and sister would leave them
at it, and our milking in the barn used to be punctu-
ated every minute by a clatter which told of a calf's
effort to start a further supply at the bottom of the
pail.

But all this, as I knew, would wear a different aspect
in winter, when frost-winds rushed through the bare
trees in late and early twilight, and skies were wild
and meadows flowerless, and only the light of cottage
windows here and there signalled the proximity of
man.

So I bought some calves and brought them up on
the cows in succession. This, besides scotching in
advance much argument with my mother as to her
milking in the winter, at the same time cheated her of
the huge labour of thoroughness that was her butter-
making. It was a good stroke.

" But why ? " she asked, realising one early morning
what the arrival of the calves meant.

" Because it pays better to turn milk into beef than
butter," I answered.

" Oh ! " she said, with feminine unconviction that

that could be the more profitable which was the less laborious.

By breakfast-time the second implication had dawned.

"But what about my butter-making?" she said, as though it were unthinkable that anything should be important enough to stand in the way of that. In the dairy the scrubbed pats, the polished churn, the scalded separator—all waiting!

"Would you have the calves fed on skimmed milk only?" I asked, knowing that the idea of robbing the young of proper nourishment would be anathema to her.

"I didn't realise—when you said you'd get some calves," she said. "How do you know it pays better?"

"The labour of butter-making is unpaid for. The price of the butter is the same as that of the cream which makes it. It is merely a way of marketing that which would otherwise be unmarketable. Young beef pays better; at least at present," I conceded.

She saw a gleam of new light. "I believe you're doing it on my account."

"It's merely a matter of £ s. d.," I said.

She disbelieved, but said no more, since in this house at least I was authoritative on agriculture. But I could see that she meant to ask Mr. Colville at the first opportunity. Luckily, it was from him the idea of the calves originated. As for his views on butter-making, he thought it about as profitable as tame-rabbit breeding.

All the same, the year or so that the family had been in the country had taught me that alongside my farming duties I had now the additional one of thwarting my mother's zealous attempts towards self-destruction through overwork. She, who had never been used to the life, had rushed at it. The spectacle of her in the rôle of farmer's wife was valiant, but to me, who had known her in other days, distressing.

XVI

ONE other thing I did before that winter, to protect
my mother from her own zeal. I moved the poultry,
which were still in the meadow which went with the
hire of Groveside, up to Silver Ley—patent houses,
non-foulable drinking-troughs, and all. There was a
fuss at this, as I feared, but the sight of my mother
labouring forth in rain and mire, as last winter, could
not be borne again.

"They need a change," I said.

"Who is going to look after them?" she asked.
"I know what these farm men are with poultry. They
feed them when they think of it, and water them
never."

"I will take charge of them," I answered. "I
shall be at work up there all day."

"They want plenty of grit too," she said.

"They shall have lots of grit," I promised.

In the end I left twelve hens behind to provide
eggs for the house. My mother's over-assiduity
caused innumerable interruptions to her day, which
became a kaleidoscope of things embarked upon and
left for other things more pressing as they turned up,
so that however hard she worked, there was always a
large debit of things unfinished which would not have
worried her so much if they had not been begun.

If a hen came straying from the field past the back of
the house, she would conclude that it was in need of
something, and go out with food or drink. The hen's

pleasure was her ample reward. The result was that the back garden ultimately became a promenade for hens, that strutted to and fro all day, slanting their heads up at the kitchen window as they passed.

Maybe I adhered too strongly to the yeoman farmer's attitude to hens as a useful means of disposing of unsaleable third-class corn, and scavengers of the stubbles and the stack-yards, where corn dropped from the sheaves carpeted the ground and would otherwise rot. At any rate, I fear I regarded her poultry methods as tiresomely domestic and suburban. As it was, I guessed she would be able to make twelve hens as fully an occupation as two hundred—only the actual labour would be less.

I had to promise to adhere to the strictly modern methods on which the others were run when I took them over to Silver Ley, and to take the eggs from the nest-boxes every day, instead of making the pleasant Sunday afternoon excursion in search of them that my former poultry-keeping there had entailed, when the hens just wandered about the yard at will. There were two nests in the cart-shed, I remember, one in a tumbril and the other in the seat of a self-binder. Then followed a climb to one perched precariously on the edge of the hollowed-out cliff of chaff in the barn. Before descending, I would pause to view the surrounding country through a chink in the boards. To the horse-yard next, where a certain hen would lay in the hay-rack. Sometimes the egg was there—a deep brown one—but often it would have fallen through into the manger and the horses eaten it. Thence, via a row of four real nest-boxes in which another hen laid on occasion, to the straw-stacks, where the bulk of eggs were usually to be found. Occasionally a hen, as though made suspicious by the fact that, however many eggs it laid, there was never more than one in the nest, would change its ground.

Sometimes I would be working in the yards, and have been at it for an hour or two, before suddenly noticing an eye glittering at me from the straw not two yards away. Or sometimes a hen would fly cackling from almost under one's feet, where it had sat unsuspected all that while, leaving an egg warm and moist.

The hens from Groveside, however, were housed in the middle of the big meadow, and rarely found their way to the yards; though they used to come half-way across it to meet me when I went with their food, like a welcoming deputation, and would turn and follow me back to it—the whole flock, till I felt myself haunted in the lonely field by the whispering of their many feet through the grass.

On account of the withdrawal of all agricultural business from Groveside, this winter was more comfortable. My mother had nothing to distract her from the house, and there her taste for adornment began to reassert itself. My sister, too, was growing up and discovering a sense of domestic amenity. The front of the house came gradually more into use again; a stove was installed in the hall. My brother, too, was now nearing sixteen, and we began to make friends among the people round about us. The strained and strenuous atmosphere of initiation relaxed; the mirage of get-rich-quick schemes was allowed to fade.

Emily Jarvis and her brother, being nearest, used

to visit us most. Between her and my father there was the bond of a mutual interest in music. He used to come to Groveside for the week-ends, and soon Saturday became a regular musical evening. My mother, always on the look-out for some small antique, in the course of explorations in Stambury had picked up old candlesticks. The dining-room looked well by candlelight, by which we dined. She would prepare, with the help of my sister, a pleasant meal, in honour of which and of Miss Jarvis I used to change my breeches and coat with frayed sleeves for a suit— one which would have been considered old in London, but which, owing to infrequent use, seemed to have regained its neatness by the mere fact of being laid carefully away.

Farming was definitely forgotten for several hours. Our dinner-time conversation was on music or the old diarists. Bach was my father's favourite and Lord Chesterfield was my mother's Bible ; so between them Emily found surely a haven of her dreams ; she who dwelt among the yeomen as a flower among corn.

Only once my mother interrupted the spell. " Is it true," she asked, " that while your brother was at the war you worked on the farm ? "

" Yes," she answered, and sensing the object of the question, added, " That was so different, somehow. One could do anything during the war. But after— well, one must be one thing or the other, if you understand what I mean."

My mother signified that she did, for had not she undergone a similar contrast recently ?

After dinner we went into the library for coffee.

Then the piano was opened, and my father began
fingering the bound volumes of music on his shelves,
murmuring, "What shall we start with to-night,
Miss Jarvis?"

Miss Jarvis would make a suggestion.

"Yes—ye-s," my father would say slowly, while he
searched for the piece. Then, after a pause, "What
about a little Bach?"

To which Emily, only too pleased for him to decide
the matter, would warmly assent. My mother took
up her sewing then, my brother his book, while I
lay back with a large and soporific pipe to doze the
evening away in the romantic coma of words grouping
themselves at the music's suggestion into sonorities
which might mean much or nothing, and half-lines
of poems which would never begin to be written, but
merely glow in fragments against the mind's inner
darkness, and vanish, like the changing pattern of
red sparks which my eyes watched on the chimney.

From even this depth, however, I was roused by the
music's increasing urgency and loudness. The notes
rushed thrilling as wind on water, or a hundred children chasing a hundred other children downstairs.
Looks passed between my mother and me. She
winked.

"You are getting faster," she called.

"No, dear, we are not," answered my father out
of the midst of the music. But then would come a
discordance—a hesitation—a break-off.

"Where are you?" asked my father, peering
closer. "I am at B here."

"Oh, I am only at E back here," answered Emily,
pointing to several bars behind. "I am sorry."

My father turned to the candle of wide girth beside him on a four-foot oak candlestick. "It's this confounded Papal illumination," he said.

My mother moved the lamp nearer, murmuring, "He gets faster and louder as he proceeds; always has done as long as I've known him."

They started level again. The four hands danced quietly on the keys; the notes trotted decorously.

"*Moderato*," said my father, leaning to the page. "*Moderato*." He had the treble and so he set the pace. "Now *allegro*," he cried, as the joyful word faced him at a turn of the page. The music leaped to it with an alacrity I have experienced in the different medium of hunting, when one comes out of the wood at last and beholds the hounds streaming away across country.

Miss Jarvis kept up wonderfully. They had reached the last bar together, the last chord—a fine finish. Now she would be able to relax and take breath. But my father, remorseless, cried, "Repeat!"

When that duet was really over for the second time, my mother, coming to the rescue, cried, "Now have a rest, Miss Jarvis."

She came to the fire, a little flushed with playing, and her eyes bright with the pleasure of the music.

But soon my father had found another piece that looked as though it promised well.

"Would you care to take the treble this time?" he asked politely.

"Certainly—but just as you like," she answered, and moved towards that seat.

"Well, let me see," murmured my father, deep in the pages.

There happened to be some slight reason after all which made it advisable he took the treble.

We also entertained the Colville shooting-parties to lunch that winter, as their land lay all round about, and Groveside was so situated as to be conveniently approached about the middle of the day, after starting from old Mr. Colville's house. Before, we used to lunch in a barn, or in an empty farmhouse. The dining-room at Groveside, with its soft brown carpet, looked palatial by contrast, and the table, even though spread with cold viands of the most substantial, too dainty for us somehow. My mother's fingers could not help adorning what they touched, even if they only put parsley about a pork pie. Flowers seemed to arrange themselves at a gesture from her hands.

At any rate, our house had never seen a gathering like this before, diverse though our friends had been. My mother soon put everybody at their ease; she could even talk a bit of farming now, for had she not milked, made butter, and kept poultry? The first was a thing that probably none of the wives of those present had ever done. She would have a word with Mr. Maglin, then answer a question of Arnold Colville's about a piece of furniture that had caught his eye, for he was in business and had dealt in old furniture in his time. Then, evading an enquiry of Jim Crawley's as to her husband's view of the political situation with, " Oh, he thinks I'm much too flippant to talk politics with," a question to Mr. Colville as to the truth about those calves. After lunch, coffee with the cigarettes—an unheard-of dalliance for us hitherto; I feared the family's arrival was going to have a softening effect, and sap our old simplicity.

Talk was loud and continuous, and we might have sat long had not Mr. Colville, the organiser of the day, taken out his watch and reminded us that we were only half-way through the shoot and it would be dark at four-thirty.

At that period he had another pupil on his farm—a boy of eighteen from London, even as I had been, and equally pale and slender, so that one felt, as others had felt about me, that it was "for his health." He had looked very blue on entering, but brightened with the warmth, and seemed to discover a home from home in our house, where he sat crouched over the fire on a club-fender even after the others had risen. It was not until they were putting on their cartridge-belts in the hall, and one looked in and said, "Come on, sir; we can't do without your help," that he reluctantly left the rosy hearth to face the frost-wind outside.

"Poor boy, he looks perished," said my mother; but I, who had been through all that, laughed unfeelingly.

"It will give him an appetite," I said.

Then we went and stood about a wood just behind Groveside—a famous place for pheasants. That was always the best drive of the day to me, for I can flatter myself I am a good shot when pheasants glide slowly from the trees for me, but not when a wind-rush of partridges sweeps by. Besides, old Suffolk ale made one feel fit for anything, and the air that kept even the twigs white all day just a refreshing coolness to flushed cheeks.

"There'll be an election before the spring," said Mr. Crawley, pausing by a gate and watching a rabbit lollop across a wood-ride. "Wheat's a guinea a coomb—something has got to be done," he added, as though that influenced the matter.

A whistle sounded. "Come on, Jim!" cried Mr. Colville, "your place is over there. The birds will be over in a minute."

"There'll be an election; you see." He went reluctantly away, to stand by himself and dream of governments falling instead of pheasants.

Among the beaters I recognised two or three men who used to be at Farley Hall. I spoke with them after the drive. One had just been turned off.

"Only five men at work there now," he said.

"But it can't be done," I said, "with five."

He shrugged. "Times are bad, we know," he replied; "but he'll find out that engines can't take the place of men on this land."

He had got another job, he said, and was moving there next week. Another of the Farley Hall men had found work on the roads; the third was Simmons, and this day's beating was the first job he had had, he told me, since I had employed him in the autumn. He looked more shrunken, and his face greyer.

I spoke of him to Mr. Colville. "That'll kill him, you see, not having anything to do," he said. "He's a man that's always been used to his beer. I gave him half a crown as I went past the other day, and I reckon that's the first drink he'd had for a month. It's a rare shame, his being out of work—I mean, a good workman such as he, a clever chap at a job."

I spoke then of the prospects of agriculture. He was still optimistic.

"Oh, we can't always expect prices to be right,"

he said ; " it means a chap's got to scheme a bit, that's all."

" What about Farley Hall ? " I asked.

He shook his head. " I told you he'd taken too big a bite, didn't I ? Of course prices and the weather have been against him too: that makes things worse."

XVII

In February there was a General Election. It was spoken of even in Benfield. Blue and yellow rival declarations appeared on barns and walls. A certain candidate who resided in the district published a bill inviting the support of the local electorate for this reason.

"Gardley Lives Here," it announced.

Opponents were quick to obtain supplies of this.

"Gardley Lives Here," was displayed on pig-sties, shepherd's huts, and ruined hovels.

"They've sent me enough paper to paper my house with," said Walter one morning. "But there, it ain't a mite o' use taking any notice of them, because you know very well they won't take any notice of we only when they want something."

I suppose one should have countered with the duties of citizenship in rustic lingo; but the sight of the candidate's hacks motoring about with mock buoyant expressions, and the mock solicitude with which they rushed to greet one in the stack-yard, were comment enough on Walter's unmoral truth.

It was now that a society I had never heard of— the Benfield Conservative Association—woke into activity. It had been a body so clandestine in its functions since last election, that seeing notice of a meeting in the school convened under its auspices, one might almost have been tempted to suspect that it existed only in the imagination of the candidate's agents.

Mr. Crawley was not its chairman; one could be sure of that. He was fiercely independent. I discovered that the next village of Sarrow had also a Conservative Association, and Selbridge too; but, as Selbridge consisted of the staff of the Willington works, and Mr. Willington was Conservative and his men well treated and earning good money, it was a case of *L'état c'est moi* with him. It appeared that there was a meeting of the Conservatives at Sarrow on the same date as Benfield's. The Selbridge Conservative Association had also hit upon the same evening for their rally. The fact that they were timed to take place at intervals of half an hour from one another, beginning with Selbridge, precluded coincidence. That a single speaker from the Stambury headquarters was going to rush from one to the other delivering his " set " speech was not an unlikely conclusion. And so it turned out. In the meantime, local men were to " nurse " the meetings, arousing support as best they might and keeping them on the simmer of expectancy until the speaker should arrive.

At Benfield school this was Mr. Raliffe's task— and no easy one, as it proved; for Benfield came last on the flying tour, and it only needed a heckler or two elsewhere, or an unfamiliarity with country byways, to turn what might at first have been a few minutes' lateness into half an hour's. Mr. Raliffe had the supporting presence of the Colvilles, who sat behind him and made a good show in attitudes of solidity and assurance for the established order of things. There was a strong attendance, for the school was *en route* to the Cock Inn, and but for scraping of feet, heavy breathing, and occasional coughs, a dumb one. Had they but done their drinking first and electioneering afterwards, I thought things might have been a bit livelier. Such a change from those glorious London times of " disturbance at back of hall." It seemed as though merely to be sitting on these benches again afflicted them with the awe of their schooldays. It might have been a prize-giving or inspector's visit. They looked as though Mr. Raliffe were going to ask, " What is the capital of Russia ? " But he wiped his glasses—merely as a matter of form, for he had nothing to read—and began to speak. He prepared us for the visit, not of the candidate, but of one of his lieutenants—the candidate confined himself to more populous parts. He was to arrive " at any moment now." A car was heard. It passed. Mr. Raliffe continued. Ten minutes later another car was heard. Mr. Raliffe paused hopefully. The sound died away. He drew a breath which sounded like a sigh, and began to repeat his reasons for the need for a Conservative Government. Nine o'clock struck. Half an hour overdue. Mr. Raliffe took out his watch as though to verify it.

" I fear the speaker is a little late," he said apologetically. " He may have been detained ; he has met with such—er—enthusiasm—everywhere."

Again a car. I could not bear to witness another disappointment, and softly let myself out by the back door. The meeting was showing its first signs of restlessness as I left, for the inn closed at ten, and that meant less than an hour now. I only hoped that the

door-latch had not scraped loudly enough to set other
minds on the idea of escape that way.

I had reached the cross-roads when a car came to a
swift stop beside me, and a bristly, colonel-like head
popped fiercely forth.

" Hi! my man, which way to Benfield ? " was the
command.

" Half a mile," I said, pointing whence I had come.

The chauffeur had overshot the mark, and had to
back to turn the corner.

" Fool! I'm half an hour late already," growled
the unamiable occupant.

The car screamed away. I noticed ribbons fluttering
on the radiator, and hoped the gentleman would get
his smile back in time for the meeting.

I heard later from Mr. Raliffe that a motion of
support was " carried unanimously."

These meetings, however, aroused the Benfield,
Sarrow, and Selbridge Liberal Associations from their
dormant condition; their agents came running
round shaking us by the hand, and next week the same
ceremony took place, this time with Mr. Jolman, the
local shopkeeper, in the chair. Benfield, I heard,
again attended in force, and all raised their hands
obediently in the same way; which is, being interpreted, " carried unanimously." Thus it might seem
that Benfield's pulse was difficult to gauge. Not at
the Cock Inn, though.

" They don't care that much for the likes of we
[spit]. They ain't never done a day's work in their
lives 'cept jaw—like a lot o' meetin' parsons. They
won't go far across the fields after ye [spit] when this
'ere votin's over, bor."

207

Election eve was market-day in Stambury, numb and cold. Snow began to flicker down at midday. It had not been a difficult prophecy. But the town was packed; for a big body of farmers had sent forth a challenge. The Stambury member had been Minister of Agriculture in the last Parliament—a Conservative. Dissatisfied with the way agriculture had been treated, and being unable to gain assurances that some kind of Protection should be given it, they suggested that the most impressive means of protest would be to turn him out. They had sent us all urgent messages to this effect, and announced a final emergency meeting on this day.

There had been one or two startling bankruptcies in the district. Men who had seemed to have substantial means had suddenly become the subject of whispers, and then sales-notices " By Order of the Sheriff," etc., had made the news indisputable. They were seen no more at the table of the Three Tuns on market-days, but still spoken of. " Poor old——, one of the best. I can't make it out." One, it was hinted had wild sons; another's wife, they said, with her large ideas was the cause of *his* ruin. The third . . . ? They sought excuses other than the trade. Trade was bad, certainly, but a man like that surely had enough behind him? Men looked at each other as though they stood on shifting sand where had been rock, and when another big farmer was seen threshing his corn-stacks directly after harvest people began to wonder about him too.

I stood in the upper hall of the eighteenth-century Assembly Rooms at Stambury by Mr. Colville's side. Through the window I watched the snow settling down across the gate-tower of the ruined abbey. It clothed St. Ursula's shoulders with a white cape as it slanted into her niche. The lamb in her arms received a thick fleece. It came like a sign mutely extolling her mystery of patience.

But a voice cried in the hot hall, " Our patience is at an end. We've waited for three years. Things have been going from bad to worse, and the Government has done nothing to fulfil its pledges to agriculture. It was those pledges that gained our votes at the last election. I now appeal to farmers to withhold their votes. The Liberal candidate has given definite undertakings to——"

The hall was full of farmers, and many of them wore the yellow ribbon of the Liberal candidate in their buttonholes. The scale of earnestness graduated from the door to the platform. About the speakers were the apostles of protest; the body of the hall was attentive and muttering, " Hear, hear ! " Towards the rear it whispered among itself, and glanced back self-consciously to the smiling group about the door, who obviously regarded the thing as an entertainment. Quips passed between them.

" What, Arthur, you turned yellow ? You make me regular ashamed of you ! "

And Arthur grinned uncomfortably to be found by his friend dabbling in politics. Mr. Colville shook his head.

" It's a good idea, surely," I suggested, " if the farmers would get together and make such a protest."

" The idea's all right, no doubt," he said, " but the Liberal man can't do any more than the Conservative, whatever he says. There's no Government will ever do anything for farming—and farmers had much better be seeing after their land."

Mr. Crawley met us just outside. "It's not enough," he said. "We want to make a real protest. I've thought of what we must do. All the farmers and all their men must march to London in their working clothes, with their tools on their shoulders, and we must hold a great meeting in Hyde Park, and then people will take some notice. Look, here are my plans."

He pressed a typed sheet upon each of us.

The space before the building was white as a virgin page, but on the Market Hill the crowds had trampled the snow to slush. There the banana vendor haranguing from the top of his van let forth, as I passed, the startling intelligence that the test of a good banana was whether you could wash your face with a piece of it as with soap. I had to pause. He was delivering quite a technical lecture on the banana in a way that still kept his crowd close about him, punctuating it by ripping a banana from the stalk in his hand and tossing it among them as a sample. The last banana and his last words went forth together, and the renouncing gesture with which he cast the stalk from him, letting his arm remain poised after it had fallen, was theatrical. But none of the bananas had come my way. I was drawn on by the counter-attraction of a man in a bathing-dress exulting to his proselytes in the snow settling upon his hairy chest. Such immunity was achieved, it appeared, by the contents of quite a small bottle which he held between finger and thumb. His roaring disturbed the proprietor of a drapery shop where I stood. He looked out, chucked up his head in scorn.

"He sells them something with a bad taste, that gives them dysentery, and they think they're cured," he muttered, and popped in again.

A motor-coach full of children waving the Conservative colours crept through the throng, all cheering might and main. Even the mountebanks had to pause. Hardly had they resumed before another, filled with children wild for Liberalism, again broke up their audience. The mountebanks have all my sympathies. Whatever they get, they work like Trojans for it.

The cinema's siren whiff of perfume lay in wait for passers-by—specimen photographs of the film showing a warm, weatherless interior world where bodies were but for clothes and the attitudes of love. For very contrast with present weather and clothes one stood at gaze a minute.

The sweet-seller, who for some reason wore a sailor's cap, leaned between his naphtha flares telling the child to thank Mummy for buying it such a lovely present, as he handed the chocolate-laden tin motor-car across.

The snow turned to drizzle. Early darkness came. Farmers who seemed to have been standing in discussion about the portico of the Corn Exchange all afternoon had moved into the teashops. The political meeting in the Assembly Rooms was over—the audience came thronging up the narrow street into the Butter Market. It, too, invaded the teashops and excited the atmosphere with controversy. Gesticulating shadows were visible behind the steamed windows as Mr. Colville and I approached and entered.

Would the farmers do it? That was the question immediate on all lips. Were they unanimous enough to throw over their candidate?

The tables looked too small for occupants whose rough-weather clothes, flung open, enveloped their chairs. Farmers of all grades—lean, quizzical sportsmen-farmers, large business-men farmers, independent country dwellers, millers, merchants and their wives—market-day was the magnet which drew them all. All day the sexes pursued their business apart; they lunched separately, but tea was the rendezvous before going home. The bustle was refreshing to them, and the air of great things afoot—the confidences hand-shielded, the deliberations at tables and in porches. The fact that all were soon to return to dark and solitary homesteads intensified the value of present light and company.

The ways between tables were blocked by people pausing to have a word with So-and-So and So-and-So. The waitresses squeezed to and fro, answering pleasantries and dodging the hand-wavings of some to friends in other parts of the room.

But to-night it was not just market comparisons but political crisis, bringing to a head the agricultural one. Was it true that So-and-So had had to face a meeting of creditors? Nobody knew how his fellow was doing; only the banks knew. In those discreet central-heated precincts the quiet seemed somehow ominous and inquisitorial after the blustering market, and awed one both with the mysterious power and the basic unreality of finance. There is a certain air of Mumbo-Jumbo about a bank, I always feel. Those bundles of notes, counted so swiftly, handed out so courteously—as many apparently as one cared to sign for—till suddenly: "The manager would like to speak to you."

"But," I had remonstrated one day to the bank manager of Stambury, of which our village bank was a branch, "the farmers hunt and shoot and don't seem to worry."

My innocent remark for a moment betrayed the manager from his smiling calm. His fist almost hit the table.

"But they've no business to," he cried, "they've no business to!" Then, regaining his former voice, he said, "Farmers can go on keeping up appearances for a long time, but we know the facts—they are all here." But he added with a smile, "However, you are one of the fortunate ones who do not have to make farming pay."

"On the contrary," my mother spoke up for us. She was with me seeing about the transfer of her account. I was there because I wanted an overdraft of £200 on the security of my farm for the purpose of buying additional stock, to avoid asking my father for any more money after recent expenses.

"You are quite mistaken," my mother said.

"That is very simply arranged," the manager said to me, acknowledging her remark with another mere smile, as though the overdraft were a pleasure. Nothing would break down the barrier of assurance of his smile. He treated us as quite a pleasant joke and a relief from sordid reality. How nicely he bowed us out! It only required that a limousine had been awaiting us at the door to make me believe that he was right, that we were in truth the fortunate ones for whom the winds are tempered, whom his clerks would ever be instant to serve with those crackling passports to the Castle of Indolence.

"Well, Alfred, what do you think of it?" asked Mr. Colville as young Jarvis came over to us where we sat at tea that election eve.

"I was thinking it'll be pretty weather to draw South Wood in on Friday after all this rain. It's up to your neck there after Christmas at any time."

Mr. Colville had referred to the political situation, with which the air buzzed; but he was quite as disposed to discuss hunting.

"I spoke to the keeper about the drain," he said. "He says he's got a fox there for us all right."

"I hope they can get him out into the open: it's such a great wood, that. By the time you've galloped round it three times in this weather your horse is dead beat."

"He's sure to break back Selbridge way; last time no one saw him. I told the master he would, and he put a whip there. But the fox slipped along the ditch, I reckon. An old dog—one of my chaps saw him—artful as the devil."

"I remember; that old mangy one—been about this country for years, I reckon."

Mr. Colville nodded. "He ought to be shot by rights. It's not healthy for the others."

Mr. Colville's father entered, carrying that kind of small bag in which men take things for a one night's stay, and in which farmers carry to market their samples, cheque-book, and all relating to their business.

" Did you go to the meeting ? " I asked.

" I thought Tendring spoke pretty well," said his son.

"Yes—oh, yes, I dare say," said Mr. Colville, Senior, sitting down and puffing a little with his exertions (he was getting noticeably older). " Yes, I went and heard them, but I don't know "—he scratched his head—" I don't know, I'm sure." He looked aside. " Ah, there's Mr. Bardwell ; I want a word with him," and he leaned to him as he came past, and spoke of more particular business. As time went on the father seemed to grow more detached from affairs in general, but the more preoccupied with his own acres.

As we rose to go, I saw Mr. Crawley trying to squeeze through to us from a far corner. But the crowd was too great, luckily, and he couldn't do it in the time. Instead, he settled in one of our vacant chairs by old Mr. Colville. Much encouragement he would get there !

I saw Emily Jarvis sitting near the door. I touched her shoulder. " Hullo ! "

" How's farming ? " she asked.

" Fine ! " I said, which Mr. Colville took ironically, and she as a defiance of her dictum about ex-London farmers.

" What, this weather ? "

" The weather doesn't matter. Drilling's over and I'm not hunting on Friday."

" A nice lazy morning then to-morrow," she provoked ; " nothing doing before breakfast."

" On the contrary," I answered, " I've got to help with the polling. I enrolled as a special constable some time ago, and yesterday our policeman said my assistance was wanted in the polling booth at Share to help conduct the business. I'm to be there by eight-thirty."

" All day ? "

I nodded. " I get ten shillings for it."

" Is that all ? "

" Ten shillings is always ten shillings," I said. " See you on Saturday for the musical evening. Good night ! "

Outside, rain glittered down swiftly in the light. Mr. Colville and I paused to turn up our coat-collars. Opposite, the cinema porch had put on its palace lustre. Mr. James, the new owner of Farley Hall, was talking excitedly to someone as we passed down the street. His companion was sheltering in a shop porch, but he himself stood on the pavement, rain streaming from his hat-brim on to his nose. So like him, I thought, not to notice the weather.

Next day was a morning of sun, and the pools and glistening mud-tracks made a double radiance of it, as though in recompense for yesterday's gloom. Leaving Walter in charge of all at Silver Ley, for the wet precluded land work, I drove down to Share. I found another special constable at the polling station (which was the school), as well as a full-dress florid sergeant and the polling officer and his clerks. I was given a blue and white armlet – rather a paltry badge, I thought, in consideration of the most solemn oath of constitutional loyalty we had made before magistrates in the town hall a day or two before.

As a child I had a book called *The Magic Wand*. It was the story of a boy who had accidentally found one, with the result that a single thoughtless wish could transport him from his suburban home into the Amazonian jungle. Already he had turned his best friend into a pig, which followed him disconsolately about, squeaking for the spell to be revoked—which was the one thing the wand would *not* do. Then in the jungle a monkey seized it, and, as they both struggled for possession, it broke. Later the boy wished himself a policeman (what boy doesn't?), and behold, he was in Ludgate Circus controlling traffic. But something was wrong. People were staring, drivers laughing. He looked down, and nearly died with shame to find that, as he had only half a wand, only half the wish had been fulfilled. From head to waist he was a symbol of authority, but from waist downwards he was still a little boy in knickerbockers.

My insignificant badge put me in a somewhat similar position, I felt.

During the first part of the morning business was extremely slack. A few came in, but many more country-folk paused at the porch, and seeing the sergeant and us waiting for them, with the officer and his clerks at a table like a tribunal, were abashed and went quickly away, the sergeant's booming encouragement of " Walk right in, please ! " merely hastening their retreat.

We came to experience real disappointment when we lost a " customer," and triumph when a hesitant one was coaxed in. I was almost disposed to stand on the pavement like a cut-price tailor, or one of those waiters outside Kew Gardens who endeavour with their napkins to gesture people in to high-teas.

It was eleven before any perceptible amount of voting began, and even then the emptiness of the hall and its official atmosphere rattled the electors out of their self-possession as soon as they set foot inside. But the sergeant was becoming expert at barring retreat the moment one was fairly in—putting one arm behind and the other demonstratively forward towards the table. Their nervousness, combined with their ignorance of the procedure, caused much confusion. By the middle of the day we were being kept busy.

"Hi, missis! Hi, stop her!" the sergeant cried to me as one countrywoman hurriedly marked her paper and escaped with it out of the hall. I had to pursue her into the street and tell her that she was to put it in the ballot-box and not in her hand-bag.

"Come along, missis, right up to the table," says the sergeant to an old lady hovering, a little suspicious of us, at the door. She enters with deliberation, looking from side to side as though half-expecting a practical joke.

"Your number, please."

"Sixty-four."

A fluttering of the pages of the register.

"You said sixty-four?"

"Yes, 64 Markham Cottages."

"But that's your address; I want your number on the register."

"I don't know that."

"Well, what is your name, please?"

"Lawrence."

"Lawrence, Joan Letitia. Is that right?"

218

The little shrivelled face nods. The drastically screwed bunch of hair, the perched hat nods. This is Joan, this is Letitia.

" Your number is 749."

The ballot-paper is torn off, stamped, folded, and handed to her.

" This way, madam," says the sergeant, indicating a booth and gently urging her thereto.

On the back of the booth is a printed sheet : " DIRECTIONS FOR THE GUIDANCE OF THE ELECTOR." She reads it, down to the specimen ballot-papers printed on it. She raises a puzzled pencil.

ALPHA
BETA
GAMMA

" No, no, madam," cries the sergeant, "you must mark the paper they have given you ; not that."

She suddenly becomes aware again of the paper in her hand.

" Oh, I see. But they do try to muddle you up so, don't they ? "

Another enters the room, asking, " Are the Conservatives in here ? "

Two young women stand giggling together shyly over their ballot-papers at a single booth. The sergeant, shocked by this violation of section 4 of the Ballot Act of 1872, thrusts them hastily apart.

" You mustn't interfere with one another a-voting."

They make large eyes and giggle.

" Now then, get along with you," he grins ; " over to that booth there, and you to this one here."

" Never known voting so slow," says the presiding

officer. " It drives me to drink." He retires behind
a curtain. We all have a glass of his good ale.

The sergeant says, " Quietest election of my time.
There was nothing till last night. Then there was a
few eggs. I got one—in the neck." He touches the
back of his neck with his hand and glances at it, so
bright yet is that memory of trickling bad egg.

A cow is driven past the open doorway. Children
hover at the porch and, greatly daring, put out their
tongues. The sergeant goes and exercises his authority
on them.

A middle-aged woman enters with an old woman
on her arm. They are given their papers. They go
together to a booth. The sergeant, zealous for elec-
toral integrity, parts them.

" Can't I mark her paper ? " asks the daughter.
" She can't see very well."

" If she can't see, the presiding officer will do it."

The old lady applies her eyes to within half an inch
of the ballot-paper, turns it this way and that, and
finally, when she has got it on end, thinks it is right
way up. This we see, but must say nothing. She is
about to mark it right through one of the candidates'
names, but pauses, losing confidence. She turns
vaguely to where her daughter might be.

" Annie, show me where——"

" Sh ! " says Annie. " I'm not allowed."

A consultation takes place as to whether the old
lady is or is not capable of marking her paper. It is
decided that the officer shall do it.

" Shut the doors."

Everybody is turned out, the doors closed and
guarded. The old lady is left standing alone with a

blind bird-like alertness and suspicion in the poise of
her head.

"Now," says the presiding officer, "you are
Hannah Young, aren't you?"

"Yes."

"Well, listen to this." He reads a form. "I,
Hannah Young . . . do hereby declare that I am
unable to read. Is that right?"

"No, I can read; it's just that I can't see very
well."

"Well, if you can't see you can't read, can you?"

"I suppose not," she answers in a tone that
regards the question as an argumentative quibble.

"Now I will mark your paper for you."

"My daughter is going to do that."

"Your daughter is not here; she's gone."

A sudden alarm in the attitude of the head.

"Gone—where?"

"It is all right. She is coming back for you," says
the sergeant soothingly. "Now, who do you want
to vote for?"

"Well, for the right man, of course," she answers
with finality.

"Yes, but who is that?"

"My daughter said she would show me."

"Your daughter is forbidden to influence your
vote, madam. You must choose one of these candidates." He reads the names.

"I think my daughter said it was the middle one
on the paper."

At length it is accomplished. The doors are flung
open.

We gaze along the quiet street. This town is a near

neighbour of the Eatanswill of Dickens fame, and the Blues and the Buffs are at it again as then. But not anywhere a drum. Not a green parasol. Not as yet a drunken man. The parties are politely aloof from each other.

I slip across to the inn. Narrowly I watch the barmaid. But it is apparent she is not putting laudanum into my drink. No one in the bar tries to make me drunk. No one tries to kidnap me and lock me in a coach-house. I return to my duties, cast down.

All morning it is a procession of the old, the decrepit, the almost bed-ridden—the fine day and the offer of a ride in a car to the polling station tempting out those who have not been out of doors, surely, for months. The halt and the blind come. Again and again the doors are closed for the presiding officer to mark a paper. In the afternoon come wives and shoppers. It is an orderly crowd, a little awed, a little nervous.

"Perhaps in the evening some'll come along a bit dizzy," suggests the sergeant almost hopefully.

"Wrong time of the week," says one of the clerks. "They haven't enough money to get drunk with. Now if it were Saturday——"

One, indeed, screws up his eyes and cries out threateningly, "You would like to know who I've voted for, wouldn't you? I heard you whispering. But you don't—no, you don't."

The sergeant says, "Tch-tch-tch!" and shepherds him away as though he were a hen.

One, who has fumbled for a long time with a pair of steel spectacles, holds up his marked paper to the sergeant's face, saying, "Is that right?" The sergeant turns his face aside, and pushes the paper from him with a renouncing gesture.

" You mustn't show me."

Some, having marked their papers, tear them in half and put them in the box. Some go to put them in the box unmarked, as soon as given them ; others would walk into the street with theirs. The sergeant's eyes are everywhere, and his preventing hand.

And once this election was determined just by shouting and a show of hands. The Eatanswill country has turned over a new leaf.

Later in the day I was relieved. As I drove homewards through Selbridge I saw the Willington girls, each at the wheel of a car with streaming Conservative ribbons, packed to overflowing with labourers and their wives who were greatly enjoying the ride. The clergyman's daughter was there also with a car, and several others of their circle were touring the neighbourhood. The competition was, I learned, who could carry the largest number of passengers to and fro in the allotted time. The clergyman's daughter complained that she got all the fat ones. It was another cheery open-air occasion.

Rodney, I found, had invaded Benfield to assist the true-blues to the voting-place there, or convert others by the simple argument of a ride in a car. I saw Mr. Colville's yard-man, Midden, clay pipe in mouth, " sitting back like the Lord Mayor and blowing his bacca," as Walter remarked, adding, " I could work that job just about all right myself."

Even Simmons had his ride, though what administration was going to help him back to work and evening beer I did not know.

Mist descended early. With evening the voting parties became vocal. The Cock and the school were near neighbours at Benfield. One bus-load passed Groveside in full song. That bus, and a car or two, finished up in the ditch that night, owing to liberal influences, surely, in the village. The next morning half Benfield limped, or had bumped heads or black eyes, and took a more conservative view of life.

Simmons, too, limped, but not on account of a spill. "It's the rheumatics," he said. "I've had 'em on and off the whole winter."

I had stopped to give him some tobacco. He was standing by the road enveloped in Mr. Colville's old driving-coat that had fallen to him at the clearing-out of Farley Hall. His neck and head poked up incongruously thin from it. He was leaning on the stile looking over towards Farley Hall and a scrannel crop of winter wheat on the twenty-acre field before him. One always seemed to pass him standing there. His pipe was empty, but he soon filled it, and actually smiled. The ounce packet I had given him must have made the immediate future seem almost rosy compared to the immediate past, his values having much diminished of late. But the rheumatics jerked his face back to ruefulness. His cottage thatch looked like a moth-eaten fur, a window was blocked with cardboard, and laths were laid bare in the gable-end.

"You need some thatch and plaster on your house, Simmons," I said, diagnosing the cause of the rheumatics.

"Aye, that get worse," he said.

"A pity," I said. "It's a good house."

"Yes, the house is all right if it was done a little

something to. But the weather comes in. Soon it'll be as much as the house is worth to mend it."

" Yes, I can see it will."

" That's what I told Mr. James. These housen will stand for donkey's years as long as you keep the weather out, but as soon as the weather gets in they're soon down. But there, it don't matter to he if it do fall down. My missis wholly go on about it. The man don't do nothing and of course I don't pay no rent. That's how things are."

I told him that he could have some milk from Silver Ley every day if he cared to walk over for it. I had a surplus at the time which I was giving to pigs.

Even had I had employment for him, he could not have taken it as he was.

It was now four and a half years since I had first traversed that road on my motor-cycle from London and turned into Farley Hall drive to become Mr. Colville's pupil there. How desolate this once populous corner seemed to have grown in that time. Three of the group of cottages were empty, with vacant windows. Simmons's was in decay. Engines had rucked the road, gardens were overgrown. Simmons's solitary figure did nothing to cheer the vista.

XVIII

Spring again, and I had as yet made nothing out of my farm, or nothing perceptible, for residence with the others at Groveside falsified my position as regards farming. At first, indeed, an attempt had been made to keep finances separate, but the inconvenience of paying, or recording payment, for everything that was taken from Silver Ley for family consumption soon broke it down. To make my fifty acres keep me, at any rate for a start, had been my one aim on taking the small farm, and I was prepared for an arduous life and a modest return as the price of independence and ownership. But all this was swallowed up by my living again with the others, for of course my father's position allowed them to live at a higher rate than I alone should have been able to afford—at any rate after the large expenses of their first few months in the country, when all available cash was needed for the material of that strenuous business attempt of ours—van, patent poultry-houses, etc.

The amount of money one will spend in expectation of profits to come! Pounds used to melt away like the pennies of the bus-journeying Londoner. It was a curious contrast to our former life. For we had always been trained to be careful of small things—in fact, one of my earliest recollections is of standing beside my mother on the steps of the Army and Navy Stores loudly protesting that I liked

one horse better than two. Which, being interpreted
in that just pre-motor era, meant that I preferred a
hansom to a bus; and my mother's instant dismissal
of the idea. It was galling to me, because I had
school friends who always seemed to ride in
cabs. I think I must have been a snob when young.
I remember shouting out, " Breast of chicken only
for me " to a waiter once. A difficult child, probably.

Yet when one is spending numbers of pounds in
the course of business, the spending of one or two on
oneself comes to seem a mere nothing.

But now it came to this, that Silver Ley was just a
home farm for the house of Groveside. All very
pleasant, of course, and lulling one back into that
" gentility " which I had abandoned. I began to look
respectable. Frayed sleeves meant that the old coat
must be given away—one never " threw away "
anything in the country. That garment fell upon the
shoulders of my man Walter. My corduroy breeches,
too, were sent to the wash, and when the time came
for them to be renewed the tailor found me a little
particular as to their cut, and craning at myself in the
glass—I, who had said just " breeches " and had
received just breeches, narrow and maybe loose at the
knees, but enduring.

"Certainly, sir," he said, classifying my new require-
ments. " What you want is a full market cut. I can
make you a nice smart pair."

And they were good, swelling out at the hips, with
a hint of the jolly sportsman. My leggings now
clasped me close about the ankles. *Sartor resartus*.
I was twenty-five.

For my sister's school friends used to come to the

house—motor down from London for tea or for a
week-end. My brother had friends at Cambridge,
and they used to motor over. It was incongruous to
have me breaking into these gatherings collarless,
unshaven, and hobnail-booted.

Once, returning from the farm thirsty for tea, I had
found that an old schoolmaster of mine and his wife
had turned up. I took them as much by surprise, I
think, as they had taken me, for there was an open-
mouthed stare as I stood in the doorway. He saw all
his efforts in me gone for naught. For I heard he
reported later that it was a pity after my education that
I should have turned myself into a labourer !

After that one took care to look round at the front
of the house or enquire in the kitchen first, till one
became lulled into this better-dressed, more super-
visory existence.

We had a car now. There were stables at the back
of Groveside. These had housed incubators when we
first came. Now a horse was purchased that my sister
might go hunting. Then another was purchased that
I might accompany her. My brother preferred the
gun and was developing into a good shot. The horses
only cost £25 each, as we did not need heavy-weights,
and of course the oats, chaff, and hay were grown on
the farm, so we did not feel the cost of their keep.
From our London days the idea of our owning horses
and car plus home farm would have appeared fantastic,
but it all came by such slow degrees, that even my
father took it for granted.

This was a very pleasant hiatus in our lives—I can
call it nothing else ; it was out of touch with the
reality of things for us. For my brother a holiday

on the eve of life, for my sister the gay whirl of the Willington circle, for me the day-dream of being a countryman of leisure. It was a beautiful taste, and lingers on my palate yet. Though I shall never be rich enough for it, I am glad of that sip of the life which I can always enjoy by proxy when I pause in my work to watch the red-coats ride by on crisp cubbing mornings and their hounds' forest of waving tails, or lean out of my cottage window to hear them going past in the dawn, even as in the song of John Peel. It still beguiles me into small extravagances— to paying half a crown for a seat on the grand stand at county shows on golden afternoons, there to watch the pedigree cattle paraded, and the horses, and to overhear fragments of the life of the tenacious remnants of the squirearchy—" Topping filly, what ?—at Lady Blanchett's party after the Hunt Ball—my herdsman considers—I've promised all the pups, I'm afraid— Sir William's Labrador retriever——"

Or sometimes spring, coming suddenly, betrays me into standing myself lunch at The Angel at Stambury on a day that is not market-day ; and I sit before the open window and sip a glass of sherry afterwards, overlooking the abbey ruins and enjoying the spacious peace of established things. Rare moments of sitting apart from the workaday world. Then it is I remember those two years of unjustified leisure which we thieved from life, and am glad of them. Stolen joys are sweetest. Moreover, it was the last time that our family were gathered together under one roof, a fact of which we were perhaps half-aware, and were loath to break the spell.

Groveside had been refined internally—a bathroom

installed and a satisfactory water-supply. My mother brought about a resurrection of the garden. For a long time it had been just mud and spear-grass, as when they arrived that November night. Walter's son, who had been employed about the back door of Groveside, was set on to it, and with the help of farm hands on wet days, we had the drive showing again and relaid the lawn. So that soon people began to know our house for its prettiness, saying, "That's a rare nice place you've got there." Before, the place had looked bleak and forbidding, as where the Traveller knocked at midnight in De la Mare's poem; but massed wallflowers, roses, gay borders, and shaven lawn transformed it for the passer-by into the ideal of sentiment.

The youth George, though otherwise dreamy, had a natural aptitude for gardening, which under my mother's inspiration became an ardour. He was known to have remarked that she was a " lovely lady to talk to," and on another occasion " the best person that ever set foot in Suffolk." Though, as he had then hardly set foot outside his native village, he was ill qualified to judge.

One of the intervals of her day would be a mid-morning chat with him on his work when the sun shone, a thing I liked better to see her at than poultry-tending.

My sister and I jogged many a mile exercising our horses—and we had some famous days with the hounds. We usually made a quartet with Alfred Jarvis and Mr. Colville to hack to the meet and hack home again. Those twilights—the multiple click-clack of our horses' hoofs filling the quiet as we trotted and walked by turns all four abreast. Sometimes we would cut across the fields, canter over the stubbles, making a breeze of the resting air, come upon a manor or old farm, red-curtained in the vale, and enclosed with the elfish gloom of trees. Parting at the cross-roads, first from Mr. Colville, who would have some advice as to the horses : " A warm bran-mash would do them good ; it's been a long jog home " ; then good night to Alfred at his gate ; and so to within view of the welcoming candlelight of our own dining-room, and the table set for early dinner.

Walter would be waiting with a lantern for the horses. We gave him a résumé of the day's sport as he began to brush them down. He always wanted to know every find, check, and kill. The last word was, " There'll be a bottle of beer for you in the kitchen," as we said good night.

In the kitchen would be found my brother cleaning his gun, or mending a rabbit net. We would sit down by the fire and stare at it with the heavy stillness of languor, swapping accounts of our day with his as we slowly got our boots into the boot-jack and kicked them off on the stone-flagged floor. Sarah would be bustling round, opening the oven door with a cloth and letting escape the sudden frizzle and fragrance of the roast.

" Here, I can't do with all you people in my kitchen," she would say, tripping up over one of the hunting-boots.

" Your kitchen ! I like that," my brother remarked, squinting down the barrel of his gun towards her.

" I won't have guns pointed at me either," she would further remonstrate.

At last we would drag ourselves upstairs for a bath and change.

And so on, till, as a finale to the season, came the point-to-point meeting—the flags, the friends, Alfred just failing to win the farmers' race ; a pound or two won or lost. Afterwards a dance.

Then on towards summer and tennis and otter-hunting. The cool plash of the hounds in the river as we stand idle under the trees listening to them and the hum of the summer day, the church tower rising out of red roofs over across the meadow. The sharp toot of the horn, the hounds away along the riverside, we following on leisurely, following the river all day by weir and lock, now walking with this friend, now with that. Lunch on the bridge by the mill, or under the shadows of the ruined castle of Share. On again towards the westering sun— our cars ? Somebody will give us a lift home. The otter ? No sign of him, but what matter ?

The show. Somebody's got to dress up and be the comic policeman. And who'll volunteer to ride the penny-farthing bike ? The latter fell to my lot this summer. In the local tailor's I asked for a high stiff collar. Hm ! Anything taller than that ?

" It's two-and-a-quarter, sir."

" Yes—I—er—I've rather a long neck."

" Two-and-three-quarters ? "

" That's better—hm ! " With my eyes raking the very top shelf, " You see, I want it for a—er very particular occasion."

" Yes, sir. Well, these "—he tips a box down—" are the very tallest that are being worn."

It was called the New Viceroy, and was to the

others as the Great West Road is to Benfield street.

Mr. Willington dug out a Sherlock Holmes kind of cap that had been worn seriously by his father. It had two peaks and a bow. Somebody provided a tie like a halter, a coat with one button high up, and check trousers.

I mounted my penny-farthing on the day, after twice leaping with comic misjudgment from the step over the handlebars as arranged. It was by no means an easy thing to steer. While one went straight ahead all was well; the difficulty was at corners. Luckily the ring was round. I felt like some kind of daddy-long-legs stuck up there, caught up on that great wheel as on a spider's web. I gathered confidence with speed, though. I acknowledged, by kissing my hand, the plaudits of the crowd. But in so doing I missed my exit. The rest of the comic procession had vanished, and I was doing the round alone. But no, for the next turn had already come in. It was horses, galloping horses.

With a mixture of real and mock terror I just missed them broadside and fled before them with unrehearsed effect. My last act was to have run down the comic policeman; I did a deft turn and charged for the blue. But by this time it was the real policeman who stood there, and we rolled into a heap together. The crowd was vociferous. Disentangling myself, I found it was my friend the sergeant of the Share polling station. Luckily he took it in good part, and we quietly visited the refreshment tent together.

And so to the first frosts again, and the horn in the dawn and the sound of the sportsman's gun. Pleasant days, with farming to fill up the gaps, and to make an excuse of business purpose for an excursion to Stambury.

"Earth has not anything to show more fair," for all that it was not to be viewed from Westminster Bridge. We almost began to feel that we were country-born.

XIX

MR. COLVILLE rode by over the fields from church. On fine Sundays he often used to go on his horse Jock to the service at Benfield Church, although actually he was now just out of the parish. Church attendance was not our strong point. My father said that he would go only that it would be a silent reflection on the rest of us if he were alone. But Mr. Maglin was not one to let irreligion stand in the way of friendship.

Mr. Colville used to pass across the meadow behind Groveside and would stop and chat with us on the way there or back.

Jock, whom he had ridden on the first day's hunting I had ever had (that was nearly six years ago now), still carried his increasing weight over ditch and sodden fallow. Every year it was, " I'll ride him just one more season."

"Well, how is he now?" I asked, that autumn morning, seeing him out on Jock for the first time after the summer. " He looks well."

"The grass has done his feet good," he replied, "but like me he doesn't get any younger. You can see by the way he stands."

The knees of his front legs were the slightest bit bent.

" He's carried you well, though."

" I shall never get another horse like him," Mr. Colville replied with emphasis. " I don't think he's made a mistake with me the whole time; and I've never known him beat."

That was true. When it came to a long run and my sister and I were asking each other, " Seen anything of Mr. Colville ? " and just concluding that " he must be a long way behind," behold him coming up obliquely, having taken his own sagacious line of country. Jock, without a trace of fatigue, would gallop past the horses of the young bloods, that had been so eager and capricious at the covert, and having exhausted themselves by almost over-riding the hounds for the first miles, were reduced by the heavy going to a trot. Jock went the same pace from the " gone away " to the kill. He knew his master and his master knew him; they both looked before they leaped. The horse had hardly a mark on his legs for all his seasons.

" I've got so used to the old horse that I shan't feel safe for a while on another."

I understood Mr. Colville's feeling, for I had had a day on Jock occasionally, and whatever you came to, you knew he would take it right, and didn't trouble even to speak to him about it, let alone " put him at it." In fact, one could have ridden him throughout a day's hunting practically without reins at all; he never pulled nor lagged, never touched a hound, and knew the country, field by field, almost as well as his master.

He knew the difference between hunting and exercising, too. If it were hunting, his head would be up and his ears cocked forward for sight or sound of the others as soon as we were out of the gate. He'd stand for ever, though.

" Look at him—just like an old cab-horse," Mr.

Colville would say, dismounting at a check, while my own mare was wheeling and pawing the ground.

But Mr. Colville's weight was increasing, and Jock's age.

"I'll ride him one more season," he said, as he stopped and talked that Sunday morning. "Donald too; he's blind in one eye," he added, as his glance fell on his retriever waiting at a little distance. "The old dog's getting stiff. Ah, well!"

Jock began to move homewards, but he reined up and added, "That's a bad job about Miss Jarvis, isn't it?"

"What?" I cried, going up to his stirrup.

"Haven't you heard? She's got to have an operation." He said this in a lowered voice.

"Serious?" I asked, surmising it from his tone.

"I reckon so."

"But she was here last night!" I exclaimed. "She seemed all right—bit quiet, that was all."

"It's been coming on, so Alfred told me, for some time. They thought it was rheumatism. Only knew for certain last week."

"Good Lord!"

"I don't know exactly what, but she's to go into the nursing-home this week some time," he said. "Young girl like that." He shifted his hat on his head, perplexed. "Pretty girl as she is——" As though beauty were the symbol of perfection throughout. I, too, illogically found it the more difficult to believe for that reason.

"Good Lord, ain't that old man dead yet?" Mr. Colville exclaimed, as old Charlie shuffled by on the road.

"He comes out every summer," I said.

"Isn't it wonderful how a chap like that goes on? I reckon his old inside must be made of leather. He's been drunk more times than all the rest of Benfield put together. And yet a nice girl——"

Charlie turned his old tortoise head and peered at us through red-rimmed eyes. He raised his gnarled stick in recognition of Mr. Colville, while his mouth opened and shut silently, as old men's do.

"Morning, Charlie. How are you doing?"

Charlie shook his head. "Ah, master, sadly, sadly," he wheezed. "I need a new pair of bellows—that's what I need." He was referring to his lungs. "Me grub don't do me no good neither—not like it used. I shan't be with ye much longer now."

"That's what he said six years ago," Mr. Colville muttered.

"Go on, you're only a colt yet," he cried to Charlie, and added in a lower voice, "There's plenty of better people that'll die before you," as with a sense of something wrong with the order of things, owing to recent news.

Next morning I was early up, riding over the fields to a cubbing meet at the kennels. Not that my mind was on the death of young foxes. But to be riding alone in the unawakened day, the gusty wind racketing in the woods, loosening leaves on me in mothlike droves before even the bleak coming of light, was to escape from the dungeon of thought as into a manifestation of that elemental wrath which seemed the torturer of life's patience. It was good, and a definite challenge, thus to meet the space and raging force without and about us, with man's soul the one clear accuser of death's waste and blindness. And if there were a God, I felt then, what soul but the coward's would tremble before Him on the last day for His persecutions? Rather creation should call Him to account. "Tried in the fire——" That facile condoning of whatever suffering mere power cared to inflict seemed then the unrealest thing about religion. I saw no reason for Job's recantation in God's reminding him that He was the stronger.

A fox-cub broke from the wood at the corner, from the death-invaded wood, but they hallooed him back again. He broke out a second time, opposite where I stood. I galloped my mare to cut him off, shouted hoarsely in my throat, and back he skeltered to his doom. I was his god, and they were the hounds of heaven that were after him. It was so good for him, so chastening, to suffer.

On my return I saw Alfred drilling some oats on one of his fields, and I rode across and asked him about his sister, while the men were at a distance.

He said, " It's a bad business."

I asked him how bad he thought it was.

" The doctor says there's no reason why the operation shouldn't be successful. He said youth's on her side, and it's not considered by any means a hopeless case and—— Oh, damn their blasted tact! Why can't they tell you what they think? "

" When is it? "

" Wednesday." He shoved the tilth about with his boot.

" Those are side-bearing oats, are they? "

" Yes."

" They go in well."

"Ground's a bit fine, though. Could do with a few clods for oats."

"After fallow?"

He nodded.

"They'll be rank. I like to put oats in after a white-straw crop. Look here, I'll take her to Stambury in our car."

Ours was a closed car; his was an open, farming one.

"That's jolly good of you."

"Not at all. Is she——?"

"Oh, no, she's up and all that. She doesn't worry much. I should be in a hell of a funk."

I remembered, as I rode home, the previous Saturday evening when she had come to Groveside for the usual musical interlude. She had seemed more than usually bright during dinner. I discovered—how shall I put it?—moments as of that flushed gaiety at Selbridge Show. But after the music she grew pensive. I thought she was tired. When I had seen her to her gate, she said, "What pleasant evenings these have been," as our hands parted from the touch of good night; though I saw no reason why they should not go on being so.

On Tuesday morning I waited with the car, for it was on that day she was to go into the nursing-home. Alfred came out with her, carrying a suitcase of her things. She seemed bright as the morning.

"It's such a lovely day. I'm so glad. The weather makes all the difference to a drive," she said. I would have helped her into the car, but she added, "Oh, I am all right," and jumped in.

"Good-bye, Alfred," she called, "and don't

forget to look after the things in the greenhouse till I come back."

"Good-bye, Emily," he answered, "and good luck."

"It is so good of you to drive me," she said. "I hated bothering Alfred. I knew he was busy trying to get the corn set while it is dry, and one of the men ill, too."

"Don't mention it. I'm only too glad to be able to help in any way."

"Oh, don't worry about me," she said. "I shall be all right."

"Yes, of course," I said. We were passing Benfield Manor. "It's a pity somebody doesn't take that place." It was still empty since Squire Lindley left it, years ago and even more overgrown.

"Perhaps you'll take it one day," she laughed.

"And not go back to London?"

"I'm beginning to believe that you really prefer the country."

"That's something, then," I said, "to have become the exception that proves your rule about Londoners."

"We'll allow one exception," she conceded, "to the general run of mankind."

"Not exceptional enough ever to be lord of Benfield Manor, though."

"Would that be the height of your ambition?"

I shook my head. "Ambitions are conceived to be realised. Call it an ideal."

"Is it really?"

"As a life it seems so to me. And I don't mean just the beguilements of it : the duties too. The rich man

241

in his castle, the poor man at his gate—what's wrong with that?"

"Oh, one could be quite happy in a cottage."

"It's because I've proved that that I think the system so good."

We had reached the top of the hill out of Benfield.

"How pretty the village looks," she said, glancing back. "Especially to-day, with the sun on it."

We dipped towards Selbridge. The Hall stood among its lawns and laurels—a contrast to Benfield's. At a distance the tall chimney smoked busily. We passed the two Willington girls on horseback. They were laughing at a joke they had between themselves as they waved.

"I ought to have got on with them better, somehow," mused Emily, pensive a minute. "I hope Alfred manages the things in the greenhouse all right," she added.

"I'm sure he will," I assured her.

"That's the only thing I'm anxious about—I've taken such care of them."

"I'll see he does."

"Thank you."

We were more than half-way there already, though I was not hurrying. Twelve miles seems very short when you know the road.

"I'm glad they had room at Stambury," she said. "It's such a nice home, I think."

"Yes, it's prettily situated."

"In fact, it's not like anything to do with illness at all," she continued; "more like a private house, with those trees and grass round it. It's something to be able to look on to a garden."

" More like home," I suggested.

" Yes, more like home," she assented, then fell silent, looking out of the window on to the fields, where new thatch showed golden among the tree-clumps about farmsteads, the busy fields full of horses and men. I began to realise then her strength, which had held her to Benfield and the denial of her dreams; which had led her out to farm-work even, because there had been nobody else to do it. Was there after all, I wondered, a deep bond between her father and herself, unperceived by the stranger? He, though walled away from the world in himself, yet seemed to understand all her communications without question. And here was she, calm and cheerful at my side. I had no illusions as to the state of funk I should have been in under those circumstances.

" I shall miss our musical evenings," she said.

" So shall we," I answered, " very much. But you'll soon be back, I expect."

" Well, fairly soon, I hope."

I did not like this conversation; like walking with her on narrow ledges of some precipitous dream scenery—we, who had loved but gentlest undulations of Suffolk and its woodlands. Our talk was but chatter, as sun-rosed mist ever thinning from over an abyss. I was glad after all that it was only twelve miles; not knowing what she was feeling as the town came in view, and my airy optimism being unable any longer to support the weight of my spirits.

We came to the nursing-home, so beautifully and carefully disguised. Birds sang, when I stopped the car, their autumn song; chrysanthemums gazed like cheerful shaggy dogs out of the windows; a nurse stood at the door, all clean and brightly welcoming. A porter took the suitcase.

"Good-bye," said Emily, "and thank you so much."

"Good-bye—or, rather, *au revoir*," I said like a fool. "See you again, soon," I added lamely. But she only smiled.

I was glad to get out in the street again among the traffic and cheerful shoppers.

On my way home I met the High Church curate of Sarrow. I went home that way because I thought I might see him. I stopped, but before I had said more than "Good-day" he remarked, "The best of being a farmer is that so much of one's business entails a pleasant motor ride!" He was a cheerful, meet-you-on-your-own-ground kind of man, as so often the High Church are. We had met at the Jarvises', and Emily and he twitted me about my farming.

"Been to Stambury?"

I nodded.

"I like Stambury, except when there's an ecclesiastical conference on," he said. "I prefer to see it full of cheerful people like yourself."

"I've just taken Miss Jarvis to the nursing-home," I said.

"What? To the—Miss Jarvis?" His voice went hushed.

"I wondered if you'd heard. I thought it would be better you heard from me than in some haphazard way."

"What is it?"

I told him what little I knew.

"When'll they hear?"

244

"To-morrow late, perhaps—the next day——"

We gazed at each other in silence.

"Thank you for telling me," he said, and turned away, but, turning back, put his hand on my shoulder. "Thank you very much." He took the field-path towards his church.

That evening I had walked down to old Mr. Colville's house in Benfield to have a settling up between us of certain small agricultural accounts that had amounted during the past year. I sat and talked for a while at his fireside, and left towards ten o'clock. As I passed the inn the door opened, and I saw Bob, the horse-keeper at Farley Hall, half carrying the limp form of Simmons, who with weak gestures was attempting to prevent him. There was a great buzz of voices from the smoky interior; but two faces especially I saw close behind Simmons, not men of Benfield, nor at all amiable. One at least was holding Simmons back. How Simmons came to be the apparently coveted prize for whom two men were at a tug-of-war I could not for the life of me imagine, but guessing that Bob's intention was the better of the two, besides getting a kind of S.O.S. look from him, I ran to the door, seized Simmons's arm from the other man's grasp, and, before he could recover from his surprise, dragged my old thatcher out into the pitch-black night.

"Reckon we shall have to carry him, master," said Bob. Simmons sagged between us, muttering incoherently. So we got him between our arms and started up the hill.

"How did he manage to get so drunk, Bob?" I asked as we put him down to rest ourselves.

"He's had a job threshing for a little mor'n a fortnight," he said, "and he was paid off this evening. I was sittin' in the pub when he came in just on his way home. That'd been a wonderful dusty job, the last stack, the wind laying wrong, it seems, and he were wholly dry, he said. I don't reckon as he'd had a drop o' nothin' to drink for ever so long, being out of a job, and he soon had a pint down and another. There was two or three strange chaps in the bar—gyppos, I reckon—and Simmons got on to talkin' to them, and like a fool he show this money. I could see they meant having that off he afore he got out o' there. They'd soon got him fuddled, so I drinks up my pint and goes to him and says, 'Come home along o' me, Simmons.' He says, 'I ain't goin' home. I just met some mates here.' So I wait a bit, and he had a drop more. Then I took him by the arm and says, 'Come on!' 'You let he alone,' them chaps said. I didn't like the looks o' them, and I pulled him over to the door quick. One of them laid hold of him to keep him there, and then chance you come along, master, and we got him out."

"Where's his money?" I said.

We felt about him. I found a note crumpled up in a ball in his trouser pocket which had also a hole in it. Bob found another two notes. I switched my torch on to them.

"That's right—three pounds," Bob said. "That's what he had, and a little odd change he spent on the drink."

"You'd better put it in your pocket and give it to his missis when we get him home," I advised.

He folded it away, and we took Simmons up again.

Though a small man, he was quite heavy enough to carry uphill. At the top we cut across the fields. The cold breeze revived our burden. He grew restless in our arms.

"I'm a'right—what you carryin' me for? I'm goin' t'walk."

We put him on his feet. "Go on, then," said Bob.

He started forward from us, but in a minute we heard a thump and crackling of the bean stubble.

"He's gone a purler," Bob said.

We picked him up. I switched the light on him.

"He's wholly scratched his face," Bob observed. He wiped the dirt away with his handkerchief, and we carried him again. When we rested, Simmons again asserted his capacity to stand on his own legs. From the way he spoke one would have imagined it was some practical joke on our part that prevented his legs from carrying him.

"Damn ye!" he cried. "Let me be!" He staggered free. "Ye won't catch me no more," he shrilled. Then, after a moment, another explosive "Blast ye!" and a splash. Silence.

"Where the hell's he now?" said Bob.

My torch revealed only a white owl winging low along the hedge.

"He's in the ditch, I'll bet," said Bob, and presently we came upon his feet poking up; his body lay along in the water. We scrambled among the brambles and hiked him out as though he himself were one of the many rabbits he had pulled out of holes in the course of his career with Mr. Colville at Farley Hall. He was in a sorry mess this time, and insensible. The only thing was to get him home as quickly as possible. So we took him up and made the best pace we could, grunting and occasionally swearing as a long bramble caught our feet. It was a long time since I had walked over Farley Hall fields. Brambles had not grown about them then, nor the hedges stretched out a yard into them. We sploshed along the rucked road and were soon nearing the light of Simmons's cottage.

"There's another of these cottages empty since last week," said Bob. "There's only two chaps besides Simmons live up here now."

We got him indoors and put him by the fire, his wife repeating, "Oh, dear! Oh, dear!" all the while as she pulled off his wet things.

A dim lamp burned on the table, which was covered with a clean, much-mended cloth. On it half a loaf of bread, some butter in a saucer, and a teacup. "A Present from Yarmouth" occupied centre place on the mantelpiece, with biscuit boxes of ornamental tin on each side. A calendar hung on a big nail hammered into the chimney brickwork. Photographs stood on a side-table on a knitted openwork cloth. A geranium on the window-sill. Two chaff bags on the brick floor by the door—a hearthrug of rag scraps.

We carried him upstairs to bed, snoring hard. In one corner of the room the ceiling was black and mouldering, with a rent in it, and underneath it a zinc bath; and underneath another plague-spot a pail.

Mrs. Simmons thanked us for getting him home, and offered to make us a cup of tea, which we refused. We left her there with the remains of her home and her husband. Nor even that little at ease which she might have been, for Bob forgot to give her the money, he told me later, so that both she and Simmons, when he woke up, took it for granted that he had lost it, and all his fortnight's labour gone for nothing. Bob said their relief when he called with it next day was a picture.

" He looked wholly sheepish ; that's a fact."

XX

GUARDED and imperfect news came of Emily Jarvis the next day and days after. And then they said she was getting better, and Alfred consulted me with pleased ruefulness about a fern which looked a little rusty about the edges. Was it yellower or greener since last week? Had he watered it too little or too much? Was this other going like it too—and this one? If so, he'd be for it when Emily came back.

"George will tell you," I said, referring to our young gardener, who was now getting quite an expert by dint of reading all the books we had on gardening, which had been unopened on our shelves since hopeful publishers had sent them out for review—the leaflets still in them asking that no notice should appear before April 6, 1912.

"What a lot of ruddy fiddle-de-dee," Alfred grunted cheerfully, leaning among minute pots of seedlings with a little green watering-can. "I wonder when she'll be allowed home," he said, spraying the dregs of the can on a cobweb and waking up the spider in a panic.

"Pity the weather isn't better."

"Yes, we shall have to take care of her."

"Your father must be pleased."

"I reckon so."

"Of course, at his time of life he doesn't show much——"

"Doesn't show anything," said Alfred. "She

seems to know what's going on in his old head. I don't."

On a day we were allowed to see her. The curate of Sarrow had left flowers; they seemed to cry jubilantly that he had got there first. Ours received second place. It was a fiendish day without, wind armed with rain, which made the room seem particularly still, and Emily lying there the very stillness of fragility. Her hand looked like alabaster, and as though it would break or melt into transparency. Alfred's voice seemed to shock that room.

"All right now?" he cried cheerfully. The idea had been to make the minimum of it all along.

"Better," she replied, mostly by smile. Her voice had no tone, no more than wind in the corn.

It had been worse, I saw, than she herself had expected—the draining away of spirit. I saw on her features the ghost of the formula of optimism that had grown up among us those days before she came here. Even that must be costing her an effort, I guessed, and longed to be able to tell her not to worry about it now; that we knew that it was as bad as could be.

My part in the visit consisted mostly in smiling— that seemed the only practicable conversation. The little I spoke, I found my voice involuntarily so low as to mate with hers.

There seemed such a very little of her left as she lay there. Not that her frame struck me as wasted, but her personality. There was that kind of radiance about her as though she had been bathing in moonlight, which some call "saint-like," "ethereal"; but to me it seemed anything but glorious, this light

that was not of our good earth. Mysticism is not in
my line. The Emily that I knew, and that could give
me yea for my yea, was crouching somewhere under
the great load of weakness. That was all my faith.
Meanwhile it was as though a voice would break her.
But Alfred chattered—about home and the things in
the greenhouse, which were in a flourishing condition,
all of them, he lied; I had caught him burying a fern,
and was saving up the information for one day when
it would be just amusing. He broke off to ask,
" Who was that stingy old mare we passed in the
passage ? "

" Sh ! Alfred, that was the matron. She's very
nice."

" Hm ! looked at me as though a double bit
wouldn't hold her."

" Don't ! I mustn't laugh," she said, and that was
the first gleam of the old Emily.

" That nurse of yours is a good-looker, though,"
he admitted.

That nurse soon returned and told us our time was
up in a quiet tone that precluded any appeal. Alfred
obeyed like a lamb.

Four weeks later Emily returned to Benfield—but
only for a short time. The doctor advised that she
should not hazard the English winter as she was. So
one morning she left our country station for the Con-
tinent. She was going to see something of the world at
last.

" Give my love to the Lake of Geneva," I said.

It was odd to think that one had ever been there,
standing on the country platform, or that there was
such a place. But the label on her box confirmed it.

The two porters had a chat about the matter, waiting
for the train to come in, with an occasional furtive
glance at her through the waiting-room window. One
came and poured paraffin on the weakly fire on her
account.

" I expect you'll make lots of friends," I said.

But when it came to the point she did not seem so
bright about leaving Benfield.

Her train steamed away on the first stage of her
journey to " the warm South," while we who had our
health and strength returned to our orbits.

This winter stands out in my memory for another
thing. It was the first season that old Mr. Colville no
longer accompanied our shooting-parties as one of the
guns. At last he had had to yield to increasing years.

" What you want, Father, is a tub-cart and a quite
sort of pony that'll stand anywhere," said Mr. Colville. " It's no use you thinking about slading all
across the fields on foot in winter any more. You
only tire yourself right out. Summer-time it's
different."

His father protested a little, but was bound to
agree partially.

" Somehow I don't seem able to get about as I
used," he said in a puzzled way. " All the spring
seems to have gone out of my legs." As he was in
the mid-seventies, this was hardly surprising.

" Yes, a tub-cart's the thing," the other sons agreed,
and resolved to look out for one. The three of them
each happened to discover one that would suit him,
independently. Two arrived almost simultaneously
from different sales, and early the next morning the
third son came driving up in one. When I called

253

there, I found the back yard full of tub-carts and the stable full of ponies. I had come to say I knew of somebody who wanted to dispose of a similar turn-out, but withheld that information, seeing the plethora.

The unwanted ones were got rid of, and now old Mr. Colville rode round with us, collecting the game, going off occasionally to look at this crop or that. But his gun he had definitely laid aside.

In retrospect I have come to regard this winter as witnessing the beginning of the break-up of that community in whose midst I had found myself on first plunging into the country from London as little more than a boy, and with the vaguest ideas as to the future. Partly age and partly hard times were the cause of this.

There was a day towards the end of the hunting season. It was one of those days that go before the spring. Bird choruses rang down to us from every coppice as we hacked to the meet. One of those days that make the true hunting man bristle, because owing to the sun the scent was sure to be bad. But when it was enough to be just ambling along the back of a great wave of corn land which served for " hill " in this country, gazing to right or to left to another far billow of this new-green of springing crops, viewing in thought the vista of summer ahead as well as the ocean of increase about me, and in the hollow of each wave a church tower and village smoke, what did the fox matter ? Little enough to me, and I'm not sure that I shouldn't have been left watching the wild life creeping and bobbing about the corner of the wood long after hounds had gone away, if I had been alone.

However, Mr. Colville was all eyes for a sight of the fox—hallooed the hounds on to it, standing in his stirrups and holding his hat on high, and was off before me. Earth went up like smoke from the horses' hoofs that day. The last I saw of him, Jock was conveying him safely across a wide ditch. Then, ten minutes later, I jumped into a field and found Mr. Colville with the rim of his hat round his neck, his face and collar grimy with earth. Jock was standing near.

Had they been by the hedge I should have understood what had happened, but they were in the middle of the level field. I rode quickly up.

"Wonder I didn't break my neck," he cried. "Never had such a thing happen to me in my life——"

"What happened?" I asked. "Are you hurt?"

"That old horse," he said, "has carried me over every hedge and ditch about here for twenty miles, and twenty times over every one without a mistake—and now he's gone and fallen down with me full gallop in the middle of a field harrowed level as a billiard-table. Full gallop, mind you—and a man of my weight. I pitched right on to my head. It's a wonder I didn't break my neck."

But luckily no damage had been done except bruises and a stiff neck. But Jock had a bad hobble. He stood facing his master rather sheepishly. We got him home slowly, taking it in turns to ride my horse and walk with him.

"He's too old for the job," said Mr. Colville, "that's the trouble. I shouldn't have ridden him this season. But it's the first time he's let me down. It's nothing to come down at a hedge, but when your horse falls down in the middle of a field——" He shook his head. "He stumbled and couldn't recover himself, I reckon." We trudged half a mile in silence, then, "I shouldn't feel safe on him ever again," Mr. Colville said, and after another half-mile, "No, I shan't ride him any more."

Jock stood in his stable many days, and the vet. came to him, but the leg didn't seem to get really right. One day when I called I found the stable empty.

"I didn't see the use of letting him be about till he died of old age," said Mr. Colville. "Old horses suffer a lot of misery with rheumatics, and it's no kindness really. But I wouldn't be here to see them take him away."

There was one other horse Mr. Colville had had whom he had cared for as much as Jock, he told me, and that one in his prime had got his leg caught between two posts, rubbing in the yard, and in his struggles to get free had broken it. He lay in the yard and could not rise.

"I wasn't going to have them messing him about," said Mr. Colville; "there was only one thing to be done. I went in and got my gun, and lay down flat in the straw opposite his head and took long aim. I can see his eyes now, looking into mine."

The sporting farmer is ever parting from old friends.

I said I had not seen Simmons lately standing about by his cottage, and Mr. Colville replied, "He's been in bed the last month, so his missis told me. It's being out of work. That'll beat a man before anything." He added, "It seems a long time ago since we were at Farley Hall, doesn't it?"

It did indeed.

In respect of prices, too, he said, "In those days if

you threshed a stack of corn and sold it, it filled a fair gap, but now you need two to go as far."

It was a really pessimistic winter for the farmers. One of the Colville brothers who was in business said, " If I found my business wasn't paying I should shut up shop. You farmers ought to do the same." He urged his father to give up some of his land, but the old man would not. The curate of Sarrow, an ironical observer of life, said, " A farmer comes and tells you corn farming is a dead loss, and next day you find him sowing wheat as hard as he can go."

All sound enough in theory, but agriculture can't put its shutters up as neatly as that. Any analogy between farming and business is unsound. The earth is like no other raw material ; it has a blind will of its own that goes on, even if the farmer doesn't.

The one consolation of Benfield was, things can't get any worse. Yet by the spring they were.

Another meeting of farmers was summoned at Stambury. The saint in her niche was in full sun this time, and a butterfly wavered before her. But the speeches were about the same, only the meeting was more crowded, and the cries of " Hear, hear," more frequent and more general. Still the farmers had to have their jokes with one another, *sotto voce*. A protest was framed to the Minister of Agriculture and carried unanimously.

Only Mr. Crawley was dissatisfied. " A great open-air mass meeting of farmers and men in Hyde Park— that's the only way," he insisted excitedly to us on the steps. " They'll not take any notice of this."

Soon after that Mr. Crawley suddenly sold his farm and went away, " to study the situation," he said.

The man who took it was a stranger to this part of the country. He soon sold it again, and for a while it was bandied about from one buyer to another, cultivation going on half-heartedly the while. The last buyer could not realise, as by then the land was getting pretty foul, and it was left in charge of a foreman and half the staff for times to improve. It too became like Farley Hall.

Rumours circulated ever more persistently about Farley Hall and its owner.

One day I went up to see Mr. James, as I wanted a field pulled up deep by steam cultivation and he did that work by contract with his engines.

He was collarless and hatless, and still full of energy.

"You are just too late," he cried when he knew what I wanted. "The engines don't belong to me any more."

"Is it as bad as that, Mr. James?" I asked.

"Yes, it is!" he said.

Signs of dilapidation were everywhere visible. "I'm sorry," I said.

"Well, I had a shot at it," he exclaimed, as though aware of my impression. "I've failed, and now everybody's up against me for letting the place go to ruination. But I might have succeeded, and then everybody would have said, 'Smart chap, that.' Trade's been wrong. We're all out for ourselves, and what's the good of a lot of old cottages to me? There's old Simmons's place—people have spoken about it. What money have I got to throw away on that? And if I had, what return should I see? Why, the rent, if he paid it, would hardly be enough to cover the rates. I can't help it—I'm in as big a hole as they are. And I'm not the only one."

And very soon he was gone. Farley Hall stood empty. Four men under Bob, the horsekeeper, attempted to carry on some sort of outward signs of cultivation while attempts were made to sell the place.

Simmons was still in his bed, and some said he would not get up from it again. The cottage looked the worse for the winter, and another, I surmised, would render it uninhabitable. I wondered which would last the longer, the house or the man.

XXI

HARVEST eve once more, and the only unease of the hour when we, as was our wont in summer, strolled forth after supper and stood waist-high in the corn, was the last echo of a breeze and the pendulous swing of heavy ears on their high stalks. Otherwise complete stillness, and a sunset brooding with apparently eternal felicity on a fruitful earth. Pause and fruition.

> Time, as he passes us, has a dove's wing,
> Unsoiled, and swift, and of a silken sound.

We had become in this life half-conscious of time. With few appointments and no trains to catch, what should it mean to us ? The hours that used to hurry so had slowed down to the drift of the seasons, glided imperceptibly into one another, and stole past us as we stood.

By what degrees had the corn through which we now waded, plucking at the ears, grown to this height and hue from the mere faint breath of green over the brown mould that had been its first undungeoning from the ground ? On no day had it seemed different from the day before or the day following. The processes of this life were so gradual, the assumption of " staying where one was " so implicit. The farmer sows corn in the autumn, and by that act he has tacitly pledged his presence there for a year ahead. If prices are bad this season, perhaps they may be good the next. That is why the farmer sows his field again and again and yet again, till really he has no hope left nor possible means of raising any more money to tide him over till the reflux of hoped-for prosperity. Then he goes bankrupt—though actually he has been bankrupt for years.

" It ain't right," Walter said, when I told him of the price I had been given for a great heap of bright barley we had been all day shovelling up and sacking and weighing in the barn. " It ain't right," he said again, pausing to view the expanse on the outskirts of which we stood that evening as he passed. I told him the current price of that also, which stood high in the field, filling it to the tops of the hedges like a lock with flood-water.

At that hour when the " holy time is quiet as a nun " and the wheatlands so resting all but murmurous on harvest eve, it did seem, as Walter's tone implied, a blasphemy, the abasing of the living gold before the dug metal, for which civilisation was storing up for itself, on account of its scorn and refinement, some lingering retribution. Perhaps the worm was already born and feeding on its heart, the insidious disease that breeds in unnaturalness.

But we—I who had been in the country seven years now, and the others six—were still trespassing in the pleasances of the Castle of Indolence, as though time never was. But how sweet the lulling of summer—the lullaby of its air—how robust the winter and its sport, that was like labour glorified.

We stood waist-high in corn, rubbing out the ears, chatting, looking at the sky, looking at the stir of the heads where a rabbit scuttled along.

" To-morrow night," I said, " this will all be lying flat." For I had told Walter to bring the reaper into the field first thing in the morning, and if there were little dew to start. But that brought a sense of time into our evening stroll—for harvest is the one happening that is sudden in the fields.

To-morrow—and then the next day the sheaves all stooked up in the stubble, leaning steeply to each other like a multitude of hands in prayer. All the fields around Groveside would be populous with them and with their far-lingering shadows. And then the creak of wagons, cries of " GEE " and " WOA " all day, and the rustling of sheaves. After that, emptiness and silence broken only by partridge-cries. And, looking on empty stubbles, one would sense the first breath of autumn.

" And then," I said, " it will be time to begin sowing for another year."

" So soon," my mother said and the others echoed.

" How many harvests have we seen ? " she considered. " This is the sixth since we came to Groveside. How differently we view it now from the way we did then."

" We didn't even know the difference between corn-stacks and hay-stacks," put in my brother.

My mother said, " The more one gets to know about the fields the more one loves them."

But my brother had a birthday shortly, and speaking of that brought us to what had been put off for so long.

" Nineteen—we must really talk over your future seriously when father comes for the week-end."

And we did, among the sheaves, and in the garden. Half a dozen ears of wheat plaited together hung above the door of the house—a token that harvest was begun, which Walter never failed to bring at the end of the first day.

The next week-end we talked again. There was one thing my brother wanted to do—that was to farm. But the prospects had become so bad in England. An uncle overseas had offered to take him on to his ranch. After further long discussions, he decided to go. But the matter did not end there. My sister too had to be thinking of earning her living. That meant London, which would leave only my mother out here in the country. The obvious thing was the relinquishment of Groveside and the taking of a house near enough to London for both my father and sister to travel to and fro each day. By the end of harvest this was the course decided upon. My brother was then already packing for America.

" And what will you do ? " asked my mother.

There was no question in my mind as to that.

" I shall stay here," I answered.

" In Groveside ? "

" No, I shall turn Walter out and go back to live in Silver Ley, just as when I started."

" That hard life ? "

" Well, it's what I chose."

" But farming is so bad now."

" I shall manage to live—till times get better."

" Not like this."

" No, not like this—more as I used to live, at Silver Ley."

" Well, it's what you know, of course."

" Besides," I said, " it's too late to start other ways of life—I'm within a year or two of thirty."

263

" It'll be lonely."

" Oh, I shall miss our life here," I admitted ; " it's been a real home after all, has Groveside."

" Yes," said my mother reminiscently, " it's wonderful how acclimatised we have become, seeing how utterly ignorant we were at the beginning. Oh, but I shall miss the view of fields from the windows," she exclaimed. " And the wood-fires. I shall even miss having a pump at the sink. They are homely somehow—these old things."

However, we should all have a last country Christmas together before going our several ways.

This was the Christmas of 1928, which, if you remember, was attended by real Wenceslas weather. Deep and crisp the snow lay round about Groveside, though not even. The wind hissed over it shrewishly all night, and by morning the familiar ways had become a miniature mountain scenery, and a sculpture in pure line of invisible tides.

So deep was the snow that the postman could not use his bicycle, but came to us on foot across the white sheet of our garden, a sack on his back and a staff in his hand ; his face red with the keen air, and altogether looking as though he had tramped from afar and might break into a carol at any moment.

One only realises fully the supremacy of the cycle when its reign is suddenly interrupted, as on an occasion of snow. One realises then, too, the reason for the dying away of footpaths in this our land. For now people are seen plodding straight for their objective across the fields, whether it is the church spire, snow-encrusted, or the smoke of a cottage chimney.

Who are they? Not travellers from far, for they would not venture out to-day—in fact, the travelling area is suddenly restricted in time as it was a century ago. These are those parish workers who, when times are normal, take the serpentine routes of by-roads on bicycles. How often have I passed them on their business, heads down against the wind, toiling on? What more apt embodiment of the phrase " nose to the grindstone " than these figures? Mr. Raliffe, the district nurse, the school-mistress, postman, police-man. All these that are in fact the unobtrusive inner structure of a parish, who " must get there " whatever the weather—it is the cycle, emblem of quiet useful-ness, that carries them to and fro.

" Cold? " I asked Walter as he blew on his hands.

" Aye, master, and so I were last night. The latch o' my window came undone, and I woke up a-shakin' worse than a rice pudden on the way to the bake-house."

That day I walked down into Benfield and found the Colville family reunion all but mustered despite snow-choked ways. The sons had fought their way from all directions to that spot. The latest arrivals were Arnold and his family. He had left his car in a drift, hired a horse and trap, but eventually had to leave that too at an inn, and then, indefatigable, led the way on foot over fields and ditches to the village. They were now changing their clothes and having hot drinks. The village, to the distant view, was partly lost in the whiteness; it was seen as a few dark fragments of itself where snow had not settled; all that was not snow on that day looked black—cottage eaves and windows, a wall, the side of a stack, tree-trunks and strips of boughs.

Old Charlie, of course, had not been seen since autumn, but smoke flowed up from his chimney. No doubt he sat safely wrapped and firelit there, dozing till the spring.

On Boxing Day in the morning the glassy air was enlivened with thin chimes, sudden and near. The village bell-ringers stood in a half-circle about the front door, where still the wheat-ears hung pecked empty by birds, plying their hand-bells.

This was an annual custom. Boxing Day was the one holiday of the labourer, besides Christmas Day, and that was how these men liked to spend it. With mistletoe in their caps, wearing greatcoats and mittens and clean boots shining like coals among the snow, they went from house to house in the parish, ringing a chime and wishing prosperity through the New Year.

We came in time to consider this quite a ceremony; because somehow we did not like just to give them a donation and drink and so farewell, but used to welcome them in as on the first occasion they had come—having beer and plum cake ready set out for them in the great kitchen. The old narrow bricks used to ring with their steel-shod feet, and their voices to vibrate with an unfamiliar depth and huskiness here within walls. Somehow, seen suddenly away from their usual background of acres and sky, the texture of their lives stood out the more. The brows that one never saw save now, when their caps were off, the wiry rebellious hair like patches of standing corn that the wind had swirled awry, their clean rough shirts and collars, blue and red striped, the heavy festooned watch-chain, the thick waistcoat without points, the leather-bound cuff, the rosy cheek, the swart hand—the roughness and cleanness and well-mendedness of their clothes, the colour of them, and the slow stir that even their small movements seemed to make about them. Their eyes were like open windows, and all the sudden fresh humours of the weather seemed to come through them. Their cheeks had been painted by the air and light. They were touched always and all days by limitlessness—by great views, winds. And they brought the stare of it in with them, somehow: it was like the light of the snow in the room.

We always invited them in—we always invited everybody in. No matter who they were, they had to mix with whomsoever they might find there. Was one abashed, was one supercilious, my mother gave them no rest, bringing them to the forefront of the conversation, and keeping them there. It was as though she delighted in weaving all the diverse strands of "class" into one woof in our rooms. And her personality worked this like magic fingers. Then she'd sit quiet and watch it working, the talk passing to and fro—a journalist friend from London and the vet. who had just been attending a lame horse; an undergraduate and Alfred Jarvis; Mrs. Willington, who had made a formal "call," and Mr. Colville, who had made an informal one. . . .

The newspaper director was thoroughly interested —so much so that my mother took his empty tea-cup from his hand, refilled it, and replaced it without him seeming to notice.

"The first thing I remember in this world," the vet. was saying, "is being taken out into the harvest field on my grandfather's farm. They were just getting the last load—in those days the barley was carted loose, and they used wide pitch-forks—and one of the men put his fork so that a prong came under each of my arms, and lifted me up like that on to the load, where his mate caught me and gave me a ride home. . . . That's how big I was. . . ."

The vet. was lean, angular, and humorous in a reserved way. He wore a check cap, a longish riding-coat that splayed out at the hips, and tight-fitting leggings. I don't know why he has so far been omitted from this account, for we often met, not necessarily on my own farm, but that of a neighbour, or on the road. He drove a high old car which had some venerable brass-work about it, scrupulously bright—a two-seater of which he was the highest point; it sloped sharply away before and behind him. It had a loose piece of iron somewhere, which tinged every time the car hit a pot-hole like the bell of a fire-engine.

He was about all hours, all days, all weathers. It had to be teeming for him to have the hood up, which converted the car into the likeness of an old lady's bonnet flapping in the wind. If anything, he seemed a little busier on Sundays (which, as every farmer knows, is the one day for any untoward events on a farm—milk-fevers, mating-fevers, breaking out of pigs, etc.). But that he was conscious of the day was evident by the fact that he always wore a bowler hat and long trousers then, though they must have incommoded him in his work. It seemed a sign that he always got up quite prepared to spend Sunday as a day of rest, for all that by nine-thirty or so there would come a call for him, and by the time he had returned, two or three more had probably accumulated. He always seemed quite happy about it.

"Don't you ever get a Sunday off?" asked my mother.

He shrugged. "I don't mind. You see, I am fond of my work. Though you get some funny jobs sometimes. It's not a bit of use anybody taking it up unless they love the work. An animal's not like a human being—it can't speak—it can't tell you where it's got a pain—you've got to find out; so you've got to understand it—you've got to have a lot of patience."

His own patience was inspiring. I have seen him faced with a colt that had torn its side on a stake, one that had never had a halter on its head till half Mr. Colville's men had managed to catch it and bring it kicking and rearing into the yard for treatment. He coaxed, lightly touching, patting, stroking, and then dodged the creature's heels by inches as it let fly.

In frosty dead of night, by dim lantern light misted with our breath, I have stooped with him over a horse whose glazed eyes looked up at us between life and death. Or it has been a Sunday afternoon, with Benfield bells ringing to church, when he has hung his bowler on a peg in the cowshed, and his coat, and rolled up his shirt-sleeves, and set about some midwifery.

And so he went his way, and still goes—week by week—by night as by day—with barns for sick-rooms, straw for an operating-table, and yokels for nurses. Good luck to him. There was always a cup of tea for him at Groveside in the afternoon when he called, but there were probably still a hundred pigs with swine-fever between him and his own fireside.

When times had become bad—and worse than bad —with farming, my mother asked him one day, "Can the farmers pay you?"

"Money's very short in the country," he replied, and then, after a pause, "I got a wire this very day from a farmer, and when he met me in the yard he said, 'Well, boy (the vet. was middle-aged !), I'm glad to see you, but I never thought you'd come.' 'Why not?' I asked. 'Well,' he said, 'you know I owe you a big bill already—and I can't pay you.' He took a pound note from his pocket. 'I can give you that on account if it's any good to you.' 'No,' I said, 'I'm feeling the pinch too, but if you can't pay me you can't, and there's an end of it till you can.'"

Later in the evening, as my mother and I sat together in the library, she said out of a silence, "There's something pathetic about that story he told us this afternoon. . . . 'Well, boy, I never thought you'd come !'"

I, too, felt that England was in a bad way that such troubles should come upon peaceable men.

But I have wandered far, very far, from the bell-ringers and our last Christmas at Groveside.

When they had had a drink of beer and some cake, and brushed the crumbs from their moustaches, coughed, and blown their noses, they laid their caps in the centre of the table and on them their bells. They stood round in a circle. Their leader murmured some technical instructions in which the word "bob" recurred. Then they rang us a chime, and another.

The enclosed air of the room tingled with their echoes as of miniature church bells, while we sat round the fire listening to the knell of our life at Groveside.

The method of the ringing was this. As soon as one man had rung his two bells he put them down on the caps. They were at once taken up by another man, maybe on the opposite side of the table, while the first man's hands stretched to pick up two others somewhere else. So this complicated and swift exchange went on, and the harmony was not of the bells alone, but of the movements of all their arms as they lifted and laid them down, till the chime was ended with a clang of unison. They said nothing all the while, but their eyes were sidelong and intently observant of one another as they poised their bells shoulder high, judging the exact moment to jerk each down with a flick of the wrist and add its note to the chain of sound. Only the leader gave occasional cries of " Bob " when it was time for some change in the order of their ringing. The air above was a swirl of the echoes of all the notes they had just played, dying into one another in a kind of tonal rainbow.

Then I was asked if I would care to have a try. This had become a yearly custom : after the first two chimes the invitation was always made, and I took up the two deep-toned bells. While the others were throughout the ringing handing their bells to and fro among them, mine was the simple duty of adding the two final notes to every round without change. Even so, I found it hard to judge the right moment ; either my notes came too close on the heels of my neighbour's, or they rang out after a little gap of silence in absent-minded haste. Nor had I improved with time, though they said I had.

My father, too, took them up, and derived a technical pleasure from listening closely to their tones one by one.

Then finally they rang us a very quick, joyful chime, all the notes tumbling over one another as though for gladness, which made me think of spring and the scattering of the multitude of flowers upon the earth again in a little time from now.

My mother amused them by crying, " Who is this Bob you keep shouting to ? I'm sure he's doing it very well."

After another drink of beer they picked up their caps, saying, " Well, we must be getting on or we shan't get round before dark. A prosperous New Year to you, sir, and to you, ma'am, and all of you." They did not know we were leaving Groveside. " Good day," they cried, and trooped off across the snow, misty-breathed in the keen air.

They had never had a shorter round, though, than this winter. Half the big farmhouses which they used to visit would have answered their ringing with blank stares to-day. The Farley Hall cottages were almost all empty.

Simmons had died the previous month. He had lain in his bed so long under his mouldering ceiling, his bodily and his earthly dwelling both equally failing him. At last he had been unable even to stretch out his hand for his pipe, which had been his life's last consolation.

His wife had gone to live with a married daughter. Now the whole upper part of the gable-end of the cottage had fallen away, and the blue-flowered wall-paper of the room whither Bob and I had carried him the last time he was drunk, stared forth upon the road. The floor had a thick white carpet of snow.

"If he hadn't been out of work," said Mr. Colville, "he might still be alive to-day."

The snow in a week became like a threadbare garment; then melted right away; and already the green points of spring flowers were appearing from the earth.

"We must go before the spring," my mother had said, and it had been generally agreed. "It would be difficult to tear ourselves away when all the flowers are out in the garden."

Already she was looking for a house near London; already my brother had sailed for America; already George, our gardener, had been engaged by a neigh-bouring squire at a wage well above the ordinary rural rates of pay. Whatever the results of the family sojourn at Groveside, it did at least enable one man to rise from the sheer plod of labour to that drawing-room of agriculture—the garden. George, by self-help and the books we gave him, thrived. When next I saw him after he left Groveside, at a June show, he was wearing a sprig of sweet-peas in his buttonhole with even more blooms on one stalk than ever before —it was like a bouquet, and impeded the movement of his head, but was generally admired by the expert. "Did you grow them yourself?" asked one. I heard him reply with dignity, "I never wear anything I don't grow myself."

But long before then I had taken the car out of the garage at Groveside for the last time, and waited with it in the road, looking at the house once again empty and with curtainless windows, while Sarah, my mother and sister locked the door, and came away. My mother gave me the key to be delivered up to old Mr. Colville. Then I padlocked the garden gate and drove them down to the station, returning to my cottage at Silver Ley, whence Walter had moved—to its once familiar and now curious silence.

XXII

By the time summer returned, I had taken up the
thread of my former life at Silver Ley as it had been
seven years ago. Yet I felt that I was resuming the
existence which had first presented itself to me after
a much less lengthy interruption. In truth I felt no
older than then; that I had been little over twenty on
closing the cottage door, and was little under thirty
on re-opening it, was a fact without inner confirmation, though it stared at me every time I dated a letter.

To the superficial view the old life seemed to go on
around me—except where the big farmhouses flashed
blank windows at the sun, and for the garden of
Groveside, blossoming in solitude and gradually
tangling again.

Emily Jarvis was of course back at the farm just
down the road, but the aunt who had come to keep
house during her illness and long convalescence still
remained, and seemed to have taken root there.

Emily had enjoyed her travels. "Oh, the vines!"
she had exclaimed on returning. "The mountain
villages."

"And the markets—did you see them?" I asked.
"The cheeses like broken cart-wheels?"

She nodded. "And the flowers on the cobble-
stones."

"The funny little trains, like a sedate scenic railway.
The workmen with their umbrellas."

"And can't it rain, too?"

" Yes, just can't it when it likes ? "

" And Bière Beauregard—or did you stick to what they call ' The Nice English Tea ' ? "

We chatted so for hours, on and off, and were poor company, I fear, for Alfred.

So all that little ledge of country between the mountains and the water glowed again for me, till it became a very lotus-land, and cheated me into a belief that there I had for awhile found perfect happiness, whereas actually the peak of my joy had been on first sight of English porters again, and English words on wagons. Though my somewhat exotic adolescence had not dared admit it, I'd enjoyed holidays in the homely English countryside much more.

But the news of the family's impending departure had taken the edge off Emily's delight in being back.

The curate of Sarrow was no less pleased than I to see her, and since her return it seemed to me that he was a more familiar figure than formerly cycling along this road. But he too was not to be with us much longer I learned one day as he stopped and spoke to me as I worked in a roadside field. I had returned to the bill-hook and plough of former days, and was drawing out a furrow even as the one I told of in the first chapter of this book. I had reached the peeled stick by the hedge that had stood for my guide, with Darky and Dewdrop, the same two horses with which my first furrow had been ploughed seven years ago.

There I paused and hailed the curate cheerfully, for this furrow was a better one than that first had been. He too was blithe, for his bicycle pointed down the road where the Jarvis chimneys stood over the trees, and it was the hour of garden afternoon tea, in which farmers don't indulge, but only ladies—especially such as on whom the shadow of past illness lies but as a more delicate grace than formerly—and gentlemen.

He told me he had been appointed to a living in the Isle of Wight, which suited him very well, for the sea was as congenial to him as the inland clay of Suffolk was antipathetic. He would be leaving Sarrow in the autumn for those parts where life went more lightly shod, and where there was a more generous leaven of residential folk.

With these pleasant prospects gilding the already golden day, he continued down the road, and I resumed my ploughing. I had dispensed with " market cut "; my breeches were now just " breeches "; my coat, in which I had attended the point-to-point meetings last year, was frayed now, but fit for long service yet on Silver Ley.

The Selbridge show-day came again—that social recognition of summer, with spring still crying a broken farewell in the cuckoo's arrested note from the far coppice, and dying in violets overwoven with long grass.

The grounds of Selbridge Manor still afforded refreshment and forgetful ease. They were, if anything, the more gracious to-day on account of the ruined cottages and empty farms one passed along the road. At the Farley Hall corner there might have been a war; the dilapidations were so like those old photographs of " behind the line." The roof-beams of one cottage stood up among low trees like the ribs of a palæolithic skeleton. Simmons's was becoming just a mound of rubble ; the upper floor of another sloped sharply to the ground.

From these things, and the future, the lion-guarded gates of Selbridge Manor afforded a sanctuary. The grounds were as perfect and, on this day, as crowded as ever.

There was gaiety and even hopefulness on that murmurous afternoon. This citadel of the old order at least still stood : Mrs. Willington with her lorgnettes going her queenly round of the stalls, other people's gardeners stooping and peering in the rose-gardens, Mr. Willington, Mr. Colville, and others of their generation walking together, not noticeably seven years older, and pooling their humour as heretofore. The vegetables in the tents were as monstrous and emblematic as ever, like the tipped-out contents of the cornucopia. I sat and watched the tennis again under the trees, and reflected how Fate had looped the thread of life, crossing this point when I had sat here before, a small farmer living alone on his holding and enjoying " a day off " before the hay-harvest. The circle was complete : I was at the same point in my second start as my first, with the same modest credit in the bank, and the future as uncertain. Only I foresaw the Res Severa, which is proverbially Verum Gaudium, shining out in more emphatic lettering than before in my mind's eye. Times were more difficult for one thing. But also I had tasted interim of the life of the sporting gentleman. The rhythm of the life of labour seemed all the more strenuous for that. All the same, I still had my window to it, even though there were no door, and sitting in the grounds of Selbridge Manor I praised in my heart the Old Squirearchy. Their pleasances, I felt, were enough to justify them, whatever they themselves had been. I had little books of their "elegant" eighteenth-century verses, bought from old shops of Stambury, in my cottage, books of their travels written by the library window of the old manor on their return. I liked them and their patrician trees, and I would rather labour in the fields in sight of them than take my chance of "gentility" in cities.

Beyond the tennis-courts five children, escaped from supervision, joined hands and ran round in a ring. Prosperity seemed to smile on us for a day.

Joan came from the court to where I sat.

"Did you win?" I asked. "I was watching that other game over there."

"Those kids—yes, I thought they'd please you," she said. "Yes, we won quite easily."

"You'll probably win the tournament again," I suggested, "as you did last year. By the way, is that your sister's *fiancé* over there?"

"Yes," she replied. "They are being married next month."

I had missed the clergyman's daughter who had once played hockey and danced with me, and asked Joan about her.

"She is married, you know."

"Yes, I know; but she said that she was going to dance and play games just the same. She was most emphatic about it."

"So she said," Joan answered, "but nobody has seen much of her since she was married—and that's nearly a year ago."

"Then what a curious thing marriage must be," I

279

reflected, and added, " As I remember, she was your
opponent in the final last year. Now you are left
supreme, for you play a better game than ever. If I
were as good at it, I expect I should be as fond of it
as you."

She strummed idly on her racquet, whose coloured
gut proclaimed it to be new this season. " Oh, well,
what else is there to do ? " she said, and yawned.

Joan and I had tea alone. Rodney Willington was
married now, too, and the former Willington vortex
of bright young people was not to be found here any
more.

Somehow the flourish of our old gaiety seemed now
set on other brows, and transfixed on ours. It
was almost a sense of being deserted by those who had
married, as though they had played us false in
conspiring to secede from our party and be all in all to
each other. Even Barbara was so won over to this
new idea as to smile only to us at our table, and go over
to an empty one and sit *tête-à-tête* with her *fiancé*.

There were tables, though, where vivacious groups
were gathered, even as ours had been. But I did not
recognise them, or only vaguely.

" Who are they ? " I asked Joan.

" Oh, just kids," she said, with her nose in the air.

All the same, two of those beat Joan and her
partner in the final of the tennis tournament, who had
been respectively in short trousers and pigtails when I
had first sat here. Seven years was not much to our
elders, but it was quite an age to us.

I met Mr. Colville at the show, but he was just
about to leave, although it was quite early in the
afternoon.

" There's a farmers' meeting at Stambury," he explained to me.

" What is it about ? " I asked.

" To discuss the state of affairs in agriculture," he answered.

" They have so many of these meetings," I commented. " Are they going to do anything ? "

" I don't know—I thought I'd go along and hear what they'd got to say. Something'll have to be done, that's one thing, or there soon won't be anybody left on the land at all. I sacked three men the other day, and if things don't improve after harvest, I shall sack three more." This from Mr. Colville was the most pointed comment on the times that I had yet heard. For he of all farmers was the one who most liked to have his farm well manned.

" The better you farm nowadays, the worse off you are," he added. " I was talking to a chap in the market the other day—he's been a farmer for years, and a successful farmer. He told me he's just sacked every man on his farm except the stock-keeper—set some down to grass and let the rest go wild. He said, ' If I can't make any money, I'm at least going to keep together what I have got, and not lose it.' He was buying some rough cattle to run on his land ; for the rest, he's just going to lie low. And there'll be a lot more do the same if things don't show some improvement, you mark my words. It's the men that are going to suffer just as much as the farmers. There's nothing to pay them with—you can't get blood out of a stone. Well, I'll go and see what they've got to say at Stambury, at all events," he concluded, getting into his car.

I heard that a resolution was unanimously adopted urging the Government to take immediate steps for the relief of agriculture. The Government, of course, was as quick to act on this recommendation as it had been to do on the others which had been carried unanimously in that upper room overlooking the ruined abbey at Stambury.

However, a few weeks later I received from local farming headquarters by post a notice in bold red print. At the same time I found on ruined cottages and tumbling barns, and almost everything that had one wall yet standing, placards, emphatic to the point of exclamation, convening a mass meeting extraordinary of farmers and farm-workers alike, to be held in the open air on Parker's Piece at Cambridge—a great demonstration, in fact, of the solidity of agricultural opinion, to impress its desperate plight. All farmers were urged themselves to attend, and to give their men every facility to do so; it was also urged that there should be no vacant seat in the car of anyone driving in on that day. Furthermore, I learned that special trains were being run from all directions to Cambridge, whose single platform looked like being more congested than ever.

It would have been the farmers' "luck" had it been pouring rain on that day, but as it happened the sky was only faintly grey, with the sun occasionally peeping through upon the town. It was indeed a mighty gathering, and though many of the parties of yokels that were converging there about the time I was approaching had already the husky voices and grinning rosiness of those for whom a little drink does a good deal, and obviously regarded the occasion

282

as a day on the spree, they swelled the circumference of that great black blot of humanity which was spilled on the green of the cricket lawns.

People were craning their necks to see over each other's heads, and guessing with their friends how many that expanse of heads represented. The reckonings varied from five thousand to fifty thousand, nor had I the vaguest notion towards which of these extremes my judgment, if called upon, should be inclined. Was this, I wondered, what a mediæval army looked like? Was this the size of the English force that faced the French at Agincourt? If so, those battles must have been much smaller affairs than boyish exuberance and coloured plates in annuals had led one to visualise. Not to mention those neat little plans in history books, which reduced all the hopes, fears, and adventure of the day to the tidiness of geometry, the forces being turned for the purposes of illustration into the semblance of sugar cubes, with a few triangles footnoted unconvincingly " Archers," or " Pikemen," and a dozen or so fleas' footprints labelled " Woods."

The crowd, which continued to grow as people filtered on to the green from all directions, was concentrated about a raised platform on which a number of people were sitting. Among them I recognised several of importance locally. Above them floated in giant lettering " God Speed the Plough," the stirring ensign of the yeomen which spans the streets of a Suffolk town when an agricultural show is being held there, and is its greeting to all who drive thither. It is a phrase I have well understood when, early abroad, a team has loomed out of the mist to me like a symbol, majestic in its solitude. The horses abreast, with manes fluttered by the wind as by the unseen resistance to their effort, but with the early gleam on them like the heraldic shimmer of chivalry making them princely ; their heads bowed, yet proudly and with the prevailing of their effort. Effort and ease mingled in their gait, the sheer downward plod beautifully compensated by the proud curve of the leg lifted again. The plough seen thus in silhouette is but the line that yokes man and horse to one purpose and links them to the soil. For between them the plough's contour curves down to where it clamps itself to the earth and cuts its way, so that it is like the root and branches of a life-bearing tree, by which man is joined to the earth for sustenance as a child is to the belly of its mother.

The Man there, with his hands to the plough, is significant in his solitude, master of earth and of the greater strength of beasts, self-contained and half-sad with ploughing his lone furrow, but answerable to none but himself. If symbols count for anything, then to visualise for a moment after that the rat-like scurryings into the tubes of London is to recollect the line, " How art thou fallen from heaven, O Lucifer, son of the morning ? " Reflection and reason modify the contrast, but the symbol remains, even though the mist-born figure who seemed little lower than the angels becomes in light of later day an ugly and uncouth old man.

The president of the Farmers' Union addressed the crowd. " President " is a word misleadingly august for these circumstances. He spoke as a farmer, and it was as a farmer he was understood. He said, " We don't say much, and we are slow to kick. We like to attend to our business rather than to meddle in politics. And because we don't make a fuss we don't always get fair play. We work hard, and we want a fair living. But our barns are in ruin; our fields are full of grass; our bellies are empty. Our men, skilled in their trade, are gone from the country; their cottages fall down; they stand idle in the towns. . . ."

The speaker had a powerful voice, and he needed it and all that amplifiers could do for it to make it carry across the crowd.

"Our bellies are empty," he vociferated again.

The metaphor hit home to the labourers about where I stood, whose bellies weren't.

"Hear, hear," the cry went up in answer.

The speaker had a brow clothed in thunder, a defiant lower lip, a fist that hammered his words home. Now I expected that something—I did not quite know what—should happen, he having stated our case in all its barrenness, and being echoed by a rumble of voices on all sides. Now surely was the orator's hour to work up the white heat of passion. But somehow the moment passed; that combustion never came; each agriculturalist looked self-consciously at his neighbour who had murmured " Hear, hear."

There was an infiltration of undergraduates among the crowd for curiosity's sake. They stood taller than the farmers, straight and lithe—they were as saplings to rugged trees. Their bodies were untried, unworn by life; their gait was easy with walking in smooth places; they were supple with running and leaping, not bowed with lifting, carrying, or the brooding watch over the plough.

They found amusement here. They cocked their heads on one side and listened, looking at each other quizzically. Two who stood near me thought the phrase about our bellies being empty very quaint—repeated it to themselves, and took it away with them to share among their friends.

They were like a different race, seen in such close proximity to the farmers and labourers : their smooth skins and clear-cut features compared to the clod-shaped, tufty faces, the angularities, the bent legs. It is strange how natural and graceful the labourer becomes in his setting of fields and at his work, and how staringly unshapely as he stands at gaze in his bad " best " clothes, on an occasion like this.

The farmers looked upon the undergraduates as wild featherheads, that tittered here. The undergraduates seemed to find the land-workers as good a show as performing bears. The gulf was as wide as the contrast of appearances.

At any rate, the students did not bring their training in critical analysis to bear on the spectacle before them ; nor did X-ray photographs, through a sonnet, of the mind of Keats, to which their professors treated them, seem to aid them to an inner comprehension of the words " God Speed the Plough." Their Pegasus spurned the earth.

Now, after several speakers had had their say, some representing the capital and some the labour of agriculture, the resolution was put to the effect that this gathering strongly deprecated the Government's persistent neglect of agriculture in the past, and insisted that immediate steps be taken to save the industry from complete collapse.

"Those for the motion. . . ." Instead of the revolutionary shout that would have best suited, I thought, the exclamation marks that had summoned us here—threatening thunder of the thousands of throats of those that laboured in vain—right hands were raised in complete silence.

"Carried unanimously," cried those on the platform, and this was noted on the protest that was to be despatched to the Government. Then a brass band struck up, and everybody sang "God Speed the Plough," and following that, "God Save the King," and that was the end of the Giant Protest Meeting. The law-abiding throng began to disperse slowly through one narrow gate townwards to tea.

At the last moment during the singing, I caught sight of Jim Crawley trying to gain access to the platform, waving a pamphlet in the face of the man who stood in his way, and hammering at it with his finger.

Of course, I remembered, it was Jim Crawley's idea after all—a small scale version of it—the idea of how many years ago? I saw him again as he had stood on the steps of the hall after that first meeting at Stambury, unfolding to us his plan.

There he was to-day, vainly trying to tell them it was his idea all along; nobody paying the least attention.

Perhaps had they after all embraced his picturesque proposal, marched to London in workaday attire from every quarter of England—in other words, had they made a great nuisance of themselves as the suffragettes did—then perhaps—treasonable as the reflection should be in this age of government of, for, and by the people—notice would have been taken of them, and something done to keep them quiet, which certainly would not be done for even thousands who constitutionally held up their hands, and quietly dispersed.

I thought it was a pity, as I went my way, that in the impetuous modern exchange of new lamps for old, the light that shines from the farmhouse window, that has been the light of the life of many generations, should be allowed to gutter unregarded for lack of oil.

I was soon in the hay-harvest. Walter and I managed it together this year, as I had only two fields to cut and cart.

Riding home on the wagon-load, I gazed over the hedge on Emily in her garden. She sat with tea set out on a table before her. She called to me as I floated by upon the hay to descend and have a cup to refresh myself after my exertions. Her invitation tempted me, for, besides the attraction of her company, I was hot and thirsty, and there was a chair in the cool shade beside her.

" I've got this wagon to unload first," I cried. For after that there was half an hour's pause for tea in the working day.

" That's all right, sir," said Walter from below understandingly ; " I can fling this load off on to the stack alone, and stamp it into the middle."

He stopped the horse, and I climbed down by the rope which bound the load, and after shaking the hay from my coat and putting it on, entered the garden.

This was better than having tea alone in the field. Emily had an album of photographs of her holiday abroad beside her, which we looked through again together. It always yielded some new recollection for us to talk over.

With the tea the servant brought out a letter for her by the afternoon post. She asked to be excused while she read it and the tea brewed

Folding it away, she bent over the cups.

"It is from a man I met over there," she said as she poured out Then, after a pause, "He asked me to marry him."

"Oh," I exclaimed, and with a glance at her hand. "So he didn't impress you."

"I liked him very much," she answered, "but that was all. He lives out there. He is a writer."

"It sounds attractive," I surmised.

"Yes, but in any case I'd rather live at Benfield," she said. "It's my real home after all. That is what going abroad taught me. It's odd, isn't it?"

"I can understand," I replied. "But when your father dies—and you know how Alfred wants to get to the grass country—— You wouldn't live here alone, would you?"

"I don't know; it depends," she said.

We had tea, and continued looking at the photographs till I heard the rattle of the wagon returning empty to the field. I rose unwillingly. "And now I must resume my work."

"Already?"

"Half an hour can be very short," I said. She glanced at her watch.

"How is farming these days?" she asked, fingering the winder.

"Hard work if one is to get a living," I answered.

"Still no regrets?"

"None but that it does not allow me to sit longer with you here."

"But otherwise it gives you enough for your needs?"

I hesitated. It was difficult at that moment contentedly to exchange afternoon tea in her garden for labour in the fields with Walter.

"Well, enough for a single person living as I do," I said.

She asked, "Do you ever wish for more?"

"Wish!" I echoed; the very word just then begot whole worlds to wish for.

"I should like at this moment to be able to think that I could ever possibly become rich," I said, looking at her.

She met my eyes, then looked down at her folded hands.

"Rich necessarily?" she enquired.

"Even comfortably off——" I stared at the garden about me as though for the faintest prospect. A familiar-shaped hat went gliding along above the top of the hedge and slowed towards the gate. The rattling of the wagon had ceased, and I knew that it was waiting for me beside the hay. "But I made my choice and I must stick to it," I said. "Good-bye."

I met the curate by the gate. "I say, don't let me break up the party," he cried, with simulated concern.

290

"You're not," I answered. I jerked my thumb towards the field across the road. "The empty must be filled."

"Well, good luck," he cried.

"And to you," I called back.

Walter and I looked at the remaining hay-cocks. "Three more loads will clear the field," we agreed, and set to work.

"Wonderful faint sort of day this is," Walter puffed, pausing to wipe his brow. "Seems to take all the heart out of a chap somehow."

We surveyed the clear but leaden-hued sky in the warm stillness.

"I reckon we shall get a downfall before long," he predicted. "It'll be fresher when it's over, that's one thing."

"Yes," I agreed, "it will be better then."

OXFORD

MORE TWENTIETH-CENTURY CLASSICS

Details of a selection of Twentieth-Century Classics follow. A complete list of Oxford Paperbacks, including The World's Classics, OPUS, Past Masters, Oxford Authors, Oxford Shakespeare, and Oxford Paperback Reference, as well as Twentieth-Century Classics, is available in the UK from the General Publicity Department, Oxford University Press (JH), Walton Street, Oxford, OX2 6DP.

In the USA, complete lists are available from the Paperbacks Marketing Manager, Oxford University Press, 200 Madison Avenue, New York, NY 10016.

Oxford Paperbacks are available from all good bookshops. In case of difficulty, please order direct from Oxford University Press Bookshop, 116 High Street, Oxford, Freepost, OX1 4BR, enclosing full payment. Please add 10% of published price for postage and packing.

LOVE AND MR LEWISHAM

H. G. Wells

Introduced by Benny Green

This novel traces the early career and unfortunate love affair of Mr Lewisham, a lowly assistant master at a provincial school. The young man constructs a grand scheme of self-education which he believes will propel him to the greatness he deserves. But his love for a medium's daughter, Ethel Chaffery, causes him first to be sacked from his schoolmaster's job, and then to fail the final exams of his course at the Normal School of Science. Love triumphs, but his grand schemes perish and Mr Lewisham ends up a sadder and wiser man.

SEVEN DAYS IN NEW CRETE

Robert Graves

Introduced by Martin Seymour-Smith

A funny, disconcerting, and uncannily prophetic novel about Edward Venn-Thomas, a cynical poet, who finds himself transported to a civilization in the far future. He discovers that his own world ended long ago, and that the inhabitants of the new civilization have developed a neo-archaic social system. Magic rather than science forms the basis of their free and stable society; yet, despite its near perfection, Edward finds New Cretan life insipid. He realizes that what is missing is a necessary element of evil, which he feels it his duty to restore.

HIS MONKEY WIFE
John Collier

Introduced by Paul Theroux

His Monkey Wife was the first novel (published in 1930) by John Collier, a British poet, short-story writer, and novelist. It tells the bizarre and moving story of Mr Fatigay, an English schoolmaster in the Upper Congo, and his intelligent and sensitive pupil, Emily, a prodigious chimpanzee. Mr Fatigay brings Emily to England as a present for his flighty fiancée, Amy, in whose establishment she must accept a position as housemaid. Emily, however, who has secretly fallen in love with Fatigay, resolves to educate herself, and before long establishes herself as a serious rival for Amy in the contest for Fatigay's hand.

'John Collier welds the strongest force with the strangest subtlety . . . It is a tremendous and terrifying satire, only made possible by the suavity of its wit.' Osbert Sitwell

THE UNBEARABLE BASSINGTON
Saki

Introduced by Joan Aiken
Illustrated by Osbert Lancaster

Set in Edwardian London, Saki's best known novel has as its hero the 'beautiful, wayward' Comus Bassington in whom the author invested his own ambiguous feelings for youth and his fierce indignation at the ravages of time.

'There is no greater compliment to be paid to the right kind of friend than to hand him Saki, without comment.' Christopher Morley

CORDUROY

Adrian Bell

Introduced by Susan Hill

In the tradition of Gilbert White, Francis Kilvert, and Flora Thompson, Adrian Bell in *Corduroy* has given us an unforgettable account of past life in the English countryside. In 1920 the city-bred author left London to work as a labourer on a farm in the depths of Suffolk. We see the country landscape and rural pursuits through his perceptive young eyes. This is the first volume of Bell's three-part memoirs, followed by *Silver Ley* and *The Cherry Tree*.

'Bell's writings are literature, and should be kept in circulation as part of the English heritage' Q. D. Leavis

IN YOUTH IS PLEASURE

Denton Welch

Introduced by John Lehmann

Denton Welch's writing, so much admired by Cyril Connolly, Jocelyn Brooke, and Edith Sitwell, has a purity of style that is completely without affectation. In this, his best novel, he gives a profoundly disturbing vision of the world through the eyes of his adolescent hero.